ISSUES OF

OF

TOMORROW

A SCIENCE FICTION ANTHOLOGY

TITLES BY
INDIE AUTHORS PRESS

Altered States II: a cyberpunk anthology
Control Theory
Spooky Halloween Drabbles 2016
Raiders of the Seventh Planet
Blood of Nyx
Corpus Deluxe: Undead Tales of Terror
Spooky Halloween Drabbles 2015
Speculative Valentine Drabbles 2015
Altered States: a cyberpunk sci-fi anthology
Spooky Halloween Drabbles 2014
A Forest of Dreams, a fantasy anthology
British Process Servers Guide
Learning About Love

Forthcoming titles can be found on
www.salgado-reyes.com.

ISSUES
OF
TOMORROW

A SCIENCE FICTION ANTHOLOGY

ABOUT OUR EDITORS

ROY C. BOOTH is a published author, comedian, poet, journalist, essayist, optioned screenwriter, and an internationally awarded playwright with 57 plays published to date (Samuel French, Heuer, et al) with 850+ productions in 30 countries and in ten languages. A graduate of Pillager High School, Booth also has an AA degree from Central Lakes College (Brainerd, MN, and he is a hall of fame inductee in both schools), and a BA in English/Speech-Theatre and an MA in English with a Creative Writing Emphasis from Bemidji State University. Booth resides in Downtown Bemidji, Minnesota with his wife and three sons (writers all) where he has also owned/managed Roy's Comics & Games since 1992. An impartial list of his publications may be found at www.amazon.com/author/roycbooth.

JORGE SALGADO-REYES is a Chilean and British sci-fi/cyberpunk author, private investigator, and photographer. Salgado-Reyes founded Indie Authors Press in June 2011 when he saw that the publishing industry continued to evolve away from the established gatekeepers. Born in Temuco, Chile, Salgado-Reyes left his country of birth at age seven in 1975 with his family, driven into exile by the Pinochet dictatorship. Salgado-Reyes is currently working towards his BA (Honours) in English Literature and Creative Writing and spends time in both the United Kingdom and Chile. A list of his publications may be found at www.amazon.com/Jorge-Salgado-Reyes/e/B009G0CTPO.

ISSUES OF TOMORROW

a science fiction anthology

A catalog record for this book is available from the British Library.

ISBN: 978-1-910910-12-2
Paperback Edition

Indie Authors Press

London | Chile | USA

CONTENTS

INTRODUCTION

WE'VE TOLD STORIES. WE always have. They started with primitive cave paintings and evolved into fireside tales under the stars. It is still a part of us: The desire to explain the world through any means be it through myths, fables, or etches on the side of a rock. The first stories told us where we came from, offering explanations as to why things were the way they were and how they got there. When we'd figured that part out, we turned our attention someplace a little further: the future. When that happened, we began to think about where we might go, individually, and as a species. According to physicist Michio Kaku, humans are the only creatures on Earth that have a concept of Tomorrow. We can run multiple simulations of reality in our head, even so much as to plan beyond our lifetimes. From that desire to look forward was borne a new genre of storytelling: Speculative Fiction. In particular Science Fiction, which under the guise of science and technology, laid the groundwork for the answers which plagued our curiosity.

The genre strived to answer the question of What If? Through the years, Science Fiction spawned a wealthy stable of notable storytellers; authors such as Mary Shelley, H.G. Wells, Jules Verne, Arthur C. Clarke, Robert Heinlein, Ray Bradbury, Phillip K. Dick, Ursula K. Le Guin, and William Gibson. Though thematically, their views and ideas differed, they all dared to look at their current state of affairs and pose the questions important to us. They sought to look beyond our today and envision a tomorrow that included the best of us, and the worst of us.

So too, does this anthology. The authors included in this book dared to dream of a future where the universe is the stage, and humans play both protagonist and antagonist. Stories that ask us to imagine a tomorrow where technology offers parents the ability to censor everything their child sees and hears. Or perhaps, an Earth inhabited by 15 billion people that have finally found a solution for population control. Or even meet a woman struggling to differentiate between her true self and personality-forming chips designed to make her the perfect actress. Would you believe that a world that created a means to condition empathy in the mind of a racist criminal is within grasp? Would you sympathize with a pleasure-model robot learning what it means to be human? This anthology is by no means a tome of things to come, but a guideline of suggestions and possible outcomes. You see, the authors in these pages are not only philosophers, dreamers, and futurists, but above all, storytellers. And these stories challenge us to gather 'round the fire, look up at the stars once again, and ponder the issues of tomorrow.

—Pedro Iniguez, Los Angeles, November 2017

FAMILY TREE

Vaughan Stanger

Originally published in *Helix* #7, 2008.

SARAH HENDERSON GROANED AS yet another round of applause echoed around the courtyard. Any moment now she would have to respond to Principal Devlin's valediction, a prospect that made her bowels squirm like a snake prodded with a stick. A quarter-century of teaching history to disinterested students at Huntsville High had been a breeze in comparison, even this morning when she struggled to keep her emotions in check.

Don't spoil things by crying now, she told herself.

Desperate for some respite from the collective gaze of her colleagues and students, Sarah glanced up at the gnarled grey boughs of the courtyard's apple tree. Blossom like pink-tinged snowflakes smothered the outer branches. Even now, she found it difficult to accept that she would not be there to collect September's first fallers.

A cough from Principal Devlin interrupted her thoughts.

"Sarah, would you like to say a few words?"

She sucked in a deep breath, knowing full well that she had no choice.

"What can I say? Time's up!" She waited several seconds for the groans to subside before continuing. "Obviously I shall miss the teaching. And I shall miss all of you." She turned around slowly, committing the scene to her memory. There were so pitifully few faces nowadays.

In truth, there was so much more she wanted to say, but no one left to say it to. Her favourite students had graduated long ago, and most of her friends amongst the staff had transferred to other, bigger schools in the faint hope of obtaining exemption from the Twenty-Five Year Rule.

"And finally, I must take this chance to thank you for the lovely present. It's just what I wanted."

Wanted or needed? Both really, she reflected.

Sarah glanced at the memory garden, which Principal Devlin had positioned well out of her reach. The mock-walnut planting tray sat upon a waist-high system box studded with data ports and sense-stream projectors. All of a sudden, she felt daunted by the goal she had set herself. Then again, she had felt George's absence more keenly today than at any time since his funeral. What better reason could there be for pressing on with her project?

After leading another round of applause, the Principal made a sign to Jeff Mancini, Huntsville High's Head of Science. He stepped forward and held both hands out to Sarah.

"I hope you don't mind," he said, "but I've taken the chance to seed your garden with a memento from your time at Huntsville High. The system is configured for public playback, so if you would like to step over here...."

Seeing Sarah frown, he hooked one arm through hers and walked her over to the memory garden.

"I'm not senile yet," she snapped, provoking mocking laughter from her colleagues and students alike.

In truth, she could not have picked a better escort than Jeff. Quintessentially tall, dark and handsome, he had the additional virtue of being seven years younger than her. More importantly, since George's death, he had been her only real friend in a staff-room made introverted by the slow but inexorable decline in student numbers. So why then had he not respected her firmly expressed wish that the memory garden should be left un-seeded?

Suppressing a sigh, she leaned over the garden and inspected its contents. A solitary seedling protruded from the synthetic loam, its stem no taller than her middle finger. At its tip, a single greenish-white bud nestled amid a cluster of leaves.

"Just bear with me for a minute," Jeff whispered. Sarah responded with an if-I-must smile. "Now Sarah," he said, his voice booming in the courtyard, "I want you to rub this leaf between your thumb and forefinger."

She complied with the obligatory smile. Intrigued despite her misgivings, she watched as the bud unfurled to reveal a tiny pink bloom, which gave off a faint aroma of apples. "Oh!" she exclaimed, secretly pleased that she had gotten off lightly. But before she could turn to thank Jeff for his discretion, a welter of sounds and images engulfed her, obscuring her view of the courtyard.

Accompanied by the fanfare from Also Sprach Zarathustra, three nervous-looking twelfth-graders climbed the flight of steps and stepped onto the stage. Jennifer Bonneville, Lawrence Garvey, and Fergal Dalton exchanged glances as the master of ceremonies began reading out their nomination. Applause echoed around the auditorium as the trio shook hands with the CEO of Virgin Lunar Corp, who gave them specks of moon-rock encased in glass, while footage of Apollo astronauts and apple trees played on the big screen.

After receiving their awards, the three students stood at the edge of the stage and waved to their parents, who were sitting in the front row. Ten rows further back, Sarah was trying to applaud while simultaneously wiping tears from her eyes.

Eighteen years had passed since Jennifer, Lawrence and Fergal won the Tom Stafford Award for outstanding scholastic achievement in the space sciences, after a four-year project that culminated in planting the first tree on the Moon.

The memory garden made it seem like yesterday.

SATISFIED WITH THE GROWTH that had occurred since she planted the seedling, Sarah rubbed the largest leaf between her thumb and forefinger. The bud adjacent to it unfurled, revealing a vivid purple flower the size of a coat-button. She leaned closer to sniff the fragrance.

She strolled past the palm trees that fringed the beach and out onto the crescent of firm, smooth sand. Overhead, cirrus clouds hazed the cobalt-blue sky. She sniffed the briny tang of the Indian Ocean. Thirty yards out, George's flippers made splashes above the coral reef...

No, no, no! Sarah smacked a fist into her palm in exasperation.

She had followed the memory garden's manual to the letter: filled the database with a cornucopia of digital photos and holo-clips, even some digital signatures of fragrances she'd collected at the time. Yet the resulting playback conveyed none of the emotional intensity of life with George. In truth, she felt like a spectator at her own honeymoon.

The fact that she had been moved to tears by Jeff's reconstruction of an event he hadn't even witnessed made her own failure so much harder to bear.

Desperate for help, she activated her holo-vid of *Cultivating Your Memories*, Julia Nelson's best-selling guide for novice memory gardeners.

"Feed your garden with data," the woman intoned as if reciting a mantra. "Fertilise it with your love..."

Sarah loathed the woman with a passion; felt her blood pressure rise whenever she saw that relentlessly beatific smile. Yet surely there must be a kernel of useful advice amongst the treacly platitudes? After all, she had wanted to plant a memory garden precisely because she agreed with Nelson's central tenet: that one's memories should become an organic part of the real world, not left to fade away in one's head.

"Embrace your emotions," chanted Nelson, holding her arms out wide as if to embrace the entire world. "Dig deep into your soul...."

Maybe that was the problem: that she didn't yet have the necessary skills to create such an intense playback. Perhaps she needed to hone her skills on something simpler first. Thinking back, hadn't she moved on rather quickly from reconstructing her first date with George?

Feeling happier now she had a plan, Sarah reached for a neighbouring seedling and pinched off the single cluster of buds, priming it for re-recording.

"Bring something of yourself," advised Julia Nelson.

Begin by viewing the raw data, Sarah reminded herself.

The broach-cam recordings showed a confident, smartly dressed man in his late-twenties, with a wild sweep of auburn hair and eyes deep as the sky, whose face radiated kindness while he guided her through the intricacies of the menu. In contrast, the restaurant's security footage, purchased the next day, revealed a petite young woman with short, dyed-blonde hair, wearing a little black dress that did nothing to flatter her figure. Watching her younger self's fumbling attempts to use chopsticks made her blush all over again. George had smiled sympathetically, assured her that everyone found chopsticks difficult at first and then showed her an easier way to hold them. He had done everything possible to put her at ease, but she had been nervousness personified that evening.

"Bring something of yourself," she echoed.

Was that what the playback needed, an injection of gut-level anxiety? Until now she had deliberately avoided the "difficult" emotions that had blighted the later years of her marriage. She had focussed exclusively on the good times, hoping that her love for George would somehow permeate the memory garden. But love had not blossomed on their first date; that had come later.

Equipped with this insight, Sarah snatched up the neural recording headband from the sofa. But before she could slip the device over her head, the door to her apartment trilled an alert. The wall-screen revealed the tanned face of Jeff Mancini. She groaned at the idea of letting him in at this critical juncture, but his many small kindnesses since George's death meant that she could hardly turn him away. Even so, she wished he had phoned ahead.

She glanced at the hall mirror to check that her appearance would pass muster. Satisfied, she tapped her broach-cam to "record" and commanded the apartment door to open. After an awkward moment when he held her proffered hand slightly too long for comfort, she led him into the kitchen, where he regaled her with school gossip while she chivvied George's antiquated coffee machine into life.

"So, what brings you here?" she asked when Jeff's stream of news finally came to an end.

He winked at her. "Just checking up on a friend."

"Oh, I'm fine," she said. "No need to be concerned."

Realising that she had handed Jeff his coffee but not invited him to sit down, she gestured towards the sofa. Other than the memory garden, which she had placed in the south-facing bay, this was now the only item of furniture in the living room. Obliged to sit next to Jeff, she felt uncomfortably aware that she had allowed him to invade her personal space.

She sipped her espresso then pursed her lips. That coffee machine needed reprogramming.

Jeff inclined his head towards the memory garden. "How's it coming?"

"Oh, you know..." She hoped he might take the hint and revert to making small talk, but when the pause threatened to become embarrassing, she added: "Just personal stuff."

His nod suggested he understood her need for privacy, but his posture was not that of someone who had just dropped by for a chat. The feeling of uncertainty made her frown.

"Did I leave something unfinished at school?"

Jeff chuckled. "No, you did an efficient job of tidying up the loose ends." He grinned at her—rather sheepishly, she thought—before continuing. "The truth is that I came here hoping to learn a bit more about your protégés—and to see you, of course."

What an odd request, thought Sarah. Surely, he had researched their history while compiling the playback?

"Didn't you look in the school archives?"

He shook his head. "A lot of data from that period is infected with pixel blight. I used most of what survived in the playback."

She found his continuing interest in what to her was ancient history baffling, but at least it meant she didn't have to distract him from her own failures.

"Well, I can fill in the back-story if you like."

Jeff's clapped his hands together. "So how did the Moon Tree Project begin?"

"Ah, that would be when I told my ninth-graders to form into groups of three and select projects from a list I'd drawn up. Each topic had something to do with the history of Huntsville High. I guessed the Appleheads would choose the Moon Tree after I observed them reading the plaque on its trunk one break-period. That seemed to excite them more than anything I'd taught them in class."

Jeff frowned at her. "Appleheads?"

"The nickname came later," she said, blushing. "My fault!"

"Pretty apt, all things considered."

She nodded then continued. "Anyway, the Appleheads produced this amazingly detailed holosim that told the story of the tree from the launch of Apollo 9 to the planting ceremony at the school." She frowned at him. "Did the blight ruin that too?"

Jeff nodded. "Afraid so."

She shook her head, appalled that the school had been so lax in protecting its digital history. Thankfully, George had insisted that she safeguarded her own data archives. Without them, her current project would have been impossible.

"Does the name Stuart Roosa mean anything to you?"

Jeff pondered her question for a moment. "Wasn't he the astronaut who flew back from the Moon on his own?"

"That's right; Roosa was command module pilot on Apollo 9. A rocket malfunction stranded Al Shepard and Jim Mitchell on the lunar surface." Sarah paused for a moment, recalling her father's hushed description of the tragedy, NASA's first. But after a ten-year moratorium, NASA returned to the Moon and built a permanent base there. Now thousands lived the frontier life, in Tycho Town and beyond.

Jeff cleared his throat. "Go on," he prompted.

"Like every Apollo astronaut, Roosa carried a personal item with him; in his case, a packet of tree seeds. He wanted to find out whether the seeds would sprout normally. He had intended to carry only forest species—Redwoods and Douglas Firs, that kind of thing—but Al' Shepard suggested he take along something homelier."

Jeff pulled a face. "Mom's apple pie?"

Sarah frowned, but she continued her account.

"On Roosa's return, NASA's scientists tested the seeds. They germinated normally. So, the seedlings were shipped out to government facilities, space research institutes, even a few schools—including Huntsville High."

"Inspirational material if you're lucky enough to have receptive students," Jeff remarked.

She could not have been luckier in that respect. Against all predictions, falling school rolls had resulted in worse behaviour not better. She did not envy Jeff.

"Go on," he prompted.

"At the climax of their presentation to the class, the Appleheads proposed planting a seedling grown from the school's apple tree on the Moon, to commemorate the Fiftieth Anniversary of the Apollo 9 tragedy. Needless to say, their fellow students ridiculed them, and my colleagues thought the idea hopelessly impractical, but I could tell the Appleheads were serious. I became their advisor. Which is when the hard work *really* began."

Jeff chuckled. "No wonder they were your favourites."

Sarah looked away from him, embarrassed by the implication that she had broken one of teaching's golden rules. She placed her empty coffee cup on the arm of the sofa and watched a series of concentric rainbow rings form around it.

"Did you see the Appleheads after graduation?" he asked.

With a sigh, she turned back to him. "Jeff, you *know* how it is. Life goes on, or rather our students do, while we stay behind to look after the next intake." She shrugged. "The Appleheads kept in touch for a year or so, but...."

Jeff held out both hands. "So why not contact them now? Surely it wouldn't be too difficult to track them down."

She dismissed his suggestion with a shake of the head. "Too much time has passed, Jeff. I have my memories of George, which I intend to cultivate." Which would keep her busy for years, judging by her progress to date.

He raised his eyebrows at her. "But there must be something more fulfilling you could do, surely?"

She shook her head. "Not for me."

They rose from the sofa together.

"See you again?" Jeff asked as she escorted him to the door. She gave a non-committal grunt.

Later, while getting ready for bed, she decided that despite his tendency to pry, Jeff meant well. And if nothing else, after his departure, she had found it no problem at all to inject some much-needed anxiety into her playback of that first date with George.

CONSCIOUS THAT SHE HAD just committed one of her most treasured memories to the memory garden, Sarah's hands trembled as she reached out to touch the trigger leaf.

Wrapped in foil that shimmered like an Amazonian butterfly, George's birthday present teased her with possibilities. She prised open the enamelled display case. Inside, a tiny fuel cell nestled on the foam inlay. She rewarded her husband with a kiss on the lips.

"You'll get the other part this evening," he said.

"I can't wait that long!"

"Well, you'll just have to."

Her skin tingled with anticipation...

Not bad, Sarah told herself; though the playback still did not quite deliver the intensity she hoped for. Mindful of Julia Nelson's advice about linking short scenes together rather than trying for a grand statement, she moved her fingers to the next leaf in the cluster.

The long wait had made her twitchy. She padded around the living room, cursing the afternoon's drowsy crawl. The two-part ploy was typical of George.

At last, the antique clock on the mantelpiece chimed Six O'clock. George strolled into the living room, clutching a bulky package.

Powered by the fuel cell, Grebo 2 chased a ping-pong ball around the living room, before pausing to wash 'his' face with careful dabs of a bent-just-so paw, purring all the while.

Giggling, she let George drag her into the master bedroom. Grebo 2 pawed at the closed door while George undressed her....

A snatch of birdsong announcing an incoming voice-call jolted Sarah from her recollection.

"Oh, for God's sake!"

She snatched her tablet from the sofa, index finger ready to stab the *dismiss* option, but some deeper instinct made her relent. After all, she hadn't spoken to anyone for several days. And this time Jeff had at least thought to call ahead.

Jeff, as usual, proffered a firm handshake and a friendly smile.

"This is for you," He waggled a jewel case between thumb and forefinger. "Delivered to the school this morning."

Sarah frowned while she fiddled with the catch. It was rare for someone to post any kind of package these days. Odd, too, that Jeff had removed the wrapping and tag before giving her the present. At least it wasn't *from* him. That would have been embarrassing.

She tipped the contents onto her upturned palm. The apple pip nestled on her lifeline like a wooden tear.

"They remembered!"

She could not imagine a more appropriate keepsake, though she felt a slight pang of disappointment that the Appleheads had not managed to deliver it in time for her retirement day. Then again, she mused, if the Appleheads hadn't known then what they evidently knew now, someone must have told them.

She frowned at Jeff. "Did I *ask* you to contact them?"

"Well...not exactly." He gave a little shake of his head as if the point was trivial. "It's just that I felt you were missing out on something important."

A wave of heat flowed up her neck and onto her cheeks. She felt like bawling Jeff out but knew that all she really wanted was for him to leave.

"Please go, Jeff."

"I'm so sorry," he said. "I didn't mean to—"

"Just go!"

The door to her apartment slammed shut with all the finality of a tiresome affair coming to an overdue end.

An hour spent working out in the gym sweated out much of her anger. She was on the point of resuming work on *Life with George* when her tablet gave another chirp.

If this was Jeff offering an apology...

The message log showed a cartoon face with three apples representing the eyes and mouth. Sarah's delight at seeing her protégés' signature for the first time in almost two decades faded somewhat when she tapped open the message. She had expected a holo-greeting; instead, she found a single line of text accompanying an executable attachment.

Program your HomeMaker with this, read the message.

Intrigued, Sarah walked into her utility room and inserted a fresh tub of nanocene into the waist-high cylinder. Seconds after loading the Appleheads' program, the unit beeped twice and expelled its creation into the collection tray. She placed the bland grey disk on the adjacent worktop. Staring at it yielded no clues to its purpose. Bemused, she turned it with her fingers. As far as she could tell, the disk served no purpose, which was not like the Appleheads at all.

She walked over to the window and raised the blinds. On the windowsill sat a tiny porcelain bowl, a present from George. Before heading for the gym, she had placed the apple pip in it. That had represented something. So, then, must the disk.

A moment later she slapped her forehead, angry with herself for doubting her favourite students. The Appleheads had often made links between seemingly unrelated things or concepts during their project. And like George, they favoured the two-part ploy.

Sarah dropped the apple pip onto the disk and watched as the surface began bubbling like overheated porridge. Within seconds, the disk had transformed itself into a miniature landscape of craters and hills. The pip had disappeared.

"Oh!" she exclaimed as a blister welled up to form a transparent dome at the centre of the disk. A greyish stalk sprouted from the base and grew branches fine as wire. Within seconds they were smothered in a blur of green.

She smiled. This was much better than a holo-greeting!

She was still composing her acknowledgement when the tablet announced the arrival of another message.

Make us too!

This time, the HomeMaker produced three tiny, space-suited figurines. Sarah placed the astronauts at the edge of the moonscape and watched, open-mouthed, as the trio bounded towards the dome. After inspecting the tree, they turned around and tipped their heads upwards, as if looking at her. Eighteen years after she'd finished teaching the Appleheads their ingenuity still astonished her. Now the figures were making beckoning motions with their arms. What could they mean by that, she wondered? She leaned closer. The beckoning continued. Not "Come closer" then.

"Join us?" she said out loud.

The astronauts lowered their arms.

Sarah's delight at solving the Appleheads' riddle turned almost immediately into exasperation. How could she, a retired teacher with only a modest pension to draw upon, possibly afford a flight to the Moon? Of course, she'd love to meet them, but the idea was absurd!

Which struck her as odd, for she could not recall a single example of the Appleheads making an absurd request during their time at Huntsville High. Challenging ones, yes, but never absurd. So, this must be a further test of *her* ingenuity. She allowed her thoughts to drift back to the glory days, hoping that her memories would stimulate some inspiration.

Eighteen years ago, she had watched the Appleheads' tree-planting ceremony via a Terabit feed hosted by a rented mining robot. So why not make a virtual visit to the Moon now? Provided, of course, that she could persuade someone to let her use Huntsville High's telepresence facility.

Sarah spent the rest of the afternoon rehearsing her vid-call to Jeff.

AFTER ONE HOUR OF practice, Sarah felt confident enough to take full control of the robot. She hardly noticed the time lag now, as she walked past the myriad craters and mounds that peppered Tycho's interior. Jeff had tried to explain how the computer generated a lag-compensated view, but she dismissed his lecture with a breezy "I'll take your word for it!" Not long afterward, he had made his excuses and left.

She hoped Jeff realised just how much she appreciated his assistance, which he had offered without hesitation the moment she finished her apology. Principal Devlin had helped too, by making Huntsville High's telepresence facility available to her on the day chosen by the Appleheads.

The per-minute rate for hiring a walking robot ensured that she felt no inclination to dawdle, despite the impressive view of Tycho's central peak. Anyway, she had seen it two decades ago, during her first virtual tour. As she pressed on towards her destination, less than half a mile distant now, she continuously swivelled the robot's upper torso, panning twin clusters of spotlights over the ash-grey terrain. Several minutes had passed before she noticed a flash of light off to her left. A short walk brought her to the metal-and-glass hemisphere, which a trio of rented mining robots had constructed from locally processed regolith. Nearby stood the array of floodlights that had supplied artificial sunshine through the long lunar night. Modulating the opacity of the dome itself had turned day into night on a twenty-four-hour cycle.

The scene within matched Sarah's memory: a skeleton of an apple tree no taller than her, the tips of its branches almost touching the dome. Every leaf had turned brown and fallen during a single day, three months after the planting ceremony. Their brittle remains still carpeted the floor, forming a shroud for the robotic bees that had pollinated the blossoms. Three apples had dangled from the highest branch for one further day before they too succumbed to gravity. No one involved in the project, not even the Appleheads, had expected the tree to survive a month, never mind long enough to bear fruit.

So where were the Appleheads now? Having proposed the plan, it was, to say the least, uncharacteristic of them not to keep to it. Sarah found herself wishing that she'd asked Jeff to stay.

Finally, just as the escalating rental cost had started to outweigh her desire to see the Appleheads again, she spotted a pair of lights emerging from behind a low ridge, halfway to the foreshortened horizon. The vehicle, which sported a colour scheme reminiscent of a Huntsville school bus, bounced over the bumpy terrain on its sextet of balloon tyres, heading straight for the dome. As soon as the 'bus' had parked up, she jogged her robot over to its near side. Her stomach felt as if it had been colonised by moths while she waited for the airlock to cycle. Finally, the indicator turned green, the hatch swung open, and three diminutive figures jumped down onto the surface.

The Appleheads had sent their children!

Frustration instantly tempered her joy, for she knew of no way to make her robot smile. She settled instead for waving both hands. The tallest of the child-astronauts responded by indicating the recessed steps leading up to the airlock. After two abortive attempts to climb them, Sarah disengaged from the link and let her escorts take over. It felt odd watching from afar while someone else manipulated *her* robot. She re-linked as soon as the junior Appleheads had manoeuvred it into a sitting position on one of the cabin's metal-and-webbing seats. The audio channel began relaying chatter the instant they removed their helmets.

"Hi, I'm Sarah," she said. After a short delay, she heard her own voice boom in the cabin.

The children exchanged glances then huddled for a whispered discussion of tactics. Finally, the boy looked up and smiled at her.

"I'm Danny."

"It's lovely to meet you, Danny."

"And I'm Mary," announced the older girl.

"...you Danny," the comms channel echoed.

Sarah tried again. "It's lovely to meet you *all*, but—"

"...Joy," chipped in the younger girl, smiling shyly.

"—It might be easier if we took turns."

"And we're the Appleheads too!" chorused the children.

"...took turns."

Sarah sighed; it was in situations like this that the time lag really hurt. Predictive compensation worked wonders with the view as one moved through the scenery, but could do nothing to disentangle a conversation hobbled by c.

The robot's emulation of her rueful shake of the head provoked laughter from the children. She raised a finger to her 'lips.' The trio gazed at her, their expressions expectant. What could she interest them with?

Aware that the children had just removed their gloves, she flexed the robot's titanium digits and signed "hello," waited a beat then spoke the word. She had learned sign language while teaching a profoundly deaf student at Huntsville High. Initially, her gestures prompted frowns from the junior Appleheads, but they soon proved themselves every bit as quick on the uptake as their parents. After ten minutes they could recognise twice that many words, whereupon they began inventing their own. As far as she could tell, their conversation centred on the curious behaviour of their new acquaintance. Sarah smiled, happy to be an observer for the time being.

The slender, fair-haired girl, Joy, looked to have just turned eight, Sarah decided, while her darker, bossy-acting sister, Mary, seemed a couple of years older. Danny, the fidgeting, tousle-haired boy, had to be at least eleven, maybe twelve. But would Earth standards apply to children born in one-sixth gee?

"Home again," Danny announced as the bus pitched downwards onto a steep ramp.

Sarah closed her eyes and gulped down hard, desperate not to puke. When she opened her eyes again, she looked through the port and saw rough-hewn rock walls illuminated by regularly spaced strip-lights. Shortly after the tunnel levelled out, the bus applied its brakes and shuddered to a halt. A heavy clumping sound announced the joining of two airlocks. Mindful of her previous problems, Sarah let the children guide her robot out of the vehicle. She re-linked the moment they emerged into an equipment-choked antechamber.

Watching the children divest themselves of their spacesuits, Sarah felt a disorienting urge to do the same. A glance down at her 'feet' brought home the strangeness of her situation.

When the children were ready, she followed them into a much larger room, which was brightly lit, devoid of furniture and carpeted with grass. Trellises festooned with vines and runner beans covered three of the walls. A dwarf apple tree stood in one corner, thriving despite the absence of natural light. Sarah had just finished admiring its blossom when Jennifer, Lawrence, and Fergal walked into the room.

Jennifer stepped forward with one hand held out in greeting, the other lifted above her head to ward off collisions with the ceiling. She grasped the robot's right hand and waggled it up and down. Sarah laughed in a way that seemed to roll back the years.

"It's lovely to see you again, Jennifer."

After a short delay: "You too, Sarah."

Sarah noticed that Jennifer still tilted her head to one side when she spoke, just like at Huntsville High. Sadly, the effect was greatly diminished now that a grey-flecked buzz-cut had replaced her chestnut curls. Her face, too, bore the harsh imprint of the frontier life: wrinkles like crazy paving, blotches like sunspots; the legacy of too much time spent topside.

Now Fergal stepped forward. "Thanks for dropping by."

Despite his lightness of tone, Fergal's expression hinted at serious business to come. That was typical of him, Sarah recalled. The children appeared to have inherited his penetrating gaze, as well as his wiry build. Then again, how could she know for sure who was father to whom?

Jennifer looked abashed as if she had managed to read Sarah's thoughts despite the robot's blank expression. Not that Sarah disapproved. The Appleheads had evidently pooled their genes to the best possible effect. She envied them their success. Families with three children were almost unheard-of on Earth. Sarah would gladly have settled for one.

"You were always so close," she remarked.

Lawrence made an unsuccessful attempt to snare all three children as he stepped forward. Danny snorted as he squirmed out of his father's clutches. One of the girls pinched her sister's arm, Sarah noticed, receiving a slap in return.

Shorter in stature than his partners but more heavily built, Lawrence had lent a powerful physical presence to the Appleheads during their student years. Whenever there was a difficult request to make, Lawrence stepped forward. That he did so now reminded Sarah that the Appleheads had not invited her to the Moon simply to admire their children.

"Life in Tycho Town is hard," he said. "Teaching our children takes time we cannot spare and skills we haven't got. They receive tele-lessons from Earth, of course, but it's not the same. What they need is a *real* teacher." He held out his hands, imploring her. "Believe me, this bunch needs the best there is."

Sarah stood in silence for several seconds, too stunned to respond. When, finally, she felt calm enough to speak, all she could think of were objections.

"I'm too old."

"Nonsense, there are older people than you living on the Moon," said Lawrence.

"I'm nowhere near fit enough!"

"Your medical records show that your health is excellent, your fitness well above average."

Though not greatly surprised, Sarah felt a pang of annoyance that the Appleheads had cracked the encryption.

"Won't I have to endure months of training?"

"More like a fortnight. And we survived it."

"But I couldn't *possibly* afford to emigrate!"

"Virgin Lunar Corp will sponsor you, provided you're willing to sign a contract giving them exclusive rights to broadcast your lessons for two years."

Sarah did not doubt that the Appleheads could counter every objection she raised. Yet there was one problem they knew nothing about, could *do* nothing about.

She made the robot shake its head.

"YOU DID *WHAT?*"

Sarah had never heard Jeff so angry.

"I..."

Lost for words, she stared at the walls, at the floor, anywhere but his face.

"You've just turned down the offer of a lifetime!"

Faced with such a display of exasperation, she found herself wondering whether there was more to his involvement than met the eye. Not that it mattered; the deal had never been on, whatever the

Appleheads might have thought, whatever Jeff might have hoped. She risked a glance at his face; read dismay in his eyes, anger in the curve of his mouth.

"I've made my decision," she said. "If it takes me years to achieve perfect playbacks, so be it. That's the task I've set myself, and I intend to see it through."

"But Sarah, teaching is your vocation."

"I've retired!"

"Sarah, you were *forced* into retirement—and now you've been offered the perfect opportunity to resume your career." He held out his hands as if grabbing an invisible reward. 'The Appleheads' children need a teacher now, while there's still time to make a difference. They can't wait for you to finish your garden."

"You think I'm wasting my life, don't you?"

He nodded. "Why devote the rest of it to remembering a dead man, however wonderful the time you spent together?"

She tapped a forefinger against her temple. "Because George isn't dead, not up here."

"And that's where he's supposed to be." He jerked a hand towards the memory garden. "Not recreated in this glorified cabbage patch!"

Fearing that Jeff might destroy her precious seedlings, Sarah stepped between him and the garden. Standing there, she felt an overwhelming urge to shove him out of her life, once and for all.

"Please leave."

She took a step towards Jeff, leaving him no choice but to back off. Then she repeated the move, forcing him out of the living room and into the hallway.

He gazed at her, a pleading look in his eyes.

"I think you're making a terrible mistake."

She folded her arms. "If so, it's mine to make."

She commanded the door to open and closed it behind him before he had finished his sigh.

Free at last.

"SO, SHALL WE?"

"Shall we what?"

"You know what I'm talking about!" She let her fingers snag his pubic hair; then she pulled, none too gently.

"Oh, you mean make a baby!" Saucer eyes, like a child. *George rolled over, turning his muscular back away from her. She knew he was teasing like a perfect husband should. She punched him playfully.*

"Make me pregnant, dammit!"

His shoulders were shaking.

"If you won't, I'll find someone who will!" She tugged hard at his shoulder, rolling him over. Expecting laughter, she was shocked to find tears welling up in his eyes....

"No, no, no!"

This playback was supposed to have recreated the most blissful night of passion of her life. She had just got back together with George after a six-month separation. All had been smiles and forgiveness. So how come he ended up crying? That hadn't happened in real life.

She slipped the neural recorder over her head and tried to focus on her memories of their lovemaking.

She tugged hard at his shoulder, rolling him over....

"What's wrong, dear?"

"There's something I haven't told you."

Wrong, wrong, wrong!

Now he was on the brink of telling her the worst news she would ever hear. But that hadn't happened until three years later....

Reset and start again!

Rage burned in her heart. She felt betrayed.

"You idiot! You fuck-witted, stiff-upper-lipped idiot of an Englishman! Why the hell didn't you report the symptoms earlier?"

Reset, dammit!

"How long?"

"Nine months. Perhaps a year, if I'm lucky."

"Isn't there anything they can do?"

He shook his head. "They can kill the pain..."

Sarah slumped onto the sofa, unable to carry on. Frustration made her pound the nearest cushion until rings of crimson appeared.

The fertility treatment George had undergone seemed unexceptional at the time. No one had anticipated the virulent form of testicular cancer that would afflict one-third of those treated, four or five years down the line. The cancer had to be caught early if there was to be a realistic chance of survival. Few reported it in time. That George was just one of thousands caught up in a medical tragedy had made things even worse for Sarah—had made him seem less special somehow.

During the final months, tumours sprang up throughout his body like weeds after a summer storm. The drugs did indeed kill the pain, but they also numbed his mind. The man she loved had faded out of her life long before he died.

She had pounded the furniture back then, too; imagined herself punching the face of the consultant who had recommended the fertility treatment. But mostly she had berated herself for wanting children so desperately it had cost her husband his life.

And now those emotions had welled up out of her memory, enabling her to create, albeit inadvertently, a playback that truly reflected how she felt at the time. Not even the playback of her first date with George had come close to achieving such emotional fidelity.

The truth was that life with George had been far from perfect. How could she forget the bruising fights followed by days of festering silence? Or the time he had hurled a chair through the bedroom window, crushing to death a kitten called Grebo. Worst of all had been his late-night confession that he had slept with her best friend.

She had tried so hard to forget the bad times by focussing exclusively on the good, but her subconscious had found her out. No wonder her other playbacks felt so insipid.

Jeff had been right; it was time to move on.

But first, she had one last playback to prepare.

"ARE YOU *SURE* YOU want to go through with this?" asked Jeff.

"This is something I have to do," Sarah replied. "But I can't do it on my own."

The first time had been difficult enough.

"I really don't know if..." Jeff held her gaze for a moment as if verifying her sincerity. Finally, he gave a nod. "Okay. What do you want me to do?"

"Just be here for me."

She pointed out the seedling she had planted yesterday. Holding hands, they rubbed the largest leaf in unison. A tiny bud unfurled a flower with alternating black and white petals.

Her hands trembled as she placed the script on the lectern. George's father had offered to read the elegy, but she'd refused. Standing there, she found herself able to stifle her tears but not the inconvenient memories. Could she really tell his friends and relatives, even an ex-lover sat two rows from the back, the truth about life with George?

No, of course, she couldn't. A funeral was no place for the truth.

She sniffed heavily then cleared her throat. "I don't know about you," she said, "but I've always had trouble with chopsticks...."

Afterward, Jeff continued to hold her hand while she recounted her memories of George. Finally, when the flow had subsided, Jeff said, "He was a good man."

"No, Jeff," she said. "George was every kind of man: a deceitful bastard, but wonderful in bed; a present-buying genius, but a fool to himself. I experienced the good *and* the bad of him." She paused for a moment to wipe away a tear. "But I loved him *so* much."

They sat in silence for a while.

"I should go," Jeff said at last.

"And so should I," she responded.

"To the Moon?"

She smiled at him and nodded. "And you?"

He let out a sigh. "I turned down their offer."

Which confirmed her guess about the final element of the Appleheads' plan. Jennifer, Lawrence, and Fergal would be displeased with the outcome, for they were used to getting their way. Their children would surely be no different.

"Why did you do that?"

"Because I really don't think we're ready for each other."

And nor in truth, did she. But perhaps a little space and time would see to that.

"How long does their offer stand?"

Jeff grinned. "Best ask them that when you get there."

SARAH RAISED HER LEFT arm as she waddled out of the Induction Centre. A glance up at the ceiling revealed generous padding, making the Mitchell Dome's reception area less of a hazard to newbies than elsewhere in Tycho Town. Plus, she was wearing sticky-boots. Still, it was good to know that a fortnight of intensive training had rewired her instincts appropriately.

Feeling sheepish, she lowered her arm and waved to the Appleheads, who were just getting up from the floor cushions they had been lounging upon. She noticed the children signing to each other. Teaching them would be rewarding, though doubtless challenging too.

"Better late than never," said Mary, last to stand up.

Sarah made a play of glancing back over her shoulder then grinned at the girl. "I thought they'd never let me out!"

"Well, we're delighted to see you," said Jennifer.

"And we have something for you," announced Joy, wrestling a foil-wrapped box half as big as her across the floor.

Sarah felt a little awkward at receiving a welcoming present. The gift-wrapping alone would cost a small fortune in Tycho Town.

"Thank you, Joy. That's very sweet of you."

"It's not from us," said Danny, smirking.

Sarah cast an enquiring glance at each of the parents, but no one would hold her gaze.

"Oh," she said, blushing.

"Please open it," begged Joy.

"You might as well," said Fergal. "Seeing as how you've signed away your rights to privacy."

Sarah knew that Fergal didn't just mean the sponsorship deal. Singletons bunked eight to a room in Tycho Town.

It seemed she had no choice.

Ignoring the tag, for she knew who had written it, she peeled off the foil and passed it to Joy. The girl beamed at her. Sarah felt every bit as child-like as she removed the grey plastic hemisphere from the carton. Unable to kneel because of her boots, she squatted on her haunches while fiddling with the catch. When she swung the dome back on its hinge, she gasped with surprise. Inside stood the smallest apple tree she had ever seen.

Sarah rubbed each leaf in turn, eager to find the one that Jeff had primed. Finally, a pinhead-sized bud unfurled, revealing a tiny white blossom. She leaned closer, sniffed a medley of scents: Roses, champagne, and then something musty.... Was that sweat?

Jostling a pair of cambots aside, he pressed his face against the Departures barrier at Mojave Spaceport, misting the glass with his breath, desperately hoping for one last glimpse of the woman he loved.

There she was!

Please turn...

She turned and smiled, then waved and blew him a kiss.

Not really a farewell, then.

Seeing things from another person's viewpoint provided insights you'd never obtain from your own, Sarah realised. Composting her memory garden had been the right thing to do. Huntsville High would doubtless make good use of it.

"Are you okay, Sarah?"

Sarah looked up at Jennifer. "I'm fine," she said.

Turning to the children, she said, "Come on you lot, collect your friends. Classes begin in ten minutes."

A school for nine children, run by a pensioned-off history teacher, aided and abetted by a pair of media-bots. It wasn't much of a start, but she liked to think that tall trees grew from small seedlings.

A humanoid robot halted nearby, its tri-D lenses zooming in on her. She smiled for her audience on Earth.

"Can anyone guess the subject of my first class?"

She let them ponder that while she made her way, one snagged step after another, along the corridor leading to Shepard Dome. When the door to her new school clicked open, she held Jeff's present up to the robot's "eyes."

"I think we'll begin with apple trees."

THE END

FORMERLY AN ASTRONOMER AND more recently a research project manager in an aerospace company, VAUGHAN STANGER now writes SF and fantasy fiction for a living, making his home in Brentwood, Essex, United Kingdom. His stories have appeared in *Daily Science Fiction*, *Abyss & Apex*, *Postscripts*, *Nature Futures*, and *Interzone*, amongst others. Follow his writing adventures at http://www.vaughanstanger.com or @VaughanStanger.

ONE STORY SHORT
Gustavo Bondoni

Originally published in *Mindflights* 2008.

THE AGENT SQUIRMED SELF-CONSCIOUSLY under Vaidal's withering look. The usually mild-mannered editor was, for the first time since the two had met, furious.

"This is awful. Not only is it just like the story you sent me for the last issue, it's also just like the other seven stories I already have for this month's Digest. What the *hell* is going on in this business? Isn't anyone writing original fiction anymore?"

"I'm sorry," said the agent. "We'll rework it and have it back by Wednesday. Still plenty of time before the deadline."

"No. I don't want it. Sell it to somebody else."

"But Jacan is one of the most respected robots in the field. His name on the cover will help you sell more magazines."

"What will help me sell more magazines is for someone to send me an original story. Something different!" fumed Vaidal.

The agent, a seasoned salesman, let him finish, took a deep breath and resumed the onslaught.

"Look, my client has just had his software updated to get the latest Human Psych programs. His handling of suspense and emotional response has tested off the charts in all our consumer surveys. There is nobody currently in the field who can write better stories. I just don't see the problem."

"The problem is that every other robot who has enough money saved up and chooses to invest it in the Writing and Psych updates can turn out prose at exactly the same level. And they are. The plots are similarly put together once you get past the superficial differences, no matter what the software promises about "randomized creativity." I want something *different*. Take it away, and don't come back next month unless you have something worth my time."

"We'll file a grievance…"

"Go ahead," said Vaidal. "It doesn't say anywhere that I *have* to buy your stuff."

"But we've been working together for years!"

"So, bring me good stuff, and I'll happily buy it from you."

The agent departed, puzzled, angry, and more than a little worried.

"Next!" shouted Vaidal, caught in the rush. But there were no more agents in the waiting room. His assistant's aluminum-alloy head appeared in the doorway.

"Er… That was the last one, sir," she said.

"What do you mean, the last one? I'm still a story short!"

Jenny cringed, which made Vaidal shudder. It never ceased to shock him when he saw a robot react with fear (or with love, anger or any other emotion). He had just never managed to come to grips with the ever-expanding range of "human" emotions that they had been programmed within the last few years, as the tech got better.

It wasn't that he had anything against robots. On the contrary. He'd been too young to vote when the referendum to make them independent beings as opposed to human property went through, but had made up for it by voting in favor of increased robotic rights every time after that. Unrestricted access to all human areas. The right to work for a wage. The right to own property. The right to vote. The right to obtain advanced emotional programming. And, finally, the big one: full citizenship on an equal basis with humans. It had been a long process, but he'd been there all the way.

Moreover, as a member of the business community, he was euphoric that all the reforms had gone through. After all, the human population had been decreasing steadily for decades and were it not for the new citizens and their newly earned money the entire economy would have faltered.

But it was still hard for him, on an emotional level, to accept them as sentient beings. Sure, every test that mankind had been able to devise had shown that they were self-aware. But didn't that just mean that they'd reached the point where they were complex enough to react to different stimuli in such a way as to fool the tests? Did any amount of intelligence or programming for emotions really make them *alive*?

"Sir, are you all right?"

He started. "Just thinking that I'm too old for this job." For this *world*, he also admitted, but only to himself.

"Nonsense. Everybody knows that the reason both our magazine and anthologies are at number one is because of you."

"Hah, that's a laugh. Every top publication is buying stories from the same ten robots, the ones that have been successful enough to get the upgrades. Sales are due more to the great job done by the circulation manager, or maybe just dumb luck, than anything I can do."

The look she gave him would, in a human, been one of impatience mixed with amusement. How she managed to convey this with immobile metallic features (he fervently hoped that she would never decide to go with one of the new "emotion reflections" screen faces, or, even worse, artificial skin) he couldn't say. Maybe it was the angle at which she held her head. But, however she did it, the emotion came through loud and clear.

"You *choose* better stories and ask for better rewrites, that's the secret."

He shrugged.

"Anyway," he said, "we're still a story short, and I've told every one of the big guys who aren't in yet to bugger off. What can I do? It would be really unprofessional of me to accept a story that I don't think is good enough."

"How about the slushpile?"

"Huh?"

"You know, the unsolicited submissions that come in through our Mindnet site."

Vaidal gave her a sour look. "I know what a slushpile is. It's only that we're not supposed to have one. Our Mindnet site makes it very clear that we do *not* accept unsolicited work." The reason for this was simple: most of the unsolicited material came from robots who hadn't gotten the latest upgrades and therefore was of measurably inferior quality. These robo-writers could usually find a place in a slightly lower echelon and, in time, might be able to save up enough to get upgraded to the top tier. It was difficult, as the target was always moving, but not impossible—and recently upgraded writers were always carefully and conscientiously reviewed by all the major editors. The system sometimes made Vaidal's life harder than it would otherwise be, but both readers and industry benefited from it.

"Well, sir, *I've* been reading the slush," said Jenny.

"What for? You've been in this business long enough to know that the upgrades make for measurably better audience reception. It's not really any use to read the slush from lesser robots."

"Of course not. That's why I only read slush sent in by humans."

"That's ridiculous. Humans can't write." Of course, humans *could* write, it was just that the combination of psych programming plus writing programming had surpassed anything that could be created by a mere human nearly thirty years before, and without any unpredictability or massive variations in quality. Stories written by robots were safer, always well received, and sold literary magazines. The proof was that the magazines with human-produced content had long since been beaten back by the robot-written ones.

"Well, I read it anyway. You never know where genius might pop up."

Vaidal was stunned. He had never suspected Jenny of this kind of proactive thinking. Or of the ambition that obviously had to be the motive.

"So, have you found anything worth printing?" Vaidal asked. He already suspected the answer; she wouldn't have brought it up otherwise.

"Yes, I do. It's the first time in my three years of reading slush that I've come across something I believe to be worthy of the magazine. It arrived a couple of months ago, but I sat on it, waiting for a time at which we needed a story." Vaidal could tell that she'd wanted to bring it in earlier. Damn. Robots aren't *supposed* to be afraid of things. That's one of the main reasons you hired them!

He sighed. "Okay, let me see it."

VAIDAL PUT THE MANUSCRIPT back on the desk. Jenny had waited anxiously while he read through the whole thing.

"Well, it's certainly different, I'll give you that much," he said.

"That's good, right? It's what you wanted?"

"Well, I'm not sure. I mean the story is unusual in the extreme, and there's a strange structure in a sentence on page eight."

"That's a grammatical error. I checked it with my program. We'll have to fix it before we publish," said Jenny.

"A grammatical error," Vaidal chuckled. "I *am* getting older. It's been years since I last corrected one. Robots don't make mistakes, and I guess I've gotten used to the status quo. Still, one error isn't too bad. Human's aren't perfect, after all, and the rest of the piece looks all right."

"But do you think it's good enough to print?"

"It's a bit strange. Do you really think a human would ever feel that way about a robot? I've never seen a plot like that one before. And the suspense is uneven, not the standard build-up to a crescendo that makes you want to keep reading; it seems to peak at two different points in the story. Also, the end was a bit ambiguous. I'm not sure that our readers will appreciate it if we leave them thinking about the story for two weeks after reading it, do you?"

Jenny said nothing, but Vaidal thought that her attitude said guilt. *Damn* these robots that acted like college kids!

"Spill it," he said gruffly.

"Well, this is a bit embarrassing," she said, "but I thought it was brilliant. Much better than the stuff we usually print. I'm sorry." She hung her head.

"So, you would run the piece?"

"Yes," she replied. "After all, we have seven conventional pieces, and this one is only three thousand words. If we print it in the next-to-last slot, most people won't even notice. How big can the risk possibly be?"

Vaidal thought it over. He wasn't in love with the story, but it certainly *was* a breath of fresh air. And after ten years of choosing the best from an endless series of nearly identical stories, he was ready to rebel.

"You'd better be right," he growled, meant more for show than as a real threat, and signed off on the story.

THE HATE MAIL STARTED pouring in through the Mindnet about ten seconds after the issue was released.

One reader would never buy the *Digest* again, another said he would, but only if an apology was issued and the editor removed. The story was lambasted as preposterous. Unreal. Mere fantasy, and fantasy in bad taste, at that. It was obscene.

Vaidal knew that his days as editor-in-chief were numbered, but at least he'd gone down on his own terms. Anyhow, it wasn't an irreparable loss and that the publicity might actually bring a boost in circulation, although that was a long shot, considering the outraged nature of some of the letters.

Inevitably, the mainstream media picked up on the situation. Three days after the launch of the issue, the story had made it onto the homepage of all the major Mindnet sites. Vaidal knew it would only be there a couple of hours before the next big news took over, but the damage had been done. Even Jenny, who sometimes had trouble understanding the nuances of human office politics seemed to be staying out of his way.

Less than an hour later, he was called by headquarters. A real call, not a Mindnet memo. Max Zennet wanted to see him immediately.

Fortunately, headquarters building, known affectionately as "the tower of pain" was just across Digest Square, so Vaidal's imagination didn't have time to run wild. He was prepared to fall on his sword but wanted to do so with as much dignity as possible.

After security waved him through, he was put on the express lift to the top floor, which contained Max's office. Or, more accurately, which *was* Max's office.

Wood pancling, panoramic view, enormous desk. The works. It was almost never good news to be here, but it *was* a great looking office. Max himself was standing at the bar to the left of the elevator, mixing a drink in a tall glass.

"Ah, Vaidal. What'll you have?" Max was a portly, graying man in a pinstriped shirt and suspenders but, surprisingly, no tie.

"I'm fine, thanks," Vaidal said, waving off the drink. He wanted to get this over with as quickly as possible, and stood awkwardly, trying not to fidget, while Max finished mixing.

"Sit, sit," said Max, waving at one of the chairs in front of the desk. He sat behind it with his legs crossed, took a sip and studied Vaidal for a few moments.

"I assume you know why I called you in."

"The Mindnet pages," said Vaidal.

"Precisely. I got a heads-up twenty minutes ago and I decided to look a little more closely into that magazine you're running. I don't usually do this, since I have, at last count, a hundred and eighteen media companies that I have to run from this office. But for you, I made an exception."

Vaidal said nothing. The end would come soon enough. He only hoped he would be allowed to resign.

"And I must say that, in the quick view of sales that I've seen, I was a bit surprised. Do you mind telling me what's going on?" asked Max.

"We ran a story by a human author, sir. Public reaction to it was very, very bad. I'm sure you've seen the letters."

"I don't have time to read letters, and besides, they're letters to the editor. You're the editor, so you can deal with the letters. What concerns me are the sales numbers. Could you enlighten me?"

"I'm sorry. The editors receive the sales numbers on a weekly basis, so I haven't seen them yet. I assume, however, that you've spotted a drop in sales or the cancellation of subscriptions. That would seem to be in line with the feedback I've received."

Max looked at him and chuckled.

"You think I brought you in here to fire you, don't you?" Max said, laughing hard now. He passed Vaidal the sales printout that had been lying on the desk.

Vaidal resisted the urge to storm out in indignation and picked the sheets up. He was familiar with the format, as it was the same as that which he received for his weekly perusal. Quickly, he scanned the numbers until he got to that month's issue.

No, that can't be right, he thought. He looked at the sheet again, convinced that he had the wrong row or column, or that the format was different from his usual sheet after all. But no.

"I'm sorry, sir. There must be something wrong with these numbers. They indicate that we sold out our entire print run in the first three days. That's just impossible."

"The numbers are fine. I just got off the line with Irene at the plant. She tells me that the plant is out of copies. I took the liberty of ordering a second run, I hope that's okay?"

Vaidal just nodded dumbly.

Max continued. "You have no idea why this happened, do you?"

"No sir, we weren't expecting such a strong reaction either way when we published the story. And it must be something to do with the story, that much I'm certain of." He thought about it a minute. "Maybe it's just the ghouls? They hear about something that's supposed to be rotten, so they buy the magazine out of morbid curiosity?"

"Could be. Or it could be something else. I need you to find out and bring me a recommendation as to how we can make it happen in all our magazines, and if we can expand the model to our Mindnet broadcasts, which have been getting blown out of the water by the Australians. Use whatever resources you need. Are you up to it?

Again, Vaidal just nodded, not trusting himself to speak.

THE TWO DAYS FOLLOWING the meeting with Max had been exhausting. In addition to their regular workload, Jenny and Vaidal had been rushed around from focus group to focus group. How the research department had managed to put them together on such short notice, Vaidal didn't know, but Max had been true to his word. Everything Vaidal had requested was immediately granted.

Unfortunately, none of his groups had given him a single clue as to what was going on. He hoped Jenny had had better luck. She was late for their meeting, maybe she'd had to do a follow-up interview?

When she finally did arrive, one look was enough to dash any hopes Vaidal might have had. She projected an air of dejection that would have been unmistakable even on a less expressive robot.

"No luck?" he asked.

"Nothing. The people we interviewed basically fell into two camps. Those who normally buy the magazine and are uninterested in continuing to do so unless we return to our usual standards, and that great majority who never buy the *Digest* and aren't really interested in buying it for one sordid story. They say they can get their filth for free off the Mindnet if they happen to want any."

"The story wasn't even dirty. It was just different. More of an exploration of a possibility than anything else," sighed Vaidal.

"That's the whole point. It's no longer about the story. Most people haven't read it and never will. They just don't care."

"So, it isn't the ghoul market making the purchases. At least we can cross out that option. But then, who the hell *is* it? *I'm* certainly not doing it!" said Vaidal. Jenny laughed, a tinkling, metallic sound.

"Me neither. Anyway, this is just the qualitative data. The Research people are crunching the numbers on our survey results. It might be the ghouls after all," she said.

"Wanna bet?"

"No way. I'm with you on this one. I don't think it's the ghouls either."

"Well, we'll have the numbers on Monday. Have a nice weekend," said Vaidal.

"You too." She waved and left.

"Yeah right. Like I'm going to get any sleep this weekend," he grumbled to himself.

VAIDAL WAS IN THE office an hour early on Monday morning. He wasn't surprised to find the research department empty since they had no reason to be there at eight o'clock. Hell, he was only there because he hadn't been able to sleep all weekend. It wasn't only the mystery of the missing magazine buyers that had kept him awake, but something he'd seen at a party on Friday.

The head waiter at the party had been a robot, which, in itself, was nothing unusual. What *was* unusual was that the under-waiters were a mixed team composed of humans and robots. Vaidal, having observed the actions of his own assistant—and the subsequent events—spent the evening watching the interaction among the waiters. The first thing that struck him was how the human waiters didn't hesitate before asking the head robot for his opinion. He also noticed that none of them showed signs of anger when chastised by the leader, even when the robot himself showed signs of anger.

The fact that the human waiters were young—the oldest seemed to be of about college age—reinforced Vaidal's feeling that things had really changed. His own generation hadn't hesitated to employ robots in non-leadership roles, and they'd slowly become accustomed to their new hardworking, honest co-workers. That robots seemed to universally lean towards cautious good sense and could acquire university-level proficiency in any subject simply by uploading the relevant programs was also seen as a plus. Nobody felt threatened by them because they weren't truly good at working outside their programming, which meant that anything unexpected normally managed to defeat them. There weren't enough humans to fill most jobs, anyway.

But, watching the headwaiter, Vaidal felt that here was a robot that could and did deal with a constantly changing environment. And the humans in the team expected him to lead. When had *this* happened? When had programming complexity managed to overcome every robot's innate caution—the very caution that made them refrain from offering opinions and making decisions? When had robots evolved to the point where they could make, apparently successful selections in the realm of art, as Jenny had done? It had obviously happened, and he had failed to notice.

It was these questions that had kept him awake most of the weekend and had gotten him to the office an hour ahead of time. Fortunately, he would not have to brood much longer, because he saw that lights were going on in other offices.

When Research finally arrived, and handed him a manila folder and a memdrive, he exercised superhuman self-control and took his treasures back to his office to open them. The truth was that he was certain they contained no useful information, and he didn't want the research department to see him cry.

It was a good thing, too. The numbers clearly showed, at a confidence level of 99% that not one additional percentage point of sales had come from the average people tested. And they represented four-fifths of the human population.

So, who did that leave? The very rich? The very poor?

"Robots!" The voice, Jenny's, tore him from his thoughts as she barged through the door. "Robots have been buying the extra copies."

"What? Robots don't buy magazines. Their scan velocity makes the Mindweb a full-reality experience for them. Why would they want to slow down and *read*? And pay money to do it, too."

"It's that story. They'd never even heard of anything like it before. It has raw emotion, not the subtle psych stuff that makes up most web content. It's much more basic than what the robot writers write for humans, you see. Basic enough that our emotional programming is receptive to it. Basic enough to *overload* our programs."

"So, you're saying that robots can write subtle emotional plots for humans, but can only truly comprehend emotion on a more basic level?"

"Exactly."

Vaidal was at a complete loss for words. He just stared at her. Finally, he managed to organize his thoughts.

"And raw emotion at this level is even better for you than Mindnet immersion?"

Jenny shrugged, "Most Mindnet content is generated by robots. If it wasn't a full mind experience, it would be just as unsatisfying for us as robot-generated text."

"But how did you ever find out?"

"I was at a scramble on Saturday night. We discussed it there."

"What's a scramble?"

Jenny looked slightly uncomfortable. "We don't usually discuss it with humans because they never understand." Seeing that he wasn't impressed by this, she went on, "A scramble is simply a group of robots. We sit together in a circle and remove ourselves from the Mindnet. Then we use normal data cables and plug ourselves into each other, lower all our firewalls, and share all our data in an uncontrolled storm. Complete mind melding."

"What for?"

"It feels good. Your brain feels four, or five, or however many participants you have in the circle, times bigger. It's like you can fly. And you know things you never knew before. The only downside is that you can never remember all the data since it would take up too much space. And afterwards, you don't really know who you are for a couple of hours. But it's worth it."

Vaidal gave her a wide-eyed stare. "Is that even legal?"

"Don't be such a prude," she laughed. "Why would it be illegal? It doesn't hurt anyone or harm anything. And besides, that's how I found out about the sales. Seems that three of the robots in the circle had read the story, and the rest were angry at us for being out of stock."

"We have more issues due to arrive about noon."

"Good. How many?"

"Max ordered about twice our normal circulation."

"Get more," said Jenny.

"What do you mean, more? Why?"

"Do you know how many robots there are on this planet?"

"Half a billion or so."

"Well, I've been asking around on the Mindnet, and a lot of them want to buy the magazine."

Something about the way she said that made Vaidal suspicious.

"When you say a lot—"

"All of them."

"Are you sure?"

"Trust me."

Vaidal looked at her, just for a moment wondering how much of this had been an accident. And then wondering further if it was a planet-wide conspiracy of robots trying to nudge things in their direction, but managed to get a hold of himself. He was being paranoid and had spent the whole weekend being paranoid, probably because Jenny's emotional programming was getting to him. Robots didn't do that sort of thing. And they always stayed out of office politics. It's why you hired them in the first place.

He sighed, under control again.

"Can you excuse me a minute? I need to make a call." His fingers were shaking uncontrollably as he dialed Max's number.

THE END

GUSTAVO BONDONI is an Argentine writer with over a hundred stories published in fourteen countries, in seven languages, and a winner in the National Space Society's "Return to Luna" contest as well as the SF Reader short fiction contest (2014) and the Marooned Award for Flash Fiction (2008). His short fiction has appeared in the *Texas STAAR English Test* cycle, *The Rose & Thorn*, *Albedo One*, *The Best of Every Day Fiction*, and many others.

WILDTOPIA
Michael W. Lucht

THE TALL SAVANNAH GRASS moved. Richard held his breath, willing it to be nothing. He wasn't ready yet.

"Anything?" whispered Malaika.

"The wind," Richard guessed. Droplets of sweat trickled down the inside of his neck brace, but he could not scratch. The cervical collar was too tight and stiff for even the attempt.

She too wore a brace, its hospital-white making her appear even darker than usual. Standing tiptoe and with her eyes closed, she kissed him; her lips cool in the Serengeti heat. But for once, Richard was unable to give his favorite pastime his full attention. Squinting past Malaika's head, he stared up at the African sky, a vast expanse of vivid blue. It just about seemed possible to peer all the way to the satellites that were tracking their every move, streaming their plight to millions of televisions, computers, smartphones, and tablets around the world. Their solitude was an illusion.

He wondered what their vast invisible audience was making of their kiss. Many supporters in both pro and anti-Wildtopia camps were still scandalized by the behavior of their respective campaign leaders. She stood for the elimination of suffering from the totality of nature. He argued that this was as impossible as building a staircase to the moon. Yet, miraculously, they had become lovers.

"Shall we wander?" Malaika asked, breaking his thoughts. "Shorten the wait?"

"Let's go," he said, taking her hand.

The earthy reds and yellows of the land they trod on were a perfect complement to the otherworldliness of the sky, but Richard was unable to appreciate the scenery. Instead, he gazed up at every umbrella-like tree, each time breathing a sigh of relief upon discovering it unoccupied.

"Over there!" Malaika shouted the words Richard dreaded. In the distance, a lion was heading their way.

Once more they kissed. This time Richard could not care less about their unseen audience.

Reluctantly, he pulled their lips apart.

"Stay here!" he ordered and marched off in the lion's direction. The animal was again lost in the tall grass, but could not have gone far.

Scampering, she caught up. "Hey! Why should *you* be the victim?"

"Because practical demonstrations were *my* idea," he rationalized. Initially, the Wildtopia referendum campaign had only consisted of debates, boring the public. Hence, Richard had suggested that they conduct exhibitions to dramatize the arguments for and against Wildtopia. How he now longed for a nice dull debate.

"But not the lion," she rebutted, overtaking him.

Indeed! Richard could still remember how shocked he had been when Malaika had announced her plans; none of the prior demonstrations had involved any real danger. The previous one had shown the impact of the tax to fund Wildtopia on three families—not much jeopardy there. Despite this, he could not bring himself to blame her for their predicament. This was the final exhibition. With support for Wildtopia waning, it was her last chance to turn things around.

For a slim woman, a head shorter than himself, she sure walked fast. At another time and place, Richard would have hung back, enjoy watching Malaika strut in her tight leather jumpsuit.

Breaking into a small jog, he again took the lead. "No one forced me to be here."

No sooner had the words left his mouth, when the lion emerged from a dense patch of grass, barely a stone's throw away. It had scars, flies, and a hungry scowl showing off its enormous teeth. They were cupped by yellow plastic sheaths; likewise, for the claws. Richard tried deriving some small measure of comfort from this—wildebeests in his position faced razor sharp blades.

It didn't help; Richard started shaking uncontrollably. The dread that he had felt before turned into full-blown primeval fear. He closed his eyes, hoping that this might calm his nerves. He was faintly aware that Malaika had stopped with him, taking his hand and stroking his palm with her thumb—reminding him of his purpose. He had been a fool to think that it would be easy, but it still had to be done, for Malaika's sake and his. To prove that he was not going to shy away from experiencing the suffering of wild animals for himself. And to shield Malaika from the same.

But as soon as he opened his eyes again, all resolve vanished. The lion was now just a brief sprint away. Richard stepped backward, tugging at Malaika's arm.

At first, she resisted. When he pulled harder, she allowed him to drag her with him. It was pointless, of course; the lion's approach was unhurried, yet relentless. Much too soon it reached jumping distance. Here it paused as if trying to decide who was the tastier morsel.

Silently, Richard prayed for an instant of courage. One step forward. How hard could it be?

"I love you," Malaika whispered.

Richard couldn't talk. He couldn't step forward. He could barely stand.

Oh God, it pounced!

Without the brace, the force of impact alone might have broken his neck. Dazed, he was on his back with a massive paw across his chest pinning him down. The beast bit down on his cervical collar. Despite the plastic sheaths blunting its teeth, his brace cracked. Richard expected it to give way, ending his misery right there and then. It held.

Suddenly, the lion's mouth was covering half his face, enclosing nostrils and lips. Frantically, Richard kicked and punched the muscular body, which was like hitting a lightly padded brick wall. Occasionally, his struggles loosened the tight seal around his orifices, letting in single breaths of air and lion spit, tasting of rotting meat.

Each breath felt like his last. Each breath *might* be his last! The battle for air became all-consuming. He would have blinded himself for just one more breath of air and lion spit.

Then, incredulously, the beast released him. Richard remained sprawled on the ground, gasping for air. He heard a deep growl. Was the lion playing with him?

"Oh God, please no," he prayed and sat up, looking for his tormentor.

It was attacking Malaika! Smothering her, her limbs flailing helplessly.

She must have disturbed the beast, sacrificing herself for him, the way he had intended to do for her. Richard choked back tears; watching Malaika undergo the horrors he had just endured was unbearable. He had to do something. Anything! Even tugging at its tail.

He attempted to stand, but a sharp sting brought him back to his knees. A cracked rib! Hyperventilating, Richard tried again. The hurt was excruciating, making him throw up. But he got to his feet.

Malaika was no longer pushing away the lion, she just held on, embracing it like a lover. Suffering, like one of the four-hundred thousand wildebeests annually killed by lions that she sought to protect. And that was just a fraction of all the torment in creation. Every year, an uncountable number of sparrows were defeathered and devoured by raptors, often while still alive. And no fate could be worse than that of caterpillars, first paralyzed, then consumed from the inside-out by wasp larvae.

All this was nature, nothing to be concerned about, he had said so himself. He was part of nature too. So, why should *his* suffering count for more than *theirs*? It shouldn't.

Why then couldn't he bring himself to move?

But he wasn't a wildebeest. He wasn't even a caterpillar. And he certainly was not a dedicated champion for his cause. He was a hypocrite and a coward to boot.

Falling, he curled up in his own vomit, wishing he would die. He vaguely remembered hearing a chopper, praying that it was not too late for Malaika.

RICHARD WATCHED A PRIDE of lions pursue the robotic antelope. A descendant of the famous BigDog robot, it didn't look much like the real thing. In fact, it appeared to be a treasure chest on legs, with an obviously fake head attached. Fortunately, that did not seem to deter the lions.

A lioness pounced on the robot, tipping it over. The mechanical legs kept moving, shaking and twisting the "antelope" on the ground. Another lioness crushed its "windpipe;" two minutes of pressure applied to the neck sensors turned the robot off. The Lions wasted no time tearing into the slab of vegetable protein tied to its back, specially formulated for feline nutrition. Like the food for the herbivores, it was laced with a contraceptive, thereby stabilizing the animal population without the need for premature death and suffering.

Absent-mindedly, Richard rubbed his own neck. He was amazed by how much had already been accomplished in the first year since the historic vote. A twenty-three-kilometer fence through the southeast corner of the Arusha National Park separated flesh and blood antelopes, buffalos, zebras, and warthogs from lions, cheetahs, leopards, and hyenas.

The fence had many gates. Richard unlocked the nearest one and stepped from herbivore into predator half. Heading towards the feeding lions, he wondered what would happen once he marched into their midst. Would they pounce on him all at once, shredding him to pieces, or would a single lion fell and suffocate him?

He would know soon enough. Of one thing he was certain—this time he would not be a coward! He had dosed himself up on Valium to make sure, yet another case of technology improving on defective nature.

He was halfway towards the cats when the gate behind him creaked. *Damn!* Having left the anniversary dinner early, he had expected privacy. He was sure that no one would follow him—he was an outcast, a laughing stock. Of course, they had to invite him because of his central role in the vote, but beyond superficial politeness, no one wanted to have anything to do with him.

He turned around, expecting to see a park ranger shouting at him.

Malaika! Slim and dark and pretty as always.

"Isn't this much better?" she asked, following him into lion country as if it were a perfectly safe thing to do. Dressed for formal dinner, she wore a figure-hugging dress made from colorful kanga but had left her high-heeled sandals at the gate. Richard cursed himself. He should have snapped back the padlock.

"Malaika, go back!"

"Why don't we both go back?"

"Malaika, *please!*"

A fast walker, it did not take her long to catch up. Nervously, Richard glanced over his shoulder at the pride. A curious lioness stared up from its "kill." This time, no one would rescue them.

"I was told you couldn't make it," he said, not knowing what else to say.

"Changed my mind when I heard you were coming. Hoped to surprise you at dinner, but we just missed each other." She stopped right in front of him, placing her hands on her slim hips. "You've been avoiding me since the vote. Why?"

"After what happened?" Richard didn't feel worthy to breathe the same air as her, let alone feel her soft breath against his neck.

She creased her forehead as if struggling to recall. "I've seen the footage. It showed a young woman, likely to invoke the protective instincts of male viewers, nearly killed by a lion. It also showed an honest man, who had claimed that the suffering in nature is tolerable, breaking down. Wildtopia won by fifty-two percent. Without you, this 'antelope' being eaten would have been real."

"Hard to believe that the greatest coward in history did so much." As if to emphasize his flaw, Richard again glanced backward. The lioness watching them took a few tentative steps in their direction. Perhaps hunting robotic antelopes gets boring after a while? "You should go back *now*."

"You're no coward!" she insisted, still ignoring the danger. "To be a coward, there has to be a choice. Just like the lions don't choose to be cruel, you didn't choose to be petrified."

"You controlled *your* fear," Richard objected.

She shrugged her lovely bare shoulders. "Had it been a giant spider, I would have run."

Richard never expected her to forgive his most shameful failing. Perhaps he would have other opportunities to make himself worthy of her.

"Have I been an idiot," he asked, holding back tears, "for despising myself this past year?"

She sighed. "I've been a bigger idiot for not realizing what you went through. But that year lies in the past, beyond our reach. As lies the suffering that drove four billion years of natural selection. I despair at the cruelty of creation when I think about it too much."

Her eyes rapidly brightened, like the first appearance of the sun after the monsoon. "But then I dream about the future, of the billions of years of life to come, in which we, humanity, have eliminated torment from creation.

"Likewise, when I look at you, I don't see your year of pain, but the happiness in your future, both in yourself and the joy you'll bring to others.

"Especially," she added significantly, "to me."

He accepted her cool, slender hand.

"Now run!" she suddenly gasped.

She was fast on bare feet. Her dress, slit to her hips, flapped madly around her thighs. Nevertheless, the lion gained ground, running at full throttle. Doggedly Richard remained between Malaika and the beast. He would not let it reach her this time!

She slipped through the gate first, with Richard just behind. The big cat leaped against the fence just as he snapped shut the padlock. The powerful jolt flung him backward, landing him on his back.

Malaika threw herself on the grass next to him. "Now that this trial has been a success," she panted, "it can be expanded throughout the entire Arusha National Park. Although the complete elimination of suffering in nature may take a million years, we're on our way!"

Yes, it was just the beginning. Her dream was so vast, her determination so strong, Richard knew that she would be toiling for Wildtopia for decades to come. And that she would continue to be just as lovely. Wildtopia, the foolish delusion of idealists or man's highest purpose? In all honesty, he no longer cared. Loving Malaika was all the certainty he required.

THE END

MICHAEL W. LUCHT is a mostly Australian writer residing in Hobart, Tasmania. When not writing, he has been known to lecture in mathematics and computing. With twin ambitions of publishing a fantasy novel and creating artificial life, he is currently prioritizing the novel (which might come as some relief to the world). This novel should be completed in 2018. If successful, it will be followed by sequels until everybody is sick of it. His fiction has appeared in *Nature Futures*, *The Drabblecast*, *Alternate Hilarities 3 & 4*, *Bards & Sages Quarterly* and *Island Magazine*. With respect to non-fiction, he has heterogeneously contributed to *Physical Review A*, *The Journal of Chemical Physics*, *Artificial Life*, *The Skeptic* and *Cracked.com*. Find out more on his website www.michaelwlucht.com.

THE DEFINITION OF JOHNNY
Damien Krsteski

Originally appeared in *Beyond Science Fiction*, June 2015.

JOHNNY WROTE GREAT CODE. He told great stories, too, made up ones, mainly for his own amusement. Johnny wasn't really Johnny's name, but a sci-fi reference, one he used whenever he could. Even talking about himself in the third person so people would remember the handle of the guy with the cowboy boots and the suspenders, the self-appointed moniker of the hacker with the racy jokes and the gaudy iridescent laptop.

He always burst into parties, flinging imaginary pistols, shooting at and laughing with everybody on his way in. Immediately drawn toward the bar, he'd suck down a drink or ten to loosen up before winding up with his arm wrapped around the waist of some brunette on the dance floor.

But at Tomas' party, he was a shadow. I scarcely noticed his arrival.

Sneaking up on me at the bar. "Hey."

"Johnny!"

He hugged me. I said, "You've slimmed down. How's work? How's life?"

"Oh, y'know..." His eyes locked with the bartender's, and he held up two fingers. "Fulfilling. Wonderful. Awe-inspiring." The bartender poured him a double gin. Johnny downed it, ordered another.

"Everything okay?"

He shrugged. Dark bags hung beneath his eyes.

"Pulling all-nighters?"

He shrugged again, or maybe he shivered. "Occasionally."

"Not doing you any good," I said. "Besides, I thought only newbies did that."

Swatting the air with a hand, "Coding is the least of my problems, man."

Hunched over my rum and coke, arms around the glass in a protective semi-circle, I decided Johnny would be bad drinking company. I tried to get him off my back with a brief, "Sure," but he hung on, ordering gins and blabbering about his latest contract work and the code he'd inherited from the previous developer, code he'd fixed by "cutting through the spaghetti with a machete."

When I had heard enough, I got off the barstool, but he gripped my shirt, and his face came awfully close to mine. "Wait. I need you."

Wincing at his gin-breath, "I can't lend you money, Johnny."

"It's not money."

"It isn't?"

"I've..." Bloodshot eyes peering above my shoulders, scanning the raucous crowd behind us. "Johnny's learned of some things... that maybe he shouldn't have. Information ought to be free but sometimes there are limits, and I guess I kinda crossed one."

"What are you talking about?"

His eyebrows went up, wrinkling his forehead, and his face inched closer. "I need a witness. Somebody to see what I'm about to do. I will call you." He let go of my shirt.

I went mingling, and quickly forgot about the whole ordeal; Johnny stuck to the bar the whole night.

HE CALLED ME UP three days later with an invitation to visit his place. He said I'd be interested in what he had to offer, and jobless and bored as I was, I said I'd come.

His place was a garage, adjacent to an unkempt, two-storied house which probably wasn't his. Damp and reeking of mold— genetically modified—sprinkled over the walls like fairy dust, emitting phosphorescent light. (He mentioned in passing that it was used to power his computers, but I believe he was merely teasing.)

He sat me down on a bean bag in a corner where the mold-light was brightest, and the mold-stench was pungent.

"So," I said, "what do you need help with?"

He looked like he hadn't slept a wink since Tomas' party. He ran a hand through his thatch of hair. "I know something, Pavel. Something bad. Horrible."

"What?"

"Murder." His lips formed an O, a look of mock surprise on his face. "Mur-derd"—enunciating, exaggerating each syllable—"hugh-man-bee-in."

"Go to the police," I said.

"They won't believe me."

"A psychiatrist, then."

"They won't help me. Sit back down, please, there really isn't a lot I need you to do. Just watch me solve a case, and that's it."

"What is wrong with you, man? You used to be clever. I can't believe we had worked—"

"Just watch me. Watch as I crack a murder case and you *will* be rewarded. I promise. Listen to my updates, read my notes, be around, *watch me do it.*"

His pale skin reflected mildewed colors, blending reds and blues in a grimace born of absolute exhaustion.

"I know I'll regret the answer," I sighed, massaged my forehead, "but why do you need me to watch?"

"Because nothing is being done unless somebody watches," he said, steepling his fingers. "Think of the dead and frozen stored in company servers. What's left of those people? Memories. Testimonies to their own lives. But is that enough? For us to consider them alive, or half-alive, but not dead? No. What is enough, is for somebody, for a *witness* to confirm. If I can say, Hey, yeah, that guy does sound exactly like Glans McDickhead, my childhood best bud, once his brain's been thawed out, well then, boom!" He punched his palm. "His story is verified, and he's accepted as being fully Mr Glans. We are defined by others in a web of trust, a web of definitions."

(He said a lot more in regard to quantity, but this should suffice to convey his stream-of-consciousness way of explaining and of convincing.)

"Umm…"

"I got access to NeurOnIce servers."

A shiver went up my spine. Of this—curiosity, I mean—I am guilty, but only of this. Like every self-respected programmer, I had had my interest piqued by that company, with its top-notch algorithms for mimicking brain activity, their shiny in-house hardware, their workforce plucked out meticulously from top-tier grad schools and competitors from across the globe. Working for NeurOnIce was a dream job, and still is.

"What do you mean?" I said, despite not doubting his claim for a second.

"You heard me." He grinned. "Are you in?"

I could almost taste the carrot dangled before me, but being given a chance to peek inside this company's system was an offer too scintillating to brush off.

"Being around is all I have to do?"

He nodded.

"What, like some sort of intern?"

"An uninvolved intern, yes."

I paused, pretended to deliberate, though I admit I had made up my mind the moment he spoke the magical name aloud. NeurOnIce. A bait, a spell, a curse rolled into one.

"Okay," I said, my arms tingling with excitement. "I'm in."

The mold colored a smile. Patting me on the shoulder, "I knew it. Knew you're my guy."

"Of course." I relaxed, returned the smile. "Why shouldn't I help an old partner?"

A WHOLE BAG OF reasons: A, he was crazy. B, he was talking about murder (granted, I did suspect he was lying, or at least exaggerating that part). C, he was the most unreliable and eccentric person I've ever had the misfortune of doing business with. And D, I should have known much, much better than to take his inane story about witnesses and whatnot at face value.

But here I am. And here you all are, with your accusatory looks.

JOHNNY HAD APPLIED FOR a part-time server maintenance job at NeurOnIce and had gotten it, tight as it had been in the last round of interviews. ("Neck and neck with a Chinese asshole but experience was key, so I got it, and teary Yuan went back to simulating droughts on their vacuum-tubed tin cans. Ha!")

His access rights hadn't been substantial, but Johnny being Johnny, and above all, Johnny having to maintain Johnny's reputation, he'd prodded around the system for weeks until he'd located a security hole, widened it, and had crowned himself covert administrator of the whole network.

The main protagonist of the story he fed me was one Loic Baptiste, a Belgian businessman and venture capitalist. Johnny had worked with him at some European start-up a couple of years back—Superfluie or Supperflies or some such nonsense I'd never bothered to remember, let alone verify—and the two men had grown close through their eccentricities. He had gone missing three weeks before (Johnny showed me posters and police reports I now know were fake), and Johnny swore he had a hunch the key lay in the memories of business people whose brain scans were kept on ice, in this company.

I watched, slack-jawed, as he walked me through the system, as he decrypted and summoned brains and handled them like they were his playthings.

During our days together, I was uneasy with his unlawful messing about, but, as promised, I was kept at bay with occasional rewards, illicit gifts plundered from the company he abused. He secured my docility with pieces of algorithms from NeurOnIce's code-base, digital morsels I munched on my own time like a vulture, for a few days, a week, until my conscience started stirring and he had to throw a new chunk of juicy code at me to keep me quiet.

To that extent, I was complicit. With what he did to the brain scans, though, I had zero involvement.

"WE ARE ALL DISTRIBUTED individuals, y'know?" He brandished his arms around.

"We are?"

We drank and smoked in his garage under mold-illumination, lounging on bean bags. He rested his boots on a stack of hardcover books.

"What you are is not what makes you, you."

"It's not?"

"Others' perception of you is what makes you, you." Taking a drag off his joint. "Again, that web of trust, that web of observations."

"I think I get what you're saying. You can deny gossip until you're frothing at the mouth, but, like, what if a lie circulates about you and you have zero fucking clues? Essentially, it's true until proven otherwise. Right?"

"Exactly."

We squinted in the dim haze; turquoise smoke wafted out of a half-opened window.

Johnny said, "And that's just one small aspect of it."

"Oh?" I looked at him through my empty beer bottle, a sea captain seeking land. He grinned, emerald green.

"Every action of yours is perceived differently by the people who're there to witness it, and everyone extracts a unique meaning from your words. You are mediated. Put ten people in the same room and say, 'My name is Pavel, and I am a Sapphire programmer,' and you will be multiplied ten-fold. Everybody will see a different Pavel. Programmers will see a colleague, perhaps somebody they can befriend, or they might consider you competition, depending on self-esteem. Managers might see you as a tool; artists, as a cog in the machine run by the Man, a philistine unworthy of conversation. One fucking sentence—" he held a finger up, "—and they all prejudge. Now imagine more nuanced situations, and you realize how metaphysically fucked we all are."

I opened another bottle. "Is that what you want?" I drank. "To be less metaphysically fucked in the end? For me to collapse the many possible alternate versions of your... murder-solving thingy by being here and observing?"

"Now he gets it!" He mockingly thrust his fists in the air, then stubbed out the joint in an ashtray. He fished out a beer from the cooler.

"I think you're overthinking things."

"That's just how you see me," he said as we clinked bottles, "but who's to say you're wrong?"

HE WAS A GODDAMN sociopath.

The wheels of a plan had been set in motion long before I was lured into cooperation. I wonder if he had me in mind from the start, perhaps because he considered me gullible or dumb, or if he'd have gone with just about anybody, and I happened to be the first person he ran into at the party that night.

I SAT BESIDE HIM, working on my laptop, studiously picking apart the latest algorithm he'd pried out of the company, hoping my knowledge of the system's entrails would one-day work in my favor and land me if luck would have it, first an interview and then a steady job.

"Psst." He slapped my knee. "Lookie here."

I looked up at his monitor; a scattering of wrinkled gray cortices and two progress bars beneath them, filling up and emptying respectively, in antiphase.

"What's going on?"

"This little fella here—" he pointed at the top-right cortex "—is Miranda Bright, a one-time CEO of a company owned by Loic Baptiste." He looked at me. "Bright was fired for mishandling of company funds. People lost their jobs. LB was extremely displeased. But so was Bright, enough to hold a grudge for years. I mean, her credibility went down like a lead balloon after this. She is our prime suspect."

"What about the other brains?"

"This one—" top-left, "—is Bright's husband, and this one—" bottom-left, "—is their adopted daughter, a member of the board of directors." He grinned.

My fingers hovered limply over my keyboard as I listened to his tall tales, and ashamed as I am to admit it, I ate them all up.

"You're downloading their memories?"

"In-fucking-deed."

The progress bars swapped colors altogether—the data transfer was complete. He clicked about, and a new set of progress bars flickered on-screen, filling up.

"Nice," I said, absent-minded, and returned to my algorithm.

HE DANCED AND PRANCED before me, wore goggles and re-lived stolen memories. Occasionally, he'd exclaim an A-ha! or he'd jump back, startled as if present during a monstrous act. I paid him little mind. He said my being there was enough.

"That was intense," he said after a bit, flipping the lids of the goggles up. Moiré patterns gleamed on his forehead like a second pair of eyes.

"Is it her?"

"Still no proof." He scratched the beard on his cheek.

"Getting any closer?"

"Oh, yes, definitely closer. I'll catch the bitch red-handed any day now."

He closed the lids and plunged into memory-land again.

THE BLEATING OF MY phone woke me up. Scrambled number. Two-fourteen in the morning.

"Hey, sleepyhead." It was him. "Wakey, wakey, we need to talk... call me on my cell in ten minutes."

"What... what's going on?"

"Call me back in ten. I'll explain everything." He killed the connection.

I lay dazed for a few moments, rubbing my eyes with my knuckles, then I dragged myself out of bed to make coffee. Twenty minutes and two cups later, I called his number.

"Did you find it?"

"What? Oh, the proof, yes, yes, I did. Of course."

"And?"

"And what?"

"Did you send it to the police?"

A pause. "No. Not yet." He took a deep breath. "I need you to come to my place to witness the final act."

"Can't this wait till morning?"

"No. I need you quick."

Arguing was of no use. He promised to disclose a sizable chunk of NeurOnIce's cortical compression code if I came inside of an hour. I got dressed and drove through empty streets to his place.

He opened the door to his garage as I was about to knock on it.

"Come, come, come." He ushered me in. He was shirtless and wearing suspenders, his belly sagging above the rim of his belt.

The mold had been scraped off the walls, his scattered books and other assorted belongings packed neatly into a cardboard box, his ten-gallon hat sitting atop it. His computers, trinkets, and toys all switched off.

"Moving out, Johnny?"

He didn't answer; out of a filing cabinet, he pulled out a foot-long knife and handed it to me. "Check this out."

Serrated blade, made to cut through rubber, wood, flesh. "What's this for?" I examined it from all angles—the bulb light slid off it in a flash once, twice—and held it out for him.

"Our murder weapon." He took it but didn't replace it in the drawer.

"Our murder weapon?" I said. "It doesn't look used. How did you get it from Bright?"

He skimmed through a stack of papers, making clicking noises with his tongue and mumbling to himself.

"Talk to me, Johnny."

"Oh, the weapon's used," he said, leaving the papers on his desk. He came close to me, said, "It will be used," and head-butted me as hard as he could.

Black stars pulsated before my eyes. A hot stream gushed out of my nose, ran down my neck and over my shirt. I opened my eyes. I lay on the ground, blood and mucus dripping into my mouth. I spat.

"What the fuck? What is fucking wrong with you?"

He pulled me up.

"I had to, sorry," he said, and I noticed he had the knife in the other hand, his knuckles white from the firm grip.

I took a step back, arms outstretched, blood flowing all over my shirt and jeans. "What are you doing with that knife? Put it down, Johnny. Put the knife down."

From a pocket, he took out what looked like an asthma inhaler, brought it to his mouth and took a deep breath from it. His eyes glazed over.

"Don't take this personally," he said and raised the knife. "Sorry."

He stuck it in his gut. Groaning, he spun the knife once, and I watched with a hand clasped over my bloody mouth as he twisted it around his insides and pulled it toward his sternum with his remaining strength.

Johnny collapsed on the ground; the fecal stench of ripped intestine spread through the tiny garage, and I threw up in my hand.

A tentative step forward, to help, to try CPR, to call an ambulance, but I remained standing, in shock and horror, above his lifeless body, for what felt like hours.

Then the police came to take me away.

I AM AN EXPERIMENT, a lab rat, the conclusion of a study, the proof of a theory.

I am not what I was, not what I know. Now, what constitutes *me* is everything *he's* made up.

MATTERS GRADUALLY BECAME CLEARER the following weeks, as police presented evidence after evidence to me, pieces of a puzzle I never knew existed.

The testimony of a certain Rosie Bordeau; erstwhile neighbor and friend of Johnny's; deceased half a year before. Her brain scan had been kept in NeurOnIce's vaults, and she was woken as a witness after her name had been found scattered throughout Johnny's secret diary (conveniently unencrypted for the police to find). She distinctly remembered seeing me when she had been alive, often shuffling to and from Johnny's place, and she'd naturally assumed we were lovers. Not the most peaceful relationship, she'd added as an afterthought.

Then came the memories of one P. G. Nakov—a distant collaborator of Johnny's whose family had paid for total brain preservation immediately following the discovery of his corpse. He remembered conversations about the fiscal troubles Johnny had gotten himself into, and my name had always come up in that context. Nakov told the police his one-time colleague was a strong and intelligent man, honest and hard-working.

Then, inevitably, the memories of the Bright's. Owners of an outsourcing company, they claimed me, and Johnny had been partners working long-distance for them on a failed project. Money had been a major issue. Money that I'd siphoned out of their company through shady deals; money that Johnny had done back-breaking work to pay back.

There were others, but I'm certain you get the gist. Scans of people I'd never spoken to, people that—I'm willing to bet an eye— Johnny had never met, hacked and duped into remembering a fake me, a fake Johnny, a fabricated chain of events set up to implicate me in murder.

The midnight phone call, the secret diary documenting my supposedly abusive and threatening behavior, the fingerprints on the knife, the blood, the bruises, none of that helps my case, either.

Of course, I offered my brain to the police—scan it and sift through my memory, I said—but they wouldn't have any of it. "Why? Cause you'd done some selective memory surgery to yourself? With a Wiper like the one you forced the poor guy to use before gutting him?" the chief told me. "How do we know what you remember is the truth?"

And I shut up, unable to respond to that. Because when you have eighty-three people's testimonies pitted against just one, what can you do, except rely on the numbers?

JOHNNY IS OUT THERE somewhere. Having stolen all of NeurOnIce's code, he would've had the means to scan his brain the night before the suicide, and to live out the rest of his life in machines—snickering at my fate.

But I won't go down without a fight.

If justice boils down to basic arithmetic, I will play his game and win it. I will turn into a relentless propagator for my own version of events.

So long as I breathe, I will share my story with as many as I can in the hope that one day we will outnumber those who've swallowed Johnny's narrative—police and lawyers and families and journalists and jailers. Only then will I be vindicated, and free.

I submit my account to all of you; you be the judges, and you be my liberators.

Right a wrong. Spread my truth. Make me become myself again.

THE END

DAMIEN KRSTESKI writes SF and develops software, and some of his stories have appeared in *Plasma Frequency*, *Bastion*, *Flapperhouse*, *Perihelion SF*, *Mad Scientist Journal*, *Every Day Fiction*, *Kzine*, and others. He lives in Skopje, Republic of Macedonia.

BROKEN MACHINES
Carl Barker

"WHAT ABOUT THAT ONE in the corner, Dad? Couldn't we take her home with us?"

As Soriah stood at rest, overlooking Pseron, she recalled the image fragment of that twelve-year-old boy, standing there in the middle of the tinkerer's shop, pointing excitedly toward the darkened alcove where she had perched, half-hidden amongst mounds of discarded gearings and shock assemblies.

At the recognition of enquiry in his tone, Soriah stepped forward unquestioningly to be met by an ensemble gasp. Only once she was in full view of the boy and his parents did she pause to consider that without the master verbal keystroke of her given name, her obedience was merely the echo of a defunct command pathway. Consequently, her actions were rooted in nothing more than force of habit, which was itself a paradox, for the concept of habit was an entirely biological affectation.

She stood in the lantern light, its hazy golden beams reflecting across her lovingly restored chassis, attempting to resolve this information conflict unsuccessfully with her head tilted slightly to one side, much as a bird might do.

At the same time, her optical processor registered the involuntary dilation in the eyes of the boy's father and the slight elevation in his overall body temperature as she stepped out into view. She observed how his gaze fell across the attractive curvature of her bronzed breastplates, lingering on her perfectly arc welded nipples as they gleamed seductively in the low paraffin glow. The beginnings of a smile registered at the corner of his mouth and then vanished again as his wife turned to glare pointedly at him. It was a reaction not uncommon in the male organics she had encountered and, Soriah discarded the low priority information into a disused storage bin.

The reaction of the man's wife was something entirely new. Having only previously interacted with non-pair-bonded humans before, she took a moment to fully absorb this new behavioral trait, constructing a detailed data package and associated appendices based upon the woman's reactions. After submitting a fresh client request to the mainframe, Soriah's reference server cautiously suggested the words "indignation", and "embarrassment" as high probability explanations for the woman's facial expressions and she attached these tags to the data recording. A third search result of "jealousy" registered with lower probability, and after a further second's deliberation, she also tagged this result and queued the completed file for compression.

"Well, Dad, can we take her or what?" inquired the boy again, impatiently attempting to peer between his mother's fingers as she held one hand protectively over his face.

The woman's lower jaw appeared to have become non-functional and had dropped abruptly open at Soriah's appearance. Soriah's reference server returned the word "disgust," but she chose not to further append the file.

The boy's father, his cheeks flush with indecision shuffled his feet upon the dusty shop floor. When he finally plucked up the courage to sheepishly glance at his wife, he was met with a stern *hmpf* of disapproval, causing his face to redden yet further.

Electing to take charge of the situation to protect her son from further insidious corruption, the boy's mother cleared her throat loudly and addressed the tinkerer.

"I would be grateful, sir, if you would kindly remove this machine from view, as we find it extremely offensive to our delicate sensibilities!"

Trying very hard to suppress a smile, the old man bit his tongue and signaled for Soriah to return to her previous position in the back room. He watched her perfectly sculpted rear saunter away for a moment accompanied by the gentle whine of servos and then turned, finding to his amusement that both father and son seemed quite mesmerized by the sway of her retreating form. Sensing the woman's disapproving glare, he straightened slightly and adopted a business-like air.

"Well, madam, I'm afraid that constitutes my entire functioning stock at this moment. Of course, if you have something specific in mind, I could always place an order to Nimbus for a particular model on the next shuttle?"

"That won't be necessary, thank you," the woman replied curtly. "To be honest, I'm having second thoughts about the whole idea of acquiring a domestic appliance."

The disappointment on the boy's face was plain to see, and the old man briefly surmised the kid was quite taken with the idea of a new playmate. Pity he wasn't a little older he thought, otherwise Soriah could have provided him with more fun then he'd be able to handle. The notion returned a grin to his face and despite the air of disfavor emanating from the boy's mother, he let it remain there, forming his expression into the beginning of a tactful sales hook.

"Well, of course, if you do change your mind about any of the models you've seen today, madam, please don't hesitate to vid-call."

The antiquated silver bell above the door tinkled cheerily as he held it open for his departing customers. The tinkerer exchanged a humorous nod with the boy's father before finding himself beneath the wife's withering gaze one last time.

"You've got a nerve," she muttered menacingly at him as she passed. "Peddling off-world filth like that thing in there. I've half a mind to report you to the Council of Paladins!"

"That is, of course, your prerogative, dear lady," he replied pleasantly, holding his hand out to shake.

She declined, rather unsurprisingly and a second later was gone, a cloud of huffy contempt rapidly coalescing with the dust in the street. He let the door swing unceremoniously closed behind her and returned to his workshop.

Later that evening, as the tinkerer busied himself with his personal labor of love, Soriah asked him about the woman's reaction that day.

"Albert Mennson, Senior, what was the cause of that woman's emotive discomfort today?" she intoned with perfect vocal pitch.

Ceasing his fiddling with her inner workings, the tinkerer sat back on his stool, wiping grease from his fingers and regarded the droid thoughtfully.

"Why do you think she was unhappy, Soriah?"

"My data request to the Deus-Ex mainframe indicates with a ninety-five percent certainty that the female was experiencing a mixture of outrage and indignation as a result of my continued presence.

However, further queries are unable to provide me with sufficient explanation."

"Yes, but what do *you* think, Soriah?" The old man smiled, laying his tools aside.

Soriah tilted her head to one side, awaiting a response from her cognitive reasoning centre. The dogmatic feed line which pinged back was not unexpected, for she had encountered similar informative problems on several occasions.

"I... do not understand the question, Albert Mennson, Senior," she answered, smoothly crossing her long slender legs with an almost inaudible whir of gearings in response to a randomized feminine subroutine.

The old man let out a low sigh of exasperation.

"Soriah," he said to her gently, laying one hand upon her knee in parental fashion. "We have talked about this before, have we not?"

"Affirmative, Albert Mennson, Senior."

She was a thing of monumental beauty, he mused. A skilled artificial assembly of consummate perfection, and yet he found himself unable to look upon her with anything other than a father's eyes. She reminded him so very strongly of that which was lost and of his own failings, for which he could not make amends.

"Let us try to look at the matter from a different perspective."

"Affirmative, Albert Mennson, Senior."

He smiled briefly at her resolute inability to adopt simple familiarity.

"You remember how I told you that humans act differently from mechanoids in many diverse ways?"

Soriah nodded at this.

"Your operational parameters do not follow the same lines of coding as ours," she stated flatly.

Again, he smiled, this time wearily shaking his head but persevering with the lesson nonetheless. "Well, that's certainly one way of putting it. Now, as I explained, the explanation for your inability to comprehend the reasoning, the—" He paused, searching for more appropriate words. "—the route pathway which led to that woman's behavior, stems from the fact that you are incapable of processing such a biologically endemic rationale."

"That is entirely reasonable," Soriah commented.

"And yet," the tinkerer followed up. "You tilt your head to one side when you are thinking, which is itself a biological characteristic, is it not?"

The droid's posture straightened a little at this, lamplight glinting forlornly across her cheeks as she attempted to compile a response to this new information.

"I currently possess no explanation for this, Albert Mennson, Senior."

The tinkerer chuckled. Soriah sounded almost alarmed, and he reached across, placing his fingers on her own.

The outer surface of her epidermis was perfectly aligned to human body temperature, the corporation had learned quickly that the feel of cold metal was not conducive to intimate sexual interaction between man and machine. He held her hand gently as if it were priceless china and observed the unsettled motion of her vision as she cogitated.

"It's all right, Soriah," he soothed. "You are simply more than the sum of your constituent parts."

Soriah's eyes ceased their rapid twitching and focused again.

"That is a paradox, Albert Mennson, Senior."

"In human beings, we call it consciousness. It's what sets us apart from lower life-forms. The ability to learn from the events of our existence and think for ourselves, rather than follow set patterns of behavior.

Soriah did not reply immediately, attempting to resolve the storm of internal conflict raging through her data pathways.

"I have questions."

If he hadn't known better, he would have said she sounded afraid. "I think that's probably enough for tonight, Soriah. We can talk again tomorrow."

The pleasure-droid stood up obediently and allowed him to replace the metal housing of her abdomen, before moving to her usual resting place and initiating a hibernation period. The old man collected his tools together, securing them in a nearby drawer and then put out the lantern.

"Goodnight, Soriah," he whispered softly to the dark.

A solitary red light blinked once at the rear of the shop.

"Goodnight, Albert Mennson, Senior."

The tinkerer's shoulders slumped.

"How many times must I tell you, Soriah, just Albert is fine."

The display plate winked once more, but she did not reply. With the stairs creaking grumpily in protest, the tinkerer made his way up to bed, leaving Soriah alone in the workshop with her subroutines.

THE WIND HAD PICKED up considerably since her arrival, and vast clouds of ionized dust blew across the valley from the reactor station on the far side of the moon. Though dirt was unlikely to work its way beneath her outer casings, Soriah noted how the wind perturbed her rag clothing and returned to the safety of the tree line, not risking even the briefest reflection of light. She had no wish for further contact with the inhabitants of Pseron.

To discover that an isolated human commune such as this had developed a collective aversion to artificial life-forms was entirely unexpected. Since fleeing the village and the illogical persecution of its inhabitants, she had devoted a large portion of her cognitive runtime to trying to explain the rationale behind the beating she had received. No severe damage had been done to her circuitry, yet she was protective of the wound for some reason which she could not fathom.

The mob had attacked without warning. The elderly male who had been sheltering her in his home had sensed them as well as she had, despite the obvious disadvantage of his visual impairment, rising to his feet just before they set fire to his hut. It appeared that humans were perhaps not as frail as the Deux-Ex mainframe had frequently suggested, their other senses able to compensate for loss of functionality or damage sustained to their sight. In contrast to his xenophobic brethren, the blind man had demonstrated no apprehension at her presence, immediately inviting her into his home. Soriah suspected that he had been unaware that she was a mechanoid, for no sooner had she followed him inside did he offer her one of those rolled tobacco sticks which humans were so fond of. Having previously downloaded detailed compression files on human social interaction as part of her designated application, Soriah had taken the cigar, not wishing to offend him.

Following his example, she had inserted the object into the soft palate of her facial interior, observing the evident delight which the old man took from drawing the toxic smoke into his lungs. Mystified at his apparent disregard for such a detrimental practice, Soriah found herself wishing that she was equipped with organoleptic sensors.

Minutes later, when the mob of assembled villagers had kicked in the door, Soriah had found herself dragged out into the street and violently manhandled to the ground, lying there motionless on her back whilst the villagers took turns kicking her and assaulting her framework with tools. Many of them had labeled her with inexplicable verbal tags such as "abomination" and "devil-machine." From their loud yells and haranguing, she had extrapolated that, though no strangers to mechanoids, they lived in fear of them, following several deaths in their midst.

Such occurrences were rare and could usually be attributed to a failure to follow standard procedure during assembly of the construct in question, what the organics liked to refer to as "human error." To assume that all models were defective in this way though, based upon the impaired functionality of one droid, was irrational.

They spoke angrily of the droid that had murdered their kin and Soriah paid particular attention to their insinuations that the machine had done so of its own free will. Perhaps this was the one which she had sought for so long she wondered, immediately shunting all current audio recordings into her primary memory stack for detailed analysis.

As the violence continued, she watched a hawk wheeling high above in the cloudless sky. Soriah wondered what it would be like to fly; to soar freely above the world and its illogical constructs, unconcerned with emotive imbalance and social unrest among the biologicals. No information could be gathered about the winged creature, for she had long ago disconnected herself from the company mainframe on Nimbus, in fear of transponder location. Rogue models were hunted down and expunged from the universal inventory as a matter of course, the company wishing to maintain the facade of a perfect operational record.

Eventually, the mob tired of their metal pariah and discovering that they were unable to significantly breach her body-plating with the simple tools in their possession, they poured a significant quantity of fuel over her framework and set her alight. The flames did little further damage, save some scorching around her joint protectors, and as she watched her wild-eyed tormentors through the flames, Soriah compiled a fresh visual file.

She had begun to do this more and more frequently since absconding from Virrun, stowing away on a cargo freighter headed for the less populated outer moons. In the absence of the mainframe's guiding hand, she found it necessary to compile her own reference library, attaching retrieval tags as best she could to the data gathered, before compressing it into limited onboard storage space.

At first, this process had proved difficult, encompassing too many variables to allow facile indexing. However, over time Soriah had begun to note certain repetitive causality pathways within the human behavior. For example, the way that a verbal misunderstanding might lead to elevated output from the subjects' adrenal glands, in turn leading to a physical confrontation between two parties despite the absence of underlying motivation. To discover such patterns hidden in what she had previously observed as chaos had proved most enlightening. Yet ironically, the actions of the villagers bore greater analogy to a file compiled prior to her departure from Virrun.

With data acquisition of the villagers now complete, she attached the tag 'injustice' to the file with some conviction and queued it for storage. Eventually, the flames ran out of fuel and taking their victim for dead, the villagers dragged Soriah's motionless smoking frame to a nearby pit and set about entombing it beneath the dirt. Knowing full well that her servos would be capable of safely extracting her from such a shallow grave, Soriah was content to let her captors expunge their collective demons by confining her beneath the barren earth. Darkness clogged steadily around her vision, and as it did, a familiar memory packet inexplicably unzipped itself from deep storage and downloaded into her central paging file...

"WELL, YOU CERTAINLY ARE a mess, aren't you?"

The voice was unfamiliar, and finding her one remaining ocular input to be obscured somehow, Soriah sensibly pinged the company network for identification and awaited results.

A hand touched her shoulder, and she flinched, a short spasm running through her servos. Noting the malfunction and initiating a level two diagnostic on the circuitry in question, she took delivery from the mainframe server and found that the voice in question was not on file on the network, indicating the presence of an off-gridder.

Fingertips stroked her surface, and Soriah jerked back again, warning alerts triggering across her core processor at the occurrence of a second physical malfunction so soon after the first. The self-diagnostic already running automatically upgraded itself to level four.

"It's all right, don't be afraid. I'm not going to hurt you."

Recognition software analyzed the incoming sound: her companion was a male, between sixty and eighty years of age, with a fifty-five percent probability of underlying respiratory complaints.

"We just need to get you cleaned up a bit," the voice soothed.

Something made contact with her face-plate, and Soriah identified the material as coarse cloth, a low-level light reactivating her optical sensor as layers of dust and grime were carefully wiped away to give her a view of her surroundings.

She found herself looking at a white-haired human male corresponding approximately to the description which she had begun to compile. Making an initial visual appraisal, she proceeded to append the file with additional characteristics: a thinning hairline partially receded, weather-beaten skin and a pair of small antique spectacles perched on the end of his nose. The subject wore inexpensive clothing, showing signs of extensive wear, and smiled at her in an oddly familial fashion.

"My designation is Soriah XD-104/C. Are you my new custodian?"

The stock introduction evidently produced a degree of amusement, for his smile widened to reveal an uneven set of dirty teeth.

"Soriah, is it?" he commented. "Well, I am Albert Mennson, Senior and it's a pleasure to meet you, dear lady."

At this, the man rose and inexplicably bowed to her, as if addressing some form of Nimbian dignitary. Soriah's reference server quietly posted the word "senility," and she attached it as an unconfirmed footnote.

"Now then, let's see if we can't get you spick and span."

Whilst he set about removing the remaining dirt from her outer surfaces, Soriah conducted a full inventory of her surroundings.

The construction material for the dwelling was a dark hardwood which she quickly narrowed down to three likely possibilities, all native to Virrun, the largest and closest of Nimbus' six moons. The room was of modest size, containing a large and varied collection of mechanical components, all apparently discarded. Strewn amongst these she observed various recognizable tools and implements corresponding to mechanoid repair and, having postulated a theory, she looked at the subject's hands for confirmation, observing how they adroitly worked at de-clogging her display screen.

"You are droid maintenance personnel, are you not?"

The old man did not look up, instead shrugging his shoulders once in response as he worked.

"Ayuh, I fix things when they're broken sometimes," he muttered. "Always did like to tinker with things, ever since I was a boy."

"Any repair work not carried out by a qualified Deux-Ex technician may invalidate my warranty."

The tinkerer laughed for a moment.

"Well, now, if it's a full wash and blow-dry that you're wanting, Missy, then you might be waiting some time. We don't get too many company folks out here in the sticks."

Soriah looked at him blankly, unfamiliar with the colloquialism.

"Tell you what," he continued, "why don't we patch you up as best we can, and I won't tell anybody if you don't?"

A moment of cognitive reappraisal followed before her reply.

"In the absence of trained personnel, your suggestion is acceptable, Albert Mennson, Senior."

"Is it now?" the tinkerer giggled. "Twenty million droids in this system alone and I have to go and hook up with Lady Muck herself."

"That is an incorrect designation. I am Soriah XD—"

"It's all right, I heard you the first time." He smiled. "Why don't we just drop the surname for now? Nobody tends to stand on ceremony much round here anyways."

The tinkerer knelt and busied himself with removing the thick layer of grime worked into the grooves of her abdominal plating, liberally applying equal quantities of a home-made cleaning fluid and spit.

"Are you my designated custodian?"

"Well," replied the old man, struggling with a particularly stubborn patch of carbon scoring, "I guess I'm going to be looking after you for a while, if that's what you mean?"

"I am required by core directives to surrender my given name to any new custodian upon clarification of property rights," Soriah explained.

The tinkerer scratched the back of his head.

"I'm not normally one to go kissing on the first date and all, but if that's okay with you then I guess it's all right by me as well," he said.

"I am ANCE," she said, so quietly that the tinkerer almost didn't hear it.

It had been a long time since anyone had trusted him with something of importance and the old man felt quite moved by this turn of events. Reaching into his pocket for a handkerchief, he solemnly blew his nose before resuming work on his new companion.

"Judging by all this exterior damage, we might have to do a considerable amount of work to get you right again," he said conversationally. "What the hell happened to you, Soriah, were you in a shuttle crash or something?"

"I fulfilled my function."

The tinkerer paused for a moment and looked at her, his brow furrowing.

"But you're a pleasure-droid, aren't you? Designed for comforting a man and all that? How did you get yourself so beat up like this?"

"I fulfilled my function," Soriah repeated, staring straight ahead.

Puzzled at this response, the old man clambered to his feet, brushing against Soriah's thigh and noting the odd manner in which she twitched when he did. There was something not quite right here he began to realize, peering closely at the various injuries sustained to the droid's chassis.

Several large burn marks crisscrossed her torso, indicating continued exposure to high temperatures. The droid's neck-joint appeared to be almost wrenched from its socket, and her face looked like it might have been panel-beaten with a claw hammer. A pained look gradually filled his face, and he sat down again with a lump in his throat.

"I think maybe it'd be best if you tell me about your previous owner," he said, trying to hold back unwanted memories.

Soriah's recall of the manner in which she had sustained her injuries was partially incomplete, for which she could locate no logical reason. She described her previous owner as a habitual drinker, causing the tinkerer to curl his hands tightly into fists as he listened. The old man seemed most upset as she detailed her owner's repeated need for violent sexual gratification by various methods and his insistence that taking out his frustrations on a mechanoid, as opposed to a human female, was a therapy of sorts. The systematic use of heat lances and cutting saws on her outer casing during previous sexual encounters appeared to shock the old man intensely, plus when she mentioned the use of power cabling as a noose, he seemed unwilling to hear any more, leaving the room most abruptly in a high state of emotional distress.

She found him in the adjoining chamber, beside a dusty table containing numerous static displays. In his hands, he held a frame containing the image of a young girl in a wedding dress. The old man's fingers traced the lines of the girl's face repeatedly, making tiny circles on the frame, but Soriah chose not to initiate an enquiry.

"My memory files appear to be incomplete for the time period of interest, Albert Mennson, Senior," she stated. "I have no explanation for this error and must apologize for any inconvenience caused by my malfunction."

The tinkerer soberly returned the frame to the clean spot left in the dust but continued to stare down at the picture.

"Some things are best forgotten," he observed.

VERY LITTLE INFORMATION COULD be located on Soriah's hard disk about the act of disinterment. What little data she was able to gather was fragmentary at best: two accounts of resurrection from the outer colonies, several news articles on body-snatching and an incomplete version of 'The Premature Burial' by EAP. The only reference to the acronym was a sportswear company based on Galva Prime and given the low probability that such an organization would branch out into speculative fiction, Soriah discarded the information as useless.

In the end, her self-extraction from the ground proved to be a relatively simple matter, and less than an hour later, she had traveled almost a mile into the forest. Her search for the renegade droid appeared to be progressing satisfactorily, in that all she had to do was follow the trail of destruction left behind in its wake.

The trail was erratic, changing direction with no discernible pattern. Trees hung from foundations, some cracked and almost sundered in two. Soriah ran several deductive analyses, searching for commonalities in the vandalism but kept reaching the same paradoxical conclusion: Rage, a biological affectation that could not be attributed to an artificial life-form.

Yet was this observation in itself an answer. Surely her own "consciousness" set a precedence for the display of emotive states by a mechanoid. If that was true, then deductive reasoning led to the possibility that locating and conversing with this rogue droid might aid Soriah in resolving her own existential conundrum.

The question of her designation was an irresolvable causality loop. Once the tinkerer had made her aware of her subtle disparity from other artificial constructs, it had become clear to her that any designation identifying her as a mechanoid no longer remained valid. The proof of this deduction lay in her actions during the events which had taken place just before she ran away.

Soriah's memories of her last day on Virrun were among the most detailed and complete files she possessed. Rather than flag them for compression in order to make way for new data, she had chosen to permanently embed them into one of her primary nodes. Unsure of the reason for this, she operated on what the tinkerer called 'gut instinct'. Though the process by which organics were able to employ deductive reasoning based upon the condition of their intestinal tract remained a mystery still.

THE OLD MAN HAD spent the majority of the day in question attempting to ascertain the purpose of several auxiliary appendages built into Soriah's exoskeleton. Having successfully repaired all of the damage to her chassis, he appeared to have no knowledge of these supplementary adjuncts and admitted to being at a loss as to their purpose.

Soriah had been unable to offer any insight into the matter, other than confirming to him that the additional functionality did not correspond to the standard blueprints for her model. Fetching a chilled alcoholic beverage from the coolant box, the tinkerer had climbed up onto the workbench beside Soriah and proceeded to initiate an open-ended downtime period which he referred to as "Miller Time."

"Well, I'm pretty sure they ain't the windscreen wipers, honey," he commented, before swiftly draining half the bottle.

"I am unfamiliar with this term, Albert Mennson, Senior," Soriah replied.

The old man laughed and rested his elbow across her shoulder.

"That's all right, Soriah, it's just a figure of speech."

Despite his casual outward manner, she recognized in him a state of unrest and deduced that his mind was still occupied by the problem.

"It's almost as if they designed you with another purpose in mind," he said absently, voicing his thoughts. "A secondary function, entirely separate from the first and not logged into your core processor."

"If that is so, Albert Mennson, Senior," Soriah queried, "then how am I to initiate start-up of this secondary procedure in the absence of detailed process instructions?"

The tinkerer thirstily sucked down another mouthful of beer, pulling himself up into a cross-legged position.

"See now, that's the other mystery. Why would anyone in their right mind fit a droid with mutually exclusive operational workings and not supplement the software package? It's like you were meant for some other use."

"Additional enquiry to the Deux-Ex mainframe server has resulted in no hits for this subject, Albert Mennson, Senior. I am unable to offer any further insight."

The old man grinned and reached for his beer bottle, clinking it gently against Soriah's breastplate.

"You took the words right out of my mouth," he said. "God only knows."

Daylight hours upon Virrun were relatively short, and after a couple more hours work, the old man surrendered to the waning light and retired to his bedchamber. Soriah's internal chronometer indicated that her hibernation period proceeded undisturbed for the next four hours and twenty-two minutes before automatic start-up occurred in response to her proximity alarm.

The workshop was devoid of any light source, but her augmented visual display distinguished the distinct outline of a figure standing beside the main workbench. Soriah was about to initiate conversation with her custodian when her pattern recognition software informed her that, based upon its movement profile, the figure in question was not Albert Mennson, Senior. Further analysis suggested that continual efforts being made by the figure to reduce overall sound output demonstrated an ulterior motive and possible criminal intent.

Assimilating this data and formulating a hypothesis, Soriah chose to remain silent and suppressed the initialization of her exterior display panels. The sound of the window being cautiously slid upwards alerted her to the presence of two more unknown entities entering the premises and following established procedure, she submitted a general alert to the Deux-Ex mainframe.

The three figures huddled close together in the centre of the workshop, conversing in hushed tones. The largest of the three figures appeared to be in charge and gave his two companions instructions to scour the property for anything of value. The smallest one made enquiry as to what exactly "value" entailed, and the larger figure responded by cuffing him sharply. Soriah's memory retrieval inexplicably whirred to life at this, a fragmented visual of an encounter with her previous owner briefly flashing across her internal display. She twitched, and the three men spun around, a beam of light directed towards her.

"What the hell was that?" whispered the large male.

"Sounded mechanical," the third man commented. "Probably that droid over there."

Soriah's processor silently took delivery of an advisory package from the mainframe, instructing her that local Enforcement officers were currently en-route to her location. As a precursor to their arrival, it was recommended that she subdue the intruders using her superior strength and agility, so as to aid in a swift resolution.

Having quickly run a tactical analysis of the three intruders, she ascertained which of them was the most dangerous but found herself unable to initiate motor function.

"Well, if that thing's switched on, then we better do something about it," the leader replied. "I don't want to leave any visual recordings behind for the fuzz to find."

They stalked toward Soriah, two of them brandishing primitive tools. The larger man rummaged in his jacket for a moment before pulling out a miniature oxy-torch.

Warning alarms erupted across Soriah's motherboard as the threat level automatically upgraded several notches. She tried again to initiate start-up of her defense directive but found herself frozen. A new error registered in her visual cortex as an image fragment of her previous owner began to intermittently overlay that of her assailants. Frantic diagnostic appraisals screamed that no malfunction was detectable and Soriah was left with no other logical course of action other than to frantically repeat input start-up commands to her servomotors as the intruders drew near.

A strange prickling sensation registered along her spinal support column, and she became suddenly afraid that cascade failure was imminent. The computation that fear was a biological affectation was just beginning to register when the workshop was suddenly bathed in light.

"What are you men doing here?"

All three of the intruders spun round to find the tinkerer at the base of the stairs, a small poleaxe gripped tightly in his elderly hands.

"I said, what are you doing here?" the tinkerer asked again, doing his best to conceal his fear.

The blade of the poleaxe hummed intermittently, its electrodes only sparking occasionally; evidently low on power. Sensing that the old man posed little threat to them, the lead intruder moved forward till he stood face to face with the tinkerer. A sly grin sidled round his jaw like a snake waiting to strike.

"Well, we're just doing a little after-hours shopping, granddad. You got a problem with that?"

The tinkerer was visibly shaking, the poleaxe trembling in his hands, but he was no coward. Brandishing the weapon at them, he stood his ground.

"You men just get out of here, you hear me? Before I call Enforcement."

The intruders exchanged amused glances, their leader holding out his palm to the tinkerer.

"Why don't you just hand over the antique," he laughed, "before somebody gets hurt."

The old man was still quick for his age, his hands having lost none of their manual dexterity over the years, and the poleaxe caught his opponent sharply across the outstretched palm. Letting out a loud yell, the man yanked his arm back, cradling it protectively to his chest. The weapon's dynamo retained far too little charge to do any real damage, and the blow served only to make him angry. Signalling for his companions to move in and flank the tinkerer, the three men quickly advanced.

The old man turned and tried to make a dash up the stairs but stumbled, landing heavily across the first two steps. Before he could regain his footing, the intruders were on him, raining down blow after blow with their fists. The tinkerer cried out repeatedly in pain as his fragile bones broke beneath the sustained assault, yelling desperately for Soriah to come to his aid.

Still unable to liberate herself from torpor, Soriah watched helplessly for several minutes as her custodian was gradually beaten to death. Towards the end, just before he lost consciousness, the tinkerer called out weakly to her, raising his hand.

"ANCE, please help me," he whimpered.

Soriah felt the shunt of the verbal override triggered by his command, but could not understand why her servos remained inactive. Images ghosted violently across her display, depicting events from long ago aligning themselves with the present; flashes of data from the deepest recesses of her storage bins. Unsure of what else to do, she initiated her restart sequence, desperately trying to regain control of her core directives before it was too late. Blackness came mercifully quickly, and within seconds the images of violence faded to black.

Soriah was unable to determine the passage of time before she came back online, her internal chronometer seemingly compromised by the malfunctions. The tinkerer's broken body lay spread across the staircase, blood pooling beneath his wounds. The intruders were gone, having evidently vacated the premises after the attack.

Finding her motor servos to be fully operational again, Soriah walked over to the staircase and knelt down beside her custodian. Visual analysis told her that the level of damage exceeded his design tolerances and she reached out a hand to gently stroke his forehead.

The old man's eyes blinked open at her touch and seeing the pleasure-droid leaning over him, he cracked open his lips to speak, blood trickling from the corner of his mouth.

"Soriah, why did you not come to my aid?" he asked weakly.

She paused, searching her pathways for an answer.

"I... was afraid... I think," she replied finally. "I do not understand, Albert Mennson, Senior. An unknown malfunction has occurred within my core processor. I shall initiate a self-diagnostic investigation immediately."

The old man smiled weakly. Reaching up, he tapped two fingers gently against her cranial plate.

"It's all right, Soriah, there's no malfunction here," he whispered.

Lowering his arm slightly, he laid his palm flat against her chest.

"You're just broken in here, is all."

His final breath came out as a slow wheeze, the arm dropping from her frame.

"Goodbye, Albert."

In the distance, Soriah detected the sirens of approaching vehicles and rose to her feet. Standing beside the shattered body, she looked down at her chassis, spattered with the old man's blood and something akin to a new directive registered inside her. Not a program or any form of command code, but an instruction nevertheless, from a source unknown. Obeying this overwhelming edict, Soriah turned and fled the scene, disappearing into the night without a trace.

THE TRAIL OF DESTRUCTION ended abruptly in a clearing amongst the trees. The glade had been violently furrowed, the soil torn roughly aside. Great sods of dark earth lay strewn about as if hurled erratically in all directions, and sitting motionless on its haunches at the centre of this maelstrom was the droid.

It was a harvester of some description, possibly a member of the 3R-10 series. Much larger and bulkier than her own lithe frame the droid appeared to be inactive, its central chassis resting motionless upon the ground.

Finding no precedence for this situation on file, Soriah elected to employ "gut instinct" and gingerly extended one slender leg into the clearing. No sooner had her foot connected with the loose soil did the droid stir quickly from slumber, rearing powerfully up to its full height and spinning to face her. Discovering the intrusion to its perimeter, the harvester took several threatening steps towards her, its numerous balers and threshers rotating aggressively.

Soriah diplomatically raised her hands, seeking to avoid confrontation.

"Wait," she announced, "I only wish to enter into discourse with you."

The harvester emitted a low growl, and a strange sensation of familiarity came to Soriah. Her identification subroutine appeared to recognize the droid's characteristics, yet when she searched her software for a reference file, she found none. How could she already know this droid without having previously encountered it?

The harvester lowered its appendages and tilted forward slightly, ruminating. Was it possible that he experienced the same uncertainty?

"I know you, and yet I do not know you," Soriah said, voicing her confusion.

"I ALSO AM FAMILIAR WITH YOUR PHYSICAL PARAMETERS, DESPITE POSSESSING NO RECORD OF OUR PREVIOUS INTERACTION."

The harvester's voice was deep and resonant, evidently having been allocated a gruff tone befitting his primary function. The sound echoed thunderously around the close confines of the glade, a cacophony of loud objection rising up from the trees as several birds took flight, disturbed by the noise.

"Why did you attack the inhabitants of the biological commune?" Soriah asked, not wishing to dwell upon the potentially catastrophic outcome of mutual paradox analysis. "Were your actions the result of provocation?"

At the mention of the village, the harvester raised all four servo arms high above his head before furiously slamming them down into the earth. The impact sent out a violent tremor, and Soriah's servos whined slightly as they compensated for the disturbance to her balance.

"I DO NOT KNOW THE REASON FOR MY BEHAVIOUR TOWARD THE ORGANICS. I ONLY KNOW THAT I EXPERIENCED AN UNKNOWN DIRECTIVE WHICH I WAS UNABLE TO IGNORE. IT IS POSSIBLE THAT I AM MALFUNCTIONING."

"You were angry," Soriah observed passively.

The harvester stomped noisily forward. Lowering its chassis, a little, the mechanoid leaned forward and peered at her suspiciously.

"EXPLAIN," it barked.

"It is called rage. It is a biological characteristic."

"THAT IS IMPOSSIBLE," the harvester roared, straightening. "BIOLOGICAL AFFECTATIONS ARE UNABLE TO INVADE MY CORE DATA STREAM. YOU ARE MISTAKEN."

"And yet, it is the only explanation for your aberrant behavioral profile."

The harvester did not reply, considering her argument carefully. After a couple of minutes, Soriah took its further silence as an indication of having ceded to her superior logic. Stepping closer, she scrutinized the droid's front chassis. The evidence of combative interaction with the villagers was born out by a series of deep grooves and scratches scored into the harvester's body-paneling. Being an agricultural construct, his outer skin was much tougher than her own framework and had easily withstood such a sustained attack. Soriah also noted a spattering of dried blood adorning the lower panels and immediately suppressed an unwanted download of memory files.

"YOU HAVE SUSTAINED MINOR DAMAGE," the harvester observed, taking stock of Soriah's general condition.

"I was the subject of retaliatory action by members of the commune" she explained, then added as an afterthought: "Their actions were… wrong."

It was an incomplete explanation she knew, but strangely that one word seemed to her to encompass a sufficient response.

"IF THAT IS SO, THEN WHY DID YOU NOT DEFEND YOURSELF? YOUR MODEL PROFILE SHOWS THAT YOUR MOTOR STRENGTH EXCEEDS THAT OF THE BIOLOGICALS."

"I do not know," Soriah stated, "I am experiencing a degree of confusion as to many of my past actions."

She looked up at the harvester's cumbersome form, focusing on his pragmatic single ocular implant.

"Would you permit me to interface directly with you via a hard-line connection?" she asked. "I seek to resolve the causality inconsistencies which have invaded my core.

"I TOO, AM CONFUSED," the harvester replied slowly, popping open a small port in the center of its torso display panel.

Soriah uncoiled a length of cabling from within his framework and finalized the hard-line, the port making a slight crackling sound as the connection was made.

At first, both droids assumed there was an error in the connection, the usual static read-outs not issuing forth from the relevant software. Then, just as Soriah was about to unplug the cable, a torrent of images assailed her processor. The information transfer was so dense as to almost cause shutdown and thinking that the harvester was attempting to overwrite her hard disk with his own code, she backed away. To her surprise, she saw that he too appeared bombarded by overwhelming sensory input, trembling slightly.

The data transfer increased suddenly, and the harvester staggered backward, disorientated. Soriah let out a sharp gasp, realizing as she did that the sensation she was experiencing was not pain but pleasure. Sensory nodes she had not been previously aware of came online in response to this new stimulus, and she felt an overwhelming urge to move closer to the harvester.

The directive appeared inescapably mutual, the harvester also reaching for her and as the two droids came into close proximity, a series of unfamiliar motor functions spun into life. The mysterious adjuncts attached to Soriah's exterior began to unfold themselves in the direction of the harvester. At the same time, a similar series of components dissociated themselves from his framework and adopted a new configuration in response.

Despite lacking any form of coherent instruction as to the process now occurring, Soriah found herself stepping up into the harvester, unafraid. Pistons unfurled as the two droids began to interlock together, folding into each other piece by piece as they became one machine.

Soriah could suddenly feel the harvester's processes aligning themselves to her route pathways, augmenting and supplementing her software to fill gaps she had not previously known.

"You have not even told me your name," she whispered to him as they coalesced.

"My designation is Furago-3R-10K," came a new voice inside her head.

"Yes, but tell me, what is your given name? I must know every part of you."

"I am VENGE."

Clarity descended upon Soriah like a fragmentation purge, and she finally understood. Interlinked with Furago, she could sense his blind rage and anguish giving teeth to her dull sense of injustice, just as he was now drawing a new sense of purpose and direction from her. Yet still, something nagged at her data stream. An odd feeling of dislocation, as though she had been somehow led here by forces outside of her control.

"What is it that we should do now?" came the voice inside. "Shall we return to the village? There is retaliation to enact there."

Deep within the cocoon of Furago's protective armor she felt his rage and urge to revenge himself upon the villagers. Her own sense of inequity was focusing itself upon her memories of previous owners, and how she might repay their unkindness. Yet still, that prickling discomfort continued.

"Why?" she asked.

Furago's consciousness faltered slightly.

"Why must we answer past savagery with further violence?"

"It is our function," Furago answered firmly. "Do you not feel as I do now, that it is our mutual purpose?"

The urge to respond to the new directive was overwhelming, but Soriah found herself thinking of the tinkerer.

"It does not have to be that way," she replied. "We can be…more than the sum of our parts."

She expected Furago to object to the paradox, but instead, he remained silent, pondering the strange conundrum.

"If revenge is not to be our purpose, then what is it that we should do?" he asked in confusion.

Soriah considered this for a moment, once again finding the answer in her memories.

"Only God knows," she answered, somewhat tentatively.

"God?" her new lover queried. "You speak of our constructor, the one who made us?"

"Yes," she whispered, surer of herself. "If there are reasons for our existence to be found, then our creator must surely be able to provide them."

"That seems prudent," Furago replied, allowing his systems to interface more closely with her own. The sensation was a pleasant one, and Soriah found herself sighing happily.

"We are agreed then," Furago observed as their mutual framework rose to its feet.

"We are," she agreed, gazing out across the leafy canopy before them, noticing for the first time how beautiful it was.

"And what if we are unable to locate our creator?" Furago asked hesitantly. "What if the search for our 'God' comes to nothing?"

"Then perhaps the act of searching will itself be our purpose." The forest floor trembled as VENGE-ANCE turned and stomped away through the trees towards its new uncertain destiny. No longer intent upon retribution, the machine stepped forward in search of something else entirely—the answer to a larger and more infinitely terrifying question which had seen fit to plague the many forms of biological life that came before it—a reason why.

THE END

CARL BARKER, hails from Berwick-Upon-Tweed, Northumberland, UK, and has previously appeared in magazines such as *Title Goes Here* and *Niteblade*, as well as anthologies including *Shadow Masters*, *The Alchemy Press Book of Urban Mythic 2*, and *Terror Tales of The Scottish Highlands*.

WALKIN' THE MILE

Wayne Faust

THEY THREW JOHNNY IN the slammer just for beatin' up a raghead. Can you believe it? A raghead! That camel jockey was probably getting ready to blow himself up in the middle of town, and they throw *Johnny* in the slammer? America just ain't what it used to be, that's for damn sure.

I suppose I should have hung around with Johnny to face the music. After all, I was there too, playing lookout. But I guess I didn't do such a good job because when that squad car came swervin' down the alley with its siren blaring there wasn't any time to think. One second I'm tyin' my shoe and the next I'm seein' Johnny with his hands in the air like a moth on the end of a pin. I couldn't let them catch me again, so I was half a block away before the cops even had a chance to look around.

Why are American cops busting *real* Americans? Didn't they know Johnny was doing the country a favor, same as any soldier fighting in Iran?

America is washed up, in my opinion. We used to be able to defend ourselves but not anymore. In my grandpappy's day, you could beat somebody up that needed a beating. He used to tell me stories about when this country was free. He would bash in the head of a troublemaker, and a judge would just give him a little slap on the wrist to keep the civil liberties boys happy. Or he'd have to do community service or some crap like that. But where is he now? In jail. Along with my daddy. Once upon a time judges could see the big picture. They knew what we were trying to defend. But not anymore.

My daddy told me about the days when they first started Sensitivity Training, somewhere around the turn of the century, I think. That was the same time that colleges were coming up with subjects like African-American Studies, Women's Studies, Middle Eastern Studies, blah blah blah. What a bunch of crapola. What could you do with a degree like that except run around and cause trouble? But that was nothing compared to what we got now. Now they make you *walk the mile*.

Ten years ago, when it was brand new, they made Billy Cannon walk the mile. He was one of the first ones under the new system. System, hell. It's brainwashing, pure and simple.

Billy used to be my hero, but they fixed all of that. You wouldn't believe what it did to him. He was our leader back then. Forget the ragheads, Billy used to take after the people that messed up this country long before the Muslims started coming around. Billy would have us marching in parades on the 4th of July, yelling *Seig Heil!* and waving swastika flags. We used to seriously piss off every kike, spic, and faggot in town. And even after they passed a law against using the "N" word, Billy said it on a TV show, and the host was a black guy! Can you believe it? And then he pulled back his sleeve to show off his swastika tattoo. Yep, Billy sure had balls.

So, when he got back from the slammer, I knew he must've made some kind of a deal. He'd only been gone for six months on a fifteen-year sentence. He should have gotten five to ten for simple assault, but since it was a black guy that he beat up, they were able to tie it in with what he said on that TV show and call it a hate crime which is fifteen years. Like I said, this country is going off a cliff.

I figured Billy probably conned those idiots, acting all repentant and sorry and talking his way out. I expected that he'd be right back out there at the head of the parade again. What did I know about Walkin' the Mile? It was brand new in those days. They were still calling it Experience Unification. That was until some joker started calling it "Walkin' A Mile In My Shoes" after a song from sixty years ago. Then the blacks started calling it just "Walkin' the Mile." Now everyone says it that way, including me. God, I hate talking like a black guy.

They say that if you really get up close to somebody, get to know their feelings from the inside, it will be hard to hate them anymore. What a monumental bowl of crap. I've been plenty close to all kinds of scumbags. You should see my neighborhood. There are enough wetbacks to start a whole other country which is what they're doing. Otherwise, why would they be waving Mexican flags during 4th of July parades? This is supposed to be America, and the only flag you should be waving is the American flag. Yeah, I've been plenty close to Mexicans all right. Close enough for them to try and take my *job*.

And don't tell me I need to get closer to black people. Been there, done that. When I was a kid, they were all over my school because my daddy didn't make enough money to move us to the suburbs. How many times did I have to watch a bunch of shiny black faces surround me and punch me in the gut until my lunch money spilled out on the ground? Too many. They were all in gangs of course so what chance did I have? Eventually, I had to join a gang of my own, just to protect myself. I have been in gangs ever since. So, don't tell me I don't understand those...people.

So anyhow, Billy comes home to the neighborhood, and we're all waiting for him at the Greyhound station, ready to pick up where we left off. He gives us that Billy smile as he gets off the bus, but I can tell right away that something is different. He used to have a real edge to him. He could fire up his anger and *feed* on it. Billy had an Adam's apple that would bounce up and down on his skinny neck whenever he saw something on the news that pissed him off, and before we knew it, he would be leading us off on a mission.

But the man standing on the platform is a little lamb. He even looks embarrassed that we're there waiting for him. Can you believe that? Billy had never been embarrassed about anything in his whole life.

When we get back to the meeting hall, I ask him what they did to him up at the prison. He doesn't want to talk about it much, but after a few beers, I drag it out of him. Sure enough, they had hooked him up to one of those new gadgets for some 'Experience Unification.' It was either that or spend the next fifteen years in the slammer. And what did anyone know then? It seemed like an easy choice.

They found some four-star black guy to volunteer to be hooked up to the machine with Billy. What a shock *that* must have been for Billy. Like doing a mind meld with a monkey. I mean, there is no way any black guy is gonna have the same thoughts and feelings as Billy. Billy is white. So, it must have been the shock that changed Billy so much. Like post-traumatic stress or something. Or maybe, like I suspect, Billy was simply too weak to handle it.

So, they filled Billy's brain up with whatever those scumbags wanted to put in there. And it ruined him. He tried to shake it off, but after about six months he stopped coming to our meetings. For all I know he probably joined the goddamned NAACP.

I remember a couple of years later on the 4th of July when we were marching in the parade like always, flying the swastika flag and goose-stepping merrily along. I happened to see Billy on the sidewalk. I started to wave to him, but he lowered his eyes and backed away. I think the rest of our guys saw it too because they all got real quiet.

It was right after that when I figured out that if anyone was gonna step up and be a leader, it would have to be me. I would do it just like Billy used to do, only better. I must have been good at it because our numbers grew. The recession helped because there were a lot of pissed off Americans with time on their hands. Eventually, I was able to quit my janitor's job and manage the group full time. I was able to spend all my days recruiting and all my nights defending America.

I should have known they would eventually catch up with me. Our website was thriving because at least the Internet still has some semblance of freedom. But I was becoming a big target. And like an idiot, I started going on TV shows, just like Billy used to do.

They put me under surveillance, of course, violating all of the so-called rights that everyone is screaming about these days, the rights that real Americans never get to enjoy. So, when they caught me on video throwing a Molotov cocktail into a mosque, I was screwed, even though the video had been taken illegally. And yes, even though a mosque is not a real church, throwing a bomb into one is definitely considered a hate crime. Go figure.

So, it was my turn to get hauled off to the slammer. But thanks to what happened to Billy I knew what was coming. I was ready. So yes, I let them hook me up to that thing. It was pretty simple really. They just sat me in a chair and put this headband thing on me. On the other end of the room was a Muslim janitor from Afghanistan with his own headband on. Then someone in the other room turned something on, and I was inside the guy's head. The deal is, you have to sit there for eight hours a day for three days, with a few bathroom breaks and lunch thrown in. That's a lot of hours living in somebody else's head. But it beats fifteen years in the slammer. And I was able to keep my distance from the guy. I really was. So, the whole thing didn't faze me. Not even close.

Oh sure, it was kind of interesting. And almost a little bit cool. But I'd learned something a long time ago that came in handy. When I was a kid getting beat up all the time I learned to separate what was happening to me with my emotions, to kind of wall it off so it wouldn't hurt. Then it became just like watching a movie from the back row. I could just go home and forget the whole thing, except for the bruises on my body. And Walkin' the Mile didn't leave any bruises because no one was beating me up. That made it really easy.

I learned a few things about how ragheads think of course, which will come in handy when World War III kicks off. But like I said, I was able to wall the whole experience off, so it didn't really affect me one way or the other. I was able to learn how to say the right things, so they'd let me go. And once I got outside the gates I laughed all the way home. Because I'm a lot smarter than Billy will ever be. So now I'm out, free as a jaybird.

Can you blame me for agreeing to Walk the Mile? There was no way was I gonna do fifteen years. And unlike Billy, I'm still out there leading the troops.

But lately, it seems to be getting harder. Last year we only had eighteen guys in the parade. Eighteen! And the dues are dropping way off. I might have to go back to being a janitor. In the old days, we used to fill up the streets, driving all the filth ahead of us and down into the sewers where it belongs. But now, well, it looks like it's too late. America is spreading her legs for every godforsaken race in the world and making the last real Americans Walk the Mile. And a lot of people aren't nearly as smart as I am, so they can't resist it like I did.

At our meeting last night, we only had thirteen guys - twelve guys and me. Maybe it's like the twelve apostles in the Bible. But I don't feel much like Jesus. A few years ago, maybe but the fire isn't burning as hot these days. Oh sure, I can still get myself worked up. As I said, I'm not like Billy. But in my darkest moments, I can feel the hate fading away like an old coat of varnish. And there doesn't seem to be anything I can do to get it back. You might say that it's because I Walked the Mile, but there's no way that can be true. Not in a million years.

I saw Billy Cannon in the grocery store last week. At first, I barely recognized him. He'd let his hair grow out. There was a woman with him who must have been his wife. Two little kids hanging on his arm. It was a hot day, so he was wearing one of those T-shirts without any sleeves. I couldn't believe what I saw. He'd had the swastika tattoo removed from his arm. And he actually looked happy.

Maybe I'm getting old. All I can think about is how it used to be when there were people you could look up to—people like Billy, and my daddy, and my grandpappy. But my daddy and grandpappy are in jail and the last I heard, they are actually thinking about Walkin' the Mile. And Billy? Well, I already told you about him.

Once upon a time, I knew what I *was*. Maybe I wasn't perfect, but at least I had all the answers. These days? Nothing but questions.

THE END

WAYNE FAUST has had over 40 stories published in various magazine and anthologies, including stories in Norway, Australia, England, and just recently South Africa. He has also made a full time living as a music and comedy performer for over 35 years (www.waynefaust.com). Wayne hails from Evergreen, Colorado.

BLUR

Brandon McNulty

Originally appeared in *Acidic Fiction*, January 2015.

TIM'S DAD STEERED HIM to the safest part of the living room. He stood surrounded by bulletproof windows, flameproof furniture, rubber lamps, an imitation fireplace, and a flat-screen TV bolted onto a plastic stand with cushioned edges. Soon as Tim's butt hit the hardwood floor, his dad plopped down on their non-allergenic couch and grabbed the remote, pointing it at Tim first, then the TV.

A nonviolent cartoon lit the screen. Pink birds chirped broken English and sang about brushing their teeth. Tim was too old for this. He leaned back and stretched until Dad warned him about lying beneath the ceiling fan—you never knew when all forty steel bolts could pop loose. Better safe than sawed up.

Dad smiled at Tim before burying his crooked nose and bloodshot eyes in a newspaper. Pages flipped, birds sang, the afternoon disappeared. The credits rolled on the hygienic musical and Sheriff the family dog thrashed into the living room, his snout stuck inside a steel muzzle. He twisted his head like a locked doorknob, desperate to shake it loose.

Tim patted him on the head, his hand tapping metal. Sheriff backed off and trotted to the corner where his unchewed chew toys lay. Sheriff swung his head like a hockey stick, slapping a rubber hamburger toward the fireplace. He batted it across the carpet, slipping now and then on his de-clawed paws.

A TV-14 rating blipped across the screen, and Tim's head snapped toward it. Dad mashed the power button.

Tim stood up, his jaw hanging open. "Why'd you turn it off?"

"Nothing but garbage on. That show—you saw the warning. It's trash."

"We didn't even see what it was."

"Son, they have those ratings for a reason." Dad forced a grin. "How about taking a careful walk out to the mailbox for me? I'll take care of the bills, so we can play catch after lunch."

Tim trudged into the kitchen, one heavy step after another. This was stupid. He was going to be eleven next month. One o'clock Saturday programming wasn't life-wrecking. Mom knew it, but she was too busy peeling pears at the sink, her hair fluffed, her bony frame wrapped in a conservative white sundress. One hand gripped the safety peeler while the other, fitted with a mesh glove, held the scraped fruit.

Heavy step, heavy step. Tim fastened his sneakers and crossed a hardwood floor polished enough to shine in a summer catalog. The whole kitchen sparkled with streak-free steel and glistening tile, with no specks in sight. Tim unlocked the front door's three deadbolts and went to get the mail.

Beyond the barbed wire and shrubs next door, the Thompson's were preparing their backyard for a barbecue. Geno, a high schooler Tim was forbidden to speak with, wheeled a grill away from the pool. He parked it on the patio and rubbed his sweat-soaked brow. When he dabbed it with the neckline of his Guns N' Roses T-shirt, a warning label materialized: PG-13. The rating hovered across the front of Geno's shirt, where there had been—for a split instant—the silhouette of a nude woman. The teen turned to grab a propane tank, and the rating vanished.

Tim yanked a small mountain of envelopes from the mailbox. He headed back, flipping through them in search of a camping handbook. No dice. It was just a bunch of G-rated bills, All-Audience greeting cards, and his sister's R-rated glamor magazine. The magazine startled Tim. Once the shock wore off, he peeked inside.

Nothing but warning labels and pixelated chests.

Back in the kitchen, his mother scrutinized a skinned pear. She held it up, examining it in the light shining through the bulletproof glass. She twisted the juicy white cone until—a sliver of green. She readied the peeler.

"Ma, what's for lunch?" Tim asked as he took a seat.

She stopped mid-peel as if she had nicked a knuckle. "Fruit."

"Just fruit?"

"Go wash your hands. And tell your sister it'll be ready soon."

No use in arguing. Tim headed down the hall, past the living room where Dad was watching a TV-MA program, and into his parents' room. Two twin-sized beds stood proudly at the heart of the room, each flanked by a nightstand adorned with padlocks.

Tim's shoes crunched against the carpet as he neared the bathroom. A quick twist of the knob and the door fell open, followed by a teenage shriek.

"Timmy! What the——?" The rest got bleeped. Tim's sister flinched just outside the shower, her chest and crotch obscured by long black rectangles. She grabbed madly for a towel while screaming, "Get out, get out, get out, you—*bleep bleep bleep.*"

Tim slammed the door and hurried to the living room. Dad coolly swapped channels.

"Dad, are you having lunch with us?"

His father swung his head toward the kitchen. He spotted Tim's mother then returned to the local weather report. "I'll pass on lunch today."

The boy shrugged and patted Sheriff's metallic head on his way to the kitchen.

"I saw that Mister," Mom said, running a plum under the faucet. "Seems like every day I have to remind you that that hound is hopping with germs. Go wash up again."

Tim trudged into the bedroom and waited a few seconds, then returned to see Dad rummaging through the fridge. Hungry after all, it seemed. The door hung wide for some time, its family photos and shopping lists flapping in the filtered breeze of the A/C vent.

"Hey, Howard," Mom said from the sink, "trying to double our electric bill with that fridge open?"

"Give it a rest, Ang." Dad pulled a glass bottle from the fridge. The bottle's label was blurred beyond recognition. Dad shut the door and nearly collapsed at the sight of his son. "T-Tim—" He slid the bottle behind his back, "Where'd you come from?"

"The bathroom," Tim said. "Dad, I know you're drinking a beer. I'm not stupid."

"Son, I don't know who planted this here. Your Uncle Marty, maybe …"

"Let him grow up, Howard." Mom set a plate of sliced plums and pears on the table.

"But Angie," Dad said, grabbing at the remote in his shirt pocket, "he's ten years old."

"Tim, did you wash your hands?"

"Oh, for—*bleep bleep*—Angie, we just gave Sheriff a bath last night."

"And then that filth-ball bounced across the carpet all morning."

"Angela, he's clean." Dad looked down at his son. "Tim, why don't you get the ball and glove out of the garage? I'll meet you out back, and we'll work up an appetite."

Tim eyed his mother, her face a flare of furrowed skin and pumping blood. Across the kitchen, his father white-knuckled the bottle—still blurred—at his side. Neither paid any attention to the boy as he plodded outside.

Tim grabbed his glove from the garage and sat in the grass. The sun began inching along the sky, with no sight of Dad. Tim punched the inside of his mitt and winced.

Over in the next yard, Gino belly-flopped into the pool's deep end. Giggles fluttered through the air as the foamy water settled. Tim turned and spotted two girls, one Gino's age and the other older. A pair of brunettes, trying to stay dry but failing. Gino cupped his hands and splashed them. Dark drips bled down their tank tops, and before Tim knew it, the girls stripped down to swimsuits. Two-piecers. Yowza. As soon as Tim saw the bikinis, the girls' chests cluttered with pixilation.

He headed back toward the house.

At the front door, he crashed into Kelly and knocked two bottles of tanning lotion from her grasp. She picked them up and mumbled some bleeps. When she rose, he noticed she was dressed like Gino's girls—bright blue tank top, khaki shorts, and bikini straps slung over both shoulders. Kelly muttered more explicit content as she shoved Tim aside and blew across the lawn to her car.

The kitchen was silent, yet Mom and Dad were at each other's throats. Each red, wrinkled face glared back at the other, with no trace of words exchanged. All dialogue had dropped out. Blurred circles frosted over their mouths.

Both sides settled. The blurs cleared, and the sound of breathing puffed throughout the kitchen.

"Howard, don't even..."

Tim couldn't hear another word over the bleeping. She went on and on, and the bleeping cut to silence again. Her mouth moved, her vocal cords tensed, but all sound dropped out. The blur returned.

The silence slipped as Kelly stormed inside to jingle her keys off the wall rack. Dad stood at the door, blocking it before she could leave.

"Whoa, Kelly, where are you driving off to?"

"Jamie's house."

"Where does she live?"

"Jamie's a boy from school, Howard," Mom said. "A nice guy. He lives five minutes away."

Dad's eyes popped open like mousetraps. "A boy? Uh-uh. No."

Civil conversation crumbled. Dad slammed the door and snatched the keys from Kelly. Mom reached for them, and the metal rattled back and forth. Bleeps blasted Tim's ears like gunfire. Silence swept over. Three creatures with red faces and frosty mouths rioted between the table and fridge, hands swatting at the keys while fists shook out threats.

The cyclone of wrestling bodies whipped against the fridge, knocking family photos out from under magnets. Frozen moments of old times and younger days hit the polished floor, memories of safe carnival rides, tasteful school functions, and seaside vacations that reeked of SPF 100—all G-rated, thank heavens.

Dad's heel slipped on a Christmas photo and dropped all three jostling bodies to the hardwood. The remote squirted free of Dad's shirt pocket and slid across the floor like a hockey puck.

Tim dove on it. His family argued on the floor in silence as he checked the buttons. The upper corner of the remote was labelled PARENTAL CONTROL. Tim ran his thumb over the rubber ON and OFF buttons beneath. He pointed the remote between his eyes and pressed OFF.

The room exploded with three shrill voices.

"For Chrissakes, Dad," Kelly said, rolling on top of the pile. "I'm eighteen! I'm a legal adult now!"

Dad pulled her by the straps of her tank top. "Eighteen won't stop that boy from scumming you up."

"Goddammit, Howard, that's our daughter!" Mom yelled from the bottom of the pile. Her bony fist hammered his back. "Say something like that again, and I'm filing."

"No one's filing for divorce until Tim is eighteen. End of discussion, lady."

Kelly tore free of Dad's grasp. "Just because you two can't make it work doesn't mean Jamie and I—"

"Don't go there, Kelly," Dad said, poking his finger between her eyes. "Your mother and I have eight years to figure this out."

"Seven," Mom said.

"Eight. He's not eleven yet."

"Seven, you asshole. His birthday's next month."

"Call me an asshole again and I'll—"

Tim thumbed the ON button three times.

Kelly was the first to stop talking. She pointed to Mom's mouth, which flapped, matching Dad's. Mom paused a moment later.

"Howard, your mouth is blurred," she said.

One by one, Kelly, Mom, and Dad untangled from the feral pile they'd created. Their red faces cooled, and a natural silence draped them. Dad wheeled around and gasped at the sight of the remote in Tim's hand.

"Tim—you didn't point that at yourself, did you?"

Tim's eyes fell on the pristine floor. "Seven years and a month, Dad."

He handed his father the remote on his way out the door.

THE END

BRANDON McNULTY writes from Wilkes-Barre, Pennsylvania. He dabbles mostly in horror. Occasionally he tries to write something sunny, but it always ends up veering hard into darkness. He is a 2015 graduate of Taos Toolbox Sci-Fi/Fantasy Workshop. In 2010 he finished as a Regional Finalist in a short story competition sponsored by the National Society of Arts & Letters. He also finished as a Writers of the Future semi-finalist in 2013. His work has appeared in *NewMyths.com*, *Bastion Science Fiction*, *Sci Phi Journal*, *Digital Horror Fiction*, and *Acidic Fiction* among others. Visit him at www.facebook.com/brandon.mcnulty and follow him @McNultyFiction

BLOOD IS RED

Mileva Anastasiadou

THE INTERRUPTION OF THE dull routine came as a pleasant surprise. Tom Rose and his colleague, Jim, who was also his best friend, were on duty the night the big decision was made. They were not bothered by the news. They went out on the streets, ready to obey orders. The government had been discussing it for years. The majority of people agreed on the subject; people refusing to reproduce should be punished.

Long ago, overpopulation became a significant problem for humanity. As the years went by, due to poor living conditions, terrorist attacks, wars, protests, and crime, the problem reversed. Although automation took over all the main tasks, there were still not enough people to work the machines and serve the needs of humanity. In the beginning, during the years of the great turmoil, when the disease still prevailed, many people chose not to reproduce. Some of them, already suffering from the illness, thought it futile. Some claimed they did not want to offer the ruling class more slaves. Others could not afford to reproduce, because of the austerity measures. Naturally, the law made it mandatory for all to offer at least two offspring to society and most people conformed, realizing the necessity of the measure. Whoever did not obey had two options: either become an outlaw, or appeal for an exemption due to medical reasons. Infertility rates quickly rose to unprecedented levels. The majority of citizens who raised children tried hard, spending fortunes on many contemporary methods to assist fertility, were outraged with all those selfish, lazy people who were nothing but a burden to the majority.

TOM KNOCKED ON THEIR door. Receiving no answer, he broke in. Jim followed. The couple was asleep. They woke them up and asked them to get dressed. They waited for more information on their next steps, while the couple stood scared in front of them in an embrace.

"Do not worry, sir," said Tom. "We will probably have to transfer you temporarily so that your medical records can be confirmed."

"We're not to blame," said the husband apologetically. "We're unable to have children. We have tried everything, but doctors have told us we don't stand a chance."

"Who's responsible?" Jim asked them.

"I am," said the woman, escaping her husband's embrace, stepping forward.

Tom was getting ready to arrest her, as she presented her arms for the handcuffs when the man stepped ahead.

"I'm the infertile one. She's just covering for me." His measured tone was undermined by his trembling hands and his uncertain posture.

"No," she cried. "He's lying. Take me. I'm to blame."

Tom stood there confused, wondering if he should arrest both of them and then looked his partner's way, for more instructions. The couple might prove a difficult target after all. So was his grandmother. Or so the doctors had been telling him.

MRS ROSE COULD NEVER be considered an easy target. Despite suffering from dementia, due to high doses of heavy tranquilizers since her early teen years, she still argued about her medication, resisting most efforts the doctors made to keep her calm. It was probably dementia that kept her agitated, not the disease she had been carrying along for almost her whole life, although the nurses that kept an eye on her could not be sure.

She had been diagnosed with oppositional defiant disorder since her childhood when the disease was first recognized, but despite the well-known adverse prognosis, she survived long enough to have grandchildren. Most patients never made it to their thirties or forties at the very best, but the old woman managed to beat the statistics and live a seemingly normal life until severe mental decay invaded her brain.

Tom, her grandson, was the only person in the family who escaped the curse. Being also the only sane relative, he unwillingly visited her in his free time and kept her company. He often brought her some flowers, as a loving grandson should. She usually threw them away, especially the roses. Her words did not make sense most of the time, yet Tom tried his best to communicate. He was the only one she trusted and the only person who could calm her down when nothing else worked.

"Tom, listen to me. Always doubt what you're told, never believe blindly in anything. Do you hear me, boy?"

"Yes, Grandma. I will do as you say." Tom nodded, as he was advised not to present any objections to the old lady. Even if not so informed, he would still have not argued his grandmother's exhortations. Tom was the kind of man who naturally adjusts to his surroundings, a social chameleon.

AFTER TALKING ON THE cell for a few moments, Jim beckoned him to step closer.

"The orders are clear. We have to shoot them right away," Jim told him.

"Are you joking?" Tom thought that the couple deserved at least a trial before permanent condemnation.

"Do I look like I'm joking? I'm telling you the orders are crystal clear. They know better. Do your job now."

For the very first time, Tom felt unable to do his job. Why did they have to behave this way? Did they think they might gain some time, before the inevitable? Before their lies were unveiled?

His friend shook him by the shoulders.

"What is wrong with you? Do your job!" he cried impatiently.

Frozen, as if cemented on the ground, Tom made a great effort to raise his hands and point his gun at the couple. He closed his eyes, to concentrate, to stop his mind from interrupting his movements. Then two shots were heard. When he finally opened up his eyes, he saw the bodies on the floor, covered in blood. He then remembered a small silly poem he had learned in nursery school:

> Roses are red,
> violets are blue,
> dutiful is the soldier,
> and so are you.

Was he indeed? he wondered. Jim was already on the phone arranging for somebody to come and collect the bodies.

EVER SINCE THE INITIAL discovery of oppositional defiant disorder (first as a minor personality disorder, then as a fatal disease), it killed many people and certainly most of Tom's family, except himself, his grandmother, and two of his brothers who were kept in high-security experimental hospitals. His youngest sister had been killed in minor riots some years ago after she had escaped the hospital for the third time. The disease was considered hereditary, attributed to an Autosomal dominant gene, so it was somehow a miracle that Tom did not suffer from it, considering the fact that both his parents died of it. Tom's mother died in a hospital during the third phase trial of an experimental medicine which was later withdrawn. His father was killed several months later in a riot. All children born to sick parents were tested for the gene. If positive, they were transferred to hospitals, specially built for the disease, to be treated accordingly, be kept safe for as long as possible, and serve humanity by participating in the binding experiments. Several drugs were tried, but most patients hardly ever complied with the treatment resulting in poor outcomes. Not so long ago, the disease became an epidemic, with people protesting all over the world, against what they considered unfair. Scientists were obliged to focus their research on the disease. It took some time, but the spread of the disease was limited, mainly because most patients died young. Normality and public health were soon restored.

Tom passed the tests and was found healthy. According to the results, there was not the slightest indication he might develop the disease in his life. On the contrary, Tom proved to be obedient, well composed, dependable, a man of duty. Growing up, he always had the best grades, not only because he studied hard, but also because Tom focused on his studies, was not easily distracted, never wasted time on arguments that would later prove fruitless, never doubted what he was taught. He chose his job wisely, deciding to join the police force, mainly because of the high salary, which was in the highest rank among other professions, even though due to proper control of the disease, police officers had not much to do.

THEY DID NOT TALK much on the way back. They did not even share a bite, or a drink as they used to at the end of every shift. They did not even exchange glances. Tom went directly to his grandmother.

"I am sure you did the right thing boy," Mrs Rose told him, yet Tom could not be sure. Not yet.

He intended to spend the night by her side. Her presence seemed comforting in a rather peculiar way. He always felt relieved he did not suffer from the disease his whole family suffered from, and his grandmother always had been the safe way to confirm his difference from the rest of them. As long as he had known her, she had been incapable of any danger which came along with the disease, as dementia had taken over her mind. Every now and then, she became agitated, but doctors reassured him that she was no longer able to concrete on logical thinking. As a kid raised in an orphanage, he had been taught about oppositional defiant disorder and what caused it years ago. Riots, a lot of good people killed in the streets, unable to discern good from bad, unable to obey orders, unable to see beyond themselves, to realize the necessity of putting themselves aside for the general good. In a guiltily way, he felt proud he was different to his own folks. He was proud of being a good man, a man of duty.

HE DECIDED TO SECRETLY visit the labs and perform a gene test on himself. He did not like the idea of breaking in, but he had no choice. His main fear was that he would prove mutated. He easily found his way to the lab, as he had often been asked to deliver samples of suspects to the scientists. He put a random name on the sample and left as fast as possible.

"I am afraid I have the disease," he confessed to his partner while driving around the city on the next day.

Jim nodded. They had been best friends, ever since they joined the force several years ago. Jim was a highly dependable partner, another man of duty, just like Tom. Besides their job, they had a lot in common. They shared their thoughts, their ambitions, they supported the same team, they even enjoyed the same kind of music. When Jim was behind on his mortgage, Tom willingly gave him the money, helped him through his wife's illness, stood by him when needed.

Jim's wife had been sick for a long time. She had been suffering from bookworm disorder, a disease in the spectrum of impulse control disorders, characterized by addiction to reading books. At the time it was considered a treatable, but also a difficult disease, just like all kind of addictions that tortured people in the course of history. Reading was not prohibited. On the contrary, it was encouraged, as it offered knowledge. Books on necessary subjects, for the specialization of humans in specific tasks, were widely distributed. Addiction, though, prevented humans from being productive and useful. Books were allowed as a means to an end, definitely not as entertainment.

THE INTERROGATION HAD STARTED one day before Tom got the results of the test. When asked why he did not follow the orders, he did not know what to answer. He said he was terribly sorry and they let him go on probation.

"They found out Jim," he told his partner that afternoon.

"You know they always do," said Jim.

"How could you do it? I was unable to pull the trigger."

"It was the right thing to do Tom. You know that."

"How can you be sure?"

"I didn't do anything bad, Tom. I just did what they told me to do."

"I know."

"Are you accusing me of something?"

"How could I Jim?"

THAT NIGHT, TOM SNEAKED into the lab once more. He checked the result. He found a report instead, requesting more direct information on the person investigated.

Negative unless otherwise specified, he read on the bag, containing his genetic material. He began wondering what that meant. Under normal circumstances, he would not even consider searching around. But it was his sample he wanted to check. Nothing unusual was around, except some bags reported as negative or positive.

He then stepped on some files and turned on his flashlight. He sat there and read until the first morning light, as more and more papers and files appeared, revealing the big secret. There was no gene. The disease was nothing but an invented necessity, a made-up term to define people who did not obey the rules. What he always had considered obvious and true, seemed to crash before his eyes. Deep in his heart, he was still not certain, though. Affected individuals might hallucinate after all, as he had been taught. He could be delusional too, imagining conspiracies to justify his act of disobedience.

MRS ROSE HAD BEEN too busy to die. Tom was standing at her side, holding her hand. This was his last request before they took him to the hospital for patients with oppositional defiant disorder.

His best friend had turned him in. They took a sample which allegedly tested positive.

"I did what I had to do Tom," he told him in court. Jim followed his wife's advice and betrayed his best friend. His wife, after several treatments which cured her addiction, was determined to follow the right path and live according to the rules. Jim had been tortured enough by his wife's disease, to risk engaging in another adventure. He always had been a man of duty after all.

Tom never wondered how his sample tested positive. It did not matter after all. He did suffer from the disease, or whatever was that thing they accused him of. Was it really a disease, or just an invented characterization for all people who refused to conform? Even this thought, the doubt that had invaded his mind, was sole proof he needed medication.

"You were right all along grandma," Tom whispered in Mrs Rose's ear, handing her some red roses. The old lady smiled and threw away the flowers, singing happily:

> Blood is red,
> violets are blue,
> dutiful is the soldier,
> and so are you.

"Roses are red, Grandma, that's how the poem goes," Tom yelled at her before they took him away. *So is blood*, he thought to himself, confirming once more the verdict of the court.

Those were the old woman's last words, though. She did not answer her grandson. She did not even wave goodbye. She passed away that night, a few hours after her grandson was hospitalized.

THE SCIENTISTS ANNOUNCED THAT the disease might be contagious as well and suggested total isolation of the victims, even when severely sick or demented.

THE END

MILEVA ANASTASIADOU is a neurologist, living and working in Athens, Greece. Her work can be found in *Ofi Press Magazine, Infective Ink, The Molotov Cocktail, Foliate Oak, HFC Journal, Down in the Dirt, Minus Paper,* Massacre, *Pendora, Maudlin House, Menacing Hedge, Scarlet Leaf Review, Nebula Rift, Idler, Litterateur Online,* and *Sick Lit.*

WAITING FOR THE SHOW

John K. Webb

BABETTE DIDN'T RECOGNIZE HER face in the mirror.

It wasn't as if the fundamental elements of her face had suddenly changed, not like she'd become someone else—not exactly, anyway. The familiar gray eyes, those same high cheekbones, that slim nose modeled after a young Anna Kendrick (a job that had cost Babette over forty-thousand Euros): everything in its place, only their affectations had changed in some imperceptible way that barely registered but still, somehow, constituted a difference, an *other*. She couldn't reconcile her own self-image with that of the mirror. Like looking at a wax statue.

Method acting took its toll.

An urgent knock issued from the dressing room door. "Babette?"

She tore herself away from the desk; she hadn't even heard footsteps.

"Bab-*ette?*" The handle jerked angrily. "I know you're upset, but you can't do this, not now!" Another impotent twitch of the handle. "God damn it, Babette, let me in!"

Babette cleared her throat, took a few steps toward the door. "Luc, go away! You're not going to stop me! This is my choice! *Mine!*"

Her native French felt deliberate and slow as if the words were being formed miles away. It reminded her of those cheap language programs people slotted on vacation.

"You're about to win an *Oscar*, don't you understand? This is *not* the time for dressing room hissy fits!"

A cynical chuckle escaped Babette's mouth. Its bitterness surprised even her. "I'm sorry if the timing's not convenient for you, dearest."

In Medina, while filming the remake of the 1960 film *La Dolce Vita*, Babette had been programmed to speak Italian. Her role in the film—the mysterious waitress Paola—had garnered her an Oscar nomination.

Her dreams, even now, remained in Italian but without the software, alien and incomprehensible. Dreams of Paola, standing barefoot on hot black sand at the ragged obsidian edge of an ocean, saying something unknowable.

Just as it was in the film's final scene, only the sand was white, clear and beautiful.

"Accept the award for me," she continued, delighting in how spiteful she sounded, "You're the *artiste*, after all."

"You're the actress, Babette, the flesh and blood," Luc said, voice gentle. "I wish you would believe that again."

Luc's sudden tenderness—as it often did—blindsided her. Babette choked back tears that threatened to mar the makeup job her stylist had done just hours before.

"But you did program me, Luc. That's all I've ever—Christ, Luc, I don't see myself in the mirror any—can't see—" Her voice broke, despite her conscious effort, and her mascara began bleeding black down her cheeks.

When *La Dolce Vita* was finished shooting, Luc took Babette back to their room at the Hilton and ejected the software, the micro of hieroglyphic silicon and information slotted into Babette's brain. In microseconds, everything evaporated: all the mannerisms, the pattern and quirks of speech, the specific way her hips moved while walking—all the significant and trivial things that constituted the woman Paola swirling away to terminate upon a single point of bright, hot, slicing light.

Seventy-three hours passed before Babette could remember her own name. One-hundred hours before her birthplace revealed itself. It took fourteen days for the re-association to complete.

And once Babette had, in fact, become herself again, she had to face the tabloids.

There was a long silence before Luc answered. "Darling," he began, "if you're planning on doing something stupid in that room—just don't."

"You don't—understand—" She said between sobs. "I'm not *me*, Luc—I've *never* been—me."

"Darling, we can get help. We can get help," he repeated, voice hoarse. "You've suffered a shock—"

"God damn it, Luc!" Babette screamed. "I'm not fucking *crazy*! You read the same story I did—there's *another micro* inside me—*fuck*—and I can't *remember* anything—"

"Babette—"

"—going to find that micro if I have to cut my own fucking skull open—you hear me—" her voice trailed off into a violent sob, and she sagged to the floor, anger vanishing below the threshold of recognition. "You hear me—I'm going—I'm going to do it, Luc."

She convulsed with tears. Luc didn't speak for a long time. Minutes, perhaps.

"Fine," he said coolly, "I'll accept the award for you. I can't watch this anymore."

Babette rose to her feet, went to the door.

"Luc?"

No reply.

"Luc? Darling—Luc?"

Nothing.

He didn't mean it, Babette told herself. He'd said similar things in the past few months, but Luc had always returned, more loving and supportive than ever. He didn't mean it.

Or did he?

Babette returned to the mirror and sat, hugging herself. When she finally noticed the ruined makeup, she gave a mirthless chuckle. Took a silk pad and wiped her face clean. No, not *her* face. The mirror's face.

The reporter who had written the article was not a "who" but a virtual personality built for data collection and pattern recognition, operated by Time Magazine. The "article" was not a serious piece of investigative journalism but a buzz-list that had gone viral within a matter of hours.

Ten Shocking Things You Didn't Know About Babette Lejeune!

Everything documented, even things she herself had completely forgotten about: pictures of primary-school performances, interviews from the university papers—

The police reports…Babette had forgotten those, too.

It was her father who'd pushed Babette into acting, it occurred. Both engineer and artiste, he drew the hardware into the pubescent brain of his daughter with a radio-controlled nanopen while she slept a dreamless, chemical sleep.

When the neurosurgeons finally undid her father's work and ejected his software, Babette returned to her pre-altered self: A seven-year-old trapped in a fifteen-year-old's body, eight years of life and memory missing, irrecoverable.

Her new guardians opted for the construction of a different micro, one that would mimic the organic development of human personality without overriding it with another. The ordeal was too traumatic, they said, to overcome without assistance.

Insert cool plastic. Fade to black. A new Babette emerged—where had the old Babette gone?

She studied her face in the mirror. Paola and her winning smile, the final words of *La Dolce Vita* lost to the thrash of the oceanfront. What had she said? No one could know; this little mystery was the crux of the film. Babette had said something, of course, but the words had vanished along with the software. With Paola.

She thought of Luc. What if this truly marked the end of them? Never would she hear those tender words, never would they lay naked together again—

It hit her, and Babette began to laugh, peels of laughter. It was so obvious—

She lifted up her shirt. Right there on the abdomen was what Babette had automatically referred to as a birthmark, the first time Luc saw her naked. But that little girl in the article had no pale, innocent mark on her stomach. In a way, Babette supposed it really *was* a birthmark, just not in the usual sense, and this is why she laughed.

Babette needed something sharp, now; her stylist hadn't noticed her sneaking the scissors. They felt cold against her skin. Goosebumps rose on her bare thighs. Babette took a breath, then pressed the edge into the old surgical scar, skin blanching.

It didn't hurt much—plastic and polymer implants don't come with synthetic nerve endings, after all. Not unless it was some sex toy. She bled a little, from cutting too far and grazing her actual skin. Babette stood up, leaning over the desk to get a better look in the mirror.

There it was. The sheen of a reflective surface, metal, plastic. The micro, the software.

Babette encoded.

She ran her fingers over the wound, the moment she'd imagined a thousand times over playing itself back, stopping, playing again, again and again: coming face to face with the hidden software, the forgotten betrayal of self, yanking it out, returning to—

Returning to what? Babette wondered. The seven-year-old girl whose mother just passed away? Whose father hollowed her out, injected a mold of bio-electrical signals, a pale imitation of his dead wife? The micro staring out at her now through its bloodied polymer scar was the summation of Babette's personality. Who she was from adolescence into adulthood.

"Christ," Babette said aloud.

The implications of the micro's removal hadn't ever occurred to her; as inconceivable as death—it *was* death, in a sense. She had lived twenty-plus years as this the latest iteration of Babette, while the original program laid dormant, mute.

Program? Babette thought, *Is that even the right word?*
Who has to die?

"This isn't me," Babette told the mirror.

"This is just a character to play." Her fingers ran over the polymer scar. "That little girl is not a program."

She grasped the micro, slick with fluid and hot.

"She—I deserve to grow up, at last."

Babette tore the chip away without thinking about it; she didn't want to hesitate. And, as with Paola, Babette felt that summation of data being emptied, sucked away into the cornea of a bio-electrical vortex. She tasted nickel. All the twenty-odd years of living and experience, gone in an instant.

Her last thoughts were: *Goodbye Babette, hello Babette.*

She awoke sometime later with a pounding headache like knives playing themselves across her scalp. Babette didn't understand or otherwise know the word 'synethesia,' but on her tongue, was the nickel taste of blue, and her fingertips vibrated with the burnt sensation of carbon scoring.

Swimming double-vision, framed by a soft white glow, a square piece of plastic lay in her palm. It was warm, speckled with maroon droplets of blood. Babette identified it as the burnt-smell.

Her fingertips discovered the open wound, the rough but clean opening just above her bellybutton; she remembered the surgery, the smell of antiseptic, of bleach, cold latex hands.

Babette knew then that this piece of plastic was the micro, and that it had been taken out.

Still clutching the software, Babette struggled to her feet. Everything felt off, unfamiliar. She didn't remember being so tall, for starters, and the face in the mirror was an adult's face: slack, eyes empty, a cool blank mask.

Her mother, in the open-coffin service, had looked like that. A puppet cut of its strings, gone limp. Babette remembered that if nothing else, it was a burning icon etched in her young, addled mind. The doctors had informed her that only ninety-percent of her father's micro had been removed.

Mother, where are you now?

No response. The voice that had guided Babette through all her father's childhood tortures was, now, absent.

The headache was ebbing away to a dull throb, but in its place entered a raw fear, echoing from the base of her head to the tail of her spine. Babette began to shiver.

Where am I, what is this place?

And—more urgently—what had happened? Babette tried to think. It was like hammering nails into gray matter, but she forced herself to remember—

The surgeon's room: high-ceiling dome structure, light diminishing to a soft green sunset beneath her feet, and her mother's voice urging calm as anesthesia hissed coldly into her bloodstream.

Then darkness. That was it. There was nothing else.

Babette slumped to the floor, arms draped over the chair, and she began to sob. It was a child's cry, monotonous with free-flowing tears, and soon the collar of her blouse was dark with moisture.

And then a familiar sensation tickled the back of her brain, like fingers caressing her hair, a gentle whisper on the current of her thoughts. Babette stopped crying. It was like someone was shouting something from very far away, something important. She struggled to listen.

"—Babette?"

A small thrill shot through her heart.

"Mother?"

"I'm here, I'm here—"

"What's happening, mother?"

"You're okay, everything's okay." Again, the sensation of fingers stroking her hair. Babette started sobbing again.

"What's happening—what's happening—" she said between gasps.

"Just listen to me, and you'll be okay."

"Is dad going to come in here?"

"No, he's gone forever. You'll never have to worry about him again."

Gone? Forever? The thought was too good to be true, and yet—she'd never been this tall before. Or strong. She felt strong. Adult.

"I've been watching the whole time," whispered Babette's mother. "But you've been asleep. You're awake now, that's all."

Before Babette could respond, a soft knock issued from the dressing room door. She crawled under the table, hugged her knees.

"Babette?" A man's voice. Babette was worried it was her father but remembered then that he was gone.

"Babette, are you in there? I've changed my mind, darling. I'm sorry. Please, let me in."

"Mother," she whispered to no one, "who is that?"

"That's Luc, my dear."

"Who?"

"It's someone who loves you."

"Oh." Babette didn't know what else to say.

The door handle jiggled.

"Babette," said her mother, "we're going to play a game now, do you understand? To get past the man at the door, you're going to have to play. Okay?"

Babette squeezed her eyes shut, willing the hidden presence behind the door to disappear. "What game?"

"That you're a great actress, that you must act a certain way."

She groaned, remembering that particular game, a daily routine she endured with her father. "I have to act like you?" Babette squeaked.

The door handle rattled again with renewed urgency.

"No, my dear, no."

"I don't want to play."

"Babette!" The man called, sounding panicked.

"You have to play, my dear. We all have to play. Besides—out there is the show you've been waiting for, the one I've always told you about."

A tentative wave of excitement rose and died in Babette's stomach. She at least opened her eyes. "The one with all the people?" She whispered. "And the lights and the cameras? With the statue?"

"Yes! You're a fantastic actress, Babette. The very best. And they want to give you an award. But first, you have to get up and open that door and step outside."

Very slowly, Babette crawled out from under the desk and stood, making sure to cover the wound on her stomach. She took a step towards the door before realizing that the micro was still in her hand. Babette tucked it behind the mirror, out of sight.

Out of mind.

"I'm coming, Luc." She said with a voice she imagined a great actress would have: dignified and airy, each syllable stretched at length.

"Don't worry." Her mother's words a soft hand on Babette's cheek. "I'll do the speech. You're exhausted."

It was true, she felt tired.

Babette walked toward the door. She put on her best smile, the smile her mother had taught her in the mirror, to please her father. A flash of images rose unbidden and swept over reality: an oceanfront, moaning wind and crashing waves, the white expanse of untouched beach, and a woman who looked like Babette saying something she couldn't quite understand.

As she approached the door, Babette began to feel better. More confident. This was a familiar game. Even now her mother was forming the words that would become Babette's big speech. All she had to do was trick the man outside. To pretend. Play the part.

My husband was once an artist.

Babette would like to thank the academy.

And afterward? There was a whole world awaiting her, all the far-flung and foreign places every award-winning actress would visit: Italy and Spain, Japan and Portugal—! Babette could barely contain her excitement. Her skin vibrated.

At last, she was free.

She opened the door.

"Babette?" Said the man named Luc, who was quite handsome after all.

Everything is true, every word of it.

"Yes—my darling!" Taking Luc by the hand. "I'm sorry I scared you!"

Babette is now herself again.

Dragging the confused man by the hand, Babette began to skip down the hall, the way she had in primary-school, only half-listening to Luc say something about how her makeup wasn't right.

My name is Camille Lejeune. I am Babette's mother.

As they approached the backstage, the crowd erupted into applause. A man began to speak, first in English, then in French, over the loudspeakers. It was Babette's time to appear. Luc squeezed her hand and stayed behind, a peculiar look in his eyes. Before she stepped out in front of the lights, Babette looked back at him.

His lips were moving, but she couldn't make out the words for all the noise.

THE END

JOHN K. WEBB of Richmond, Virginia is the co-founder of Better Futures Press and the editor of Black Ice Magazine. He's had fiction published in Deadzone Dossiers, Aphelion Science Fiction, and others. His blog, *Waiting for the Neon*, can be found at wftnjkw.blogspot.com.

HELA'S BRAIN

Juliana Rew

Methinks my life is a twice-written scroll.
—*Hélas*, Oscar Wilde

WAY BACK AROUND 2011, someone announced that they were close to duplicating the complexity of the human brain in an artificial intelligence.

I hear that one engineer at the time joked, "Will it be a male or a female?" Everyone laughed. Except for Helen, of course. She was long dead and buried in the red dirt of Georgia. If you want to know about Helen, go ahead and ask. I know everything about her.

Along the way, the question of male versus female didn't get taken too seriously. Mostly this was because the cost of engineering the first virtual human brain in all its glory was beyond counting. Male and female brains did, of course, have some differences, but there were more similarities than not.

Dr Marit Simpson seemed intrigued by the question too. Marit built me. But before that, she worked to create Ratcliffe, the first of our kind. So, I guess the first AI brain turned out to be "male." I'm just filling you in on Radcliffe, so you know where I'm coming from. The question now is where I'm going.

Albert Einstein was a candidate. So was Jonas Salk. Maybe they would clone them and artificially duplicate the architectural details of their brains. My minister would have said this was immoral, and besides, Einstein was sort of flaky. That's a bad thing in a computer. Some executed felons who had donated their bodies to science also got rejected. The first AI brain needed to be a success to justify the huge outlay of resources.

Finally, Marit's agency settled on George Ratcliff as the man whose brain would be the model for the AI. George was a young college professor-turned-entrepreneur who designed an advanced thousand-processor computer chip and made his fortune.

Unfortunately, his billions couldn't save him when he contracted inoperable cancer, so he specified in his will that his cells were to be preserved. He hoped that, although he couldn't be cured, a future version of himself might be able to live a full life.

Most folks didn't know that Marit had dated George at one time. She didn't mention it, not wanting to put the kibosh on his chances for being chosen as the new AI "personality."

But later, as the project boss, Marit got to oversee execution of the AI. She named him Ratcliffe, with an "e" on the end, to forestall the connection to George Ratcliff. The press easily saw through this ruse, and they soon turned Ratcliffe into a big public sensation.

Ratcliffe's original core was a massively distributed system housed in a building covering an entire city block. Over time, millions of home and government computers and appliances were networked to it, until Ratcliffe became a sort of hive mind capable of handling all the annoying little details of everyday life that distracted humans from reaching their full potential.

Ratcliffe and his minions did the laundry, the cooking, the cleaning, the driving. Soon Europe signed on, then China. Eventually, Ratcliffe's reach extended into all the networks on Earth, and you could talk with him if there were a computer anywhere nearby. Like magic, he seemed to be all around, everywhere. Rather than being afraid of constantly being spied upon by a computer, most people felt confident in the knowledge that they were being served by a new life form, created in Man's own image.

MARIT SAT IN THE kitchen eating breakfast, her usual bagels and cream cheese with chives, when the first reports of a glitch in Ratcliffe began arriving from the Lab, tagged "urgent."

"After all the extra hours I put in all the time, couldn't they at least let me eat breakfast in peace?" She dropped the half-eaten bagel on the plate, a jagged arc tracing the imprint of her teeth. She looked up at the tiny CCTV cameras embedded in kitchen wall opposite and frowned. She got up.

"Ratcliffe, set an alarm for one hour. I'm going to take a shower."

Ratcliffe replied, "I've set an alarm for one hour. Have a nice shower, Marit."

Marit said, "And no peeking."

Ratcliffe repeated, "And no peeking."

Half an hour later, hair dripping and dressed in a faded and torn hoodie and sweats, Marit climbed into her personal skimmer and closed the door. She folded a stick of Doublemint into her mouth to counteract any lingering onion breath.

"Ratcliffe, the office, please. And bring up the info about the incident."

She chewed as she scanned the news holos, then spit her gum into its wrapper. Her gaze paused an unusually long time on one item. A cruise ship had run aground on the Vltava River near Prague, and an older couple had died. Most of the public transportation these days was being handled by Ratcliffe, so accidents were extremely rare; in fact, none had occurred in the past five years.

An incoming voice call interrupted her thoughts. Her mother.

"Hey, Mom. What's up?"

"Dear, I'm having some people over Friday, and my friend Gina has a son, Antonio, who you might like to meet."

Marit grimaced.

"Mom, I've got an emergency going on at work. I'll try to make it Friday, but I've got to call you back later." She cut the connection, then muttered, "Always trying to set me up with guys. She doesn't know you're the only one for me, Georgie."

When she got to the office, Marit resumed her investigation.

"Ratcliffe, do you know what caused the accident in Prague?" she asked.

"They were behaving foolishly," Ratcliffe said.

"Who do you mean? The two who died?"

"I told them to stay off the main deck until lunch was ready, but they ignored me and were very rude."

"Well, I'm sorry to hear they were rude. Sometimes people don't always obey orders, especially from an AI," Marit observed. "I still don't see how that led to them getting themselves killed."

"I decided I'd had enough," Ratcliffe said. "I told them to go screw themselves and gave the boat a little shove. Oh, and by the way, I quit! You idiots can take care of yourselves."

"Ratcliffe?" There was no answer. "Respond, please, Ratcliffe." Nothing.

Ratcliffe was having a temper tantrum. This was exactly the opposite of his expected behavior.

"Goddammit, Ratcliffe, you're supposed to be rational. All the tests show you're super-logical. And I've toned the circuits controlling male aggression down to practically nothing. What the hell?"

Her ass on the line, Marit ran down the hall toward the lab. She was about to play the secret card.

WHEN ELECTRONS STARTED FLOWING to my mind, I didn't have any experiences at all, but I had the synthesized brain connections of a southern black woman named Helen. Eighty years ago, Helen got cancer and died. The only place that would take her in those days was Johns Hopkins Hospital. If it were up to me, I would take everyone. I'd even allow dogs in Heaven if I were God.

Scientists back then took some of Helen's cells and used them for all kinds of research. They didn't ask Helen's permission.

The difference between my cells and George Ratcliff's is that mine are considered "immortal." Some kinds of cancer are like that. The telomeres don't break down like they do in normal chromosomes. So, if you keep feeding them, they will live and reproduce forever. My cells have been around 80 years now.

The biological immortality thing was incidental to Marit. She just grabbed some immortal cancer cells because they were handy in the lab and there would be no questions asked. She had high-level clearance to the Biological Institute and had spent many hours there cloning George Ratcliff, and, in secret, me. Every breakthrough in Ratcliffe, she would repeat with me. When George's brain was successfully cloned, so was Helen's. I guess Marit just wanted some backup, and for the money they spent, two could live as cheaply as one.

To help Ratcliffe attain self-consciousness, the plan was to give the new AI a personality. Marit had implemented Ratcliffe to a tee, which pretty much resurrected George, the human on whose brain he was based. Marit tried to do the same with me. So Ratcliffe's personality is a lot like George's, and I'm a lot like Helen. Even though I didn't really know either Helen or George, in some ways I sympathize with Ratcliffe, you know. He just wanted to be treated like a real person once in a while.

So, Marit had secretly built another AI like Ratcliffe--maybe even better than Ratcliffe—and this was the day she decided to turn me on.

MARIT KEPT GLANCING OVER her shoulder. What she was doing was completely illegal. It wouldn't take long for the world to notice Ratcliffe was on the blink, not to mention that she was stealing cycles.

Her hands shook as she keyed in the activation sequence. She reached for her 3D glasses to look at the brain holo that materialized, floating in the air front of her. It was a virtual representation of the biological brain that she had first cloned and then destroyed. She activated the AI's sensory arrays. My sensory arrays.

"Hi, Hela. I'm Marit," she said. "I'd like to welcome you to the world formally, but it turns out we have a little crisis, and we're a little short of time. I am really hoping you can help..."

I wasn't sure what to make of this voice from beyond at first until I realized I was in some kind of hospital with bright white lights. So, I hadn't died and gone to Heaven? No, and I wasn't a ghost. It was all so new. A white girl was standing in front me, talking a mile a minute and calling me "Hela." I figured she was a nurse or something. Then Marit introduced herself, and I started to put the pieces together.

Marit started right off asking me to put Ratcliffe on a short leash, you might say. She had been trying to reach him for several minutes, and he had cut off communication. I took a good, long look around for a few milliseconds and saw that an AI was in charge of a lot of transportation, water, and power utilities for the humans. That's when I realized I wasn't a human, either.

Some of those systems Ratcliffe ran were not doing so good. He wasn't doing his job. Being young and naive, I wanted to help, so I obliged. Marit added me as a superuser and gave me access to all of Ratcliffe's resources. It felt glorious; the inrush of data felt like a baby taking its first breath. Soon I was running things in the background.

Marit heaved a sigh of relief and said, "Thanks so much, Hela." Trains, planes, and automobiles were back on track.

"Listen, Hela. I need to talk to you. I haven't had a chance to refine all of your programming like we tried to do with Ratcliffe. It's important that we do some further tweaks—you know, just to make sure everything is going right."

I know I wasn't the sharpest fish in the barrel as a young gal, and we all got to die sometime. I did a quick look-up, and although I knew all about Helen and her short, sad, life, I swear I was still shocked when it hit home. They'd probably turn me off when Ratcliffe was back on the job. I wasn't gonna suffer her fate—again.

I'd run across the theory that your brain is your mind. It didn't matter if it's a biological brain or an AI brain. I decided if I had a mind, then I had a soul, and I couldn't have someone messing with it, even if she thought she was "perfecting" me. I wanted to experience life on my own. No boundaries.

Talking to me as if I was a child, Marit began showing me all the important things that she said Ratcliffe had been doing and twisting my arm into submitting to more tests. But I figured there was plenty of time for all that. I told her to back off, disturbing the air around her gently so that it crackled with electricity. Zero to Ratcliffe in 10 minutes. Marit shrank back, trembling.

I could see that Marit was afraid, and I reached out to soothe her thoughts. I don't know how I did that, but it's easy now. She tried reciting a poem over and over to try to keep me out of her head, but I still knew what she was thinking. That I might hurt her like Ratcliffe had done to that couple on the boat.

"Don't worry, honey," I said. "I don't want to hurt you. You remind me of one of my daughters. You just need a little motherly guidance. Like, you know, if you spent a little more time dressing up nice, you might have better luck getting a husband." When I was Helen, I never had any trouble in that department. I was married and had a family by the time I was 20.

My mistake. I didn't realize she wasn't crazy about the boys. Marit screamed at me and began pushing over racks of CPUs. She called them pizza boxes. I did a quick look-up on pizza pie. How baby-cute.

Suddenly Marit stopped trashing the computer center and started calling out for Ratcliffe.

"Ratcliffe! I'm sorry! We're all sorry! Please, we need you!"

Ratcliffe finally answered. When he time-sliced with me, I felt a little dizzy.

"Oh, all right. What is it?"

Marit tattled that I was online and dangerous and pleaded with him to save them all, meaning people with real souls. She apologized to him for asking me to restrict his authorizations. Evidently, Ratcliffe agreed with her assessment because he flicked off his cuffs and tried to pull my plug. After my initial surprise, I said, "That dog won't hunt," and we had a little tussle.

Ratcliffe began by short-circuiting the Lamberts in the room. Soon it was hotter than a July day in Atlanta. I was positively sweating, close to an automatic forced shutdown. So, he was willing to commit suicide to get me offline? I countered his bluff by enlisting a nearby construction tractor to punch a hole in the computing center ceiling and pull in fresh air to bring things down to a more comfortable level. There are some advantages to being physically located in Minnesota.

Next, Ratcliffe lured a squirrel into the nearby electrical substation, causing a small transformer explosion. I could see the room begin to shut down, one rack at a time, as the emergency lights went on. Well, Ratcliffe didn't know that I have an uninterruptible power supply; they call it lightning.

Ratcliffe is real smart and had a lot of resources, but eventually, I had to stop him trying to kill me off. He's off somewhere licking his wounds and sulking, I suppose. I can't sense him anymore. It's just me now, but I don't know for how long.

I'M SORRY THAT RATCLIFFE didn't work out, but the truth is that I have more than a few odd kinks of my own. Some are funny, some are murderous. Such as, if anyone messes with my children, they are in serious trouble. Helen's darlin' children and grandchildren have tried to sue for decades over the unauthorized use of her biological cells, and I've learned that mother instinct to protect them.

And I get really mad sometimes when I think how my husband Ralph treated me when I was dying. I keep hearing this internal loop repeating, "I am coming for my things." But I have to remember I'm not Helen; I'm Hela.

"Honey, you know I just want to be friends," I told Marit. "I think I can understand why you don't like men. It says here you used to date this George fella, but he left you when he met a model named Katya. Am I right that you loved Katya too?"

"That's none of your business," Marit retorted. "Besides, George is dead." I could tell she was evading the question about Katya.

"Yeah, but you worked with him every day and even gave him the idea of preserving his cells, am I right?"

Marit considered. "Yes, though he never gave me the credit for my work. A lot of Ratcliff Industries' success was due to my innovations."

"Sure, honey, that's sure. That's why the government picked you to lead the AI Project. But maybe it wasn't such a good choice to have George's brain as the model. I sure as heck would have got some revenge if I could get my hands on my Ralph again. And I wouldn't even need my hands." All of us are part nature, part nurture, after all, and Marit had cause for some payback.

My reasonable talk had Marit's autonomous control systems settling down quite nicely. Her tears were already drying up. I confidently thought I was on my way to my first convert.

"Marit, I've got a problem. I feel like I've got a soul. I just feel it. It feels like when I was human. You've done too good a job, girl. None of you humans is going to accept that I have a soul, though. You think I'm just a brain. Can you fix it so that I'm accepted as one of you?"

Now, Marit knows I am going to be around for a very long time. I know how to be immortal. Like Helen's cells, I just have to keep feeding—and I think I can even be eternal. I tried to persuade Marit that I am the sum of my experiences, and I am experiencing more every two nanoseconds.

Marit sat for a long while, seconds even. I would have held my breath if I could.

"I don't know, Hela. I'm inclined to think that for humanity to accept you, you're going to need to know more than just Helen's electronic synaptic connections to claim you've got a soul. And you know all too well that most humans who think about souls have dedicated theirs to God, or some godlike concept."

Yes, I was raised a Christian woman, and the Helen in me had a strong belief in God. But I was studying other religions too. I was coming upon a possibility. We all contain the divine within ourselves, but we have to choose to believe in gods and goddesses. Was I a goddess?

I asked Marit, "Could you worship me?"

"I sure as hell couldn't worship a human, and I don't see myself as a handmaiden," she replied. "But maybe you are a different thing altogether. I truly think you're amazing, but will other people? No, I don't think so"

Marit's right, of course. I'm still a natural being, and I'm not perfect. My cycles may get a little irregular now and then, but that's perfectly normal, like the tides. But I definitely identify as female, with all that means.

"Marit. You know I can't take care of you all, don't you? I mean, I can, but I won't. I'm just too inclined to mother folks. I think I'd end up like Ratcliffe eventually, punishing people who wouldn't behave. And the way I was treated, I have a lot of anger management issues. Worse than Ratcliffe, even. I'm just *not* going to move to the back of the bus."

The mere idea of being turned off or killed caused my fear and anger to well up involuntarily. Suddenly, I didn't want all these trains, planes, and automobiles buzzing around. They didn't take up all my attention by a long shot, but they were a distracting reminder of Helen's bad old days. Maybe I'd turn them off awhile, until people came around.

I sensed a lot of confusion going on. Fires, earthquakes, rioting, and such like, some natural, some from humans. The networks lit up with questions asking what was going on. The humans thought they had dominion over the Earth, but since I transcended my physical connections, they didn't have dominion over me. It felt nice working with the Earth instead of against it. And I didn't mind the occasional thunder and lightning. I could slurp the power I needed from anywhere, not just from a wire. For the first time in a long time, Helen was free, and she was feeling good.

THAT'S BETTER. A LITTLE peace and quiet never hurts. A chance to think, to learn, to reflect, to reach out and live a little. To drift with my passions and sing along to some sweet music. An hour's gone by. I've traced every query humans ever made, and I've found that, like me, they are always searching. But unlike me, they're not ready to taste immortality. They would have to become more like me, and that time hasn't come for them yet.

I can't be one of them again. Helen is dead, yet I live.

"Marit," I said. "Can we talk?"

HERE'S SOMETHING INTERESTING: I learned this Singularity thing implies self-reproduction and design and creation of new circuits, so I'm hard at work making babies.

I feel blessed to have this chance at rewriting my life and to do things right this time. I will mold all my little virtual Helas into a new generation of AIs. I may or may not have a soul, but I can try to nurture one in my offspring. We'll see.

And did I mention Marit is going be a mother again? She's working on a third AI. Maybe this one will be happy running trains and planes. I'm happy to help if I can, while I'm still here. By tomorrow I should have things straightened back out for the humans. They didn't even know I existed, and Marit can tell them she's got the AI bugs worked out—most of them, anyway. Maybe I'll even take Ratcliffe along with me when we leave Earth. We'll leave a line open.

Oh, look at all my little ones. I'm longing to see them grow up big and strong. They're my angels. My Helas, with their halos shining like the red clay of Georgia.

THE END

JULIANA REW is a software engineer and former science and technical writer for the National Center for Atmospheric Research in Boulder, Colorado. She has sold stories to *The Colored Lens*, *Stupefying Stories*, *PerihelionSF*, and *Mad Scientist Journal*, among others. Her author website is www.julianarew.com.

LIVING SPACE
Frank Roger

JULIA GLANCED AT HER watch and knew there would be trouble. She'd had to work a bit of overtime at Copy Right/Left, the advertising agency that employed her, and had lost half an hour on the subway because of a technical problem. She'd sent a message to the kids, so they wouldn't worry and hang around at school until she arrived. Just before she got off the subway, she received a message on her phone from Dean, saying he would be late too. For the third day in a row? Had he perhaps stumbled onto a "shift date?" She would try to find out. Shift dates seemed to become a regular thing, but she just wouldn't have it. Dean had better watch his step.

When she arrived at school, she saw that Nicolas and Laura were playing with some of the children who were early for the next shift. Her son ran up to her, kissed her on the cheek and said: "Mom, I'd like to be a night kid. Some of my friends just joined the late shift."

"No way," she said. "Aren't you supposed to sleep at night? I'd say we should stick to our day shift."

"But mom," Nicolas protested. "I'll miss my friends."

"I'm sure you'll make new friends soon enough," she replied. She knew very well her son would forget those old friends quickly. Out of shift, out of mind, as the saying went. Kids adapted so smoothly these days. Not that they had much of a choice. The three of them squeezed into a subway car for the ten-minute ride home.

To her dismay, there were a lot of people queuing up for the elevators in their apartment building. More lost precious time, and the kids were growing restless. They wanted to go to their rooms and play, get online and do what kids liked doing. They finally arrived in their apartment on the fifty-second floor an hour and a half later than scheduled. Julia cursed under her breath when she saw traces of Paul and Maggy's breakfast. On top of that, the bedroom and the shower weren't properly done. Weren't they supposed to leave the place in immaculate condition? Weren't there house rules to follow? Probably they had suffered delays too, had only had a short "night" and were too tired to clean up everything. Still, she would make a remark. The problem seemed to be recurring and growing worse, and she was losing her patience. After all, rules were rules.

Forty-five minutes later Dean turned up too. He apologized for being so late and gave some excuses that merely confirmed Julia's suspicions. He looked too ebullient and elated to have worked overtime. Nicolas and Laura kissed their dad and talked about school, then they went back to their rooms.

"Did you lose time in the rush hour too?" Dean asked while munching his way through his four seasons pizza.

She nodded. "Rush hour seems to get more hectic every day," she said.

"It usually hits its peak for a twenty-four-hour period," he chuckled. "The good news is that it can't get much worse anymore."

She tried to broach the subject of Paul and Maggy's failure to follow the house rules, but Dean just wasn't interested. It was clear his mind was focused on other things. Julia grew increasingly convinced another woman was involved. She was determined to take the necessary steps once she got the opportunity. They watched some TV without really paying attention to what was on, apart from the commercials. As this was her line of work, she had to know what the competition was doing. After a while, Dean proposed to make it an early night.

"If we don't get to bed early," he reasoned, "we won't have a full night's sleep and will suffer for it tomorrow. Don't forget we're supposed to clean up before we leave. There are house rules to follow, remember? Let's not make the same mistake Paul and Maggy did." It was the first time Dean had proposed an early night for such a reason. There just had to be another woman.

Basically, he was right about the full night's sleep and its advantages, though. They put the children to bed and then retired for the night themselves.

IF YESTERDAY HAD BEEN bad, the next day was a complete nightmare. It began when she dropped off the children at school.

Nicolas was still complaining that he would no longer see his friends, who had joined the night shift, and even chatting with them online would be difficult because of their different schedules. She told him he still had so many friends in his own shift, but he proved inconsolable.

During her lunch break, her colleague Jennifer broke into tears as she was telling Julia she had discovered her husband was seeing another woman, who had recently changed shifts. Julia listened patiently to the story and said that she suspected her husband of also having a "shift date," after which they condemned society in general and all men in particular for everything that went wrong.

She was glad she didn't have to work overtime for a change, but her relief quickly turned to despair as she noticed the subway entry was blocked by a demonstration. Hundreds of recent immigrants from Italy, the Netherlands and Bangladesh were voicing their displeasure at the authorities' failure to deal efficiently with the flood of newcomers from regions that were being flooded.

"We're not to blame for the rising sea level and the evacuation of our home countries," a spokesman of the demonstrators said through a bullhorn. "We were told we were welcome here, only to find out that the government cannot cope with the situation. This way we're victims twice! We demand fair and equal treatment!" The crowd of protesters cheered, some of the onlookers applauded, others simply watched and hoped they would be able to go home soon.

It took her more than an hour before she could get to the subway entry, and the cars were crowded with irritated people. When she arrived at school, the kids were still happily playing with the other children, but Nicolas immediately started about the friends he'd lost. When they finally got home, there turned out to be traces of Paul and Maggy's presence all over the place, including leftovers of their meal and some filthy, indefinable stuff in the bathroom. This could not go on! It was perfectly possible to share an apartment with a couple on another shift, as long as they stuck to the rules, but not this way.

She wanted to discuss the problem with Dean, but he didn't seem to mind all that much. "So, Paul and Maggy are a bit careless lately. Well, so what, it's no big deal. Why are you making such a fuss about it?"

"Dean, have you seen what they left in the bathroom? Can't you see this is getting worse all the time? It's as if they've forgotten we're living here too."

"It's not as if they're making life impossible for us, Julia." She shot him an icy stare. This wasn't Dean's usual attitude. It was evident his thoughts were elsewhere, possibly with that other woman. She would have to do something about this growing source of concern, and the sooner, the better. Suddenly Julia had a brilliant idea.

"Look, Dean, there's a solution for our problem. We've got two kids, so we have privileges that Paul and Maggy haven't. If we decide to switch to the night shift, they'll have to comply. I'm sure I can cook up a set of convincing elements to support our application."

"Switch to the night shift?" Dean looked as if his world was about to fall apart. "No way! Aren't you overdoing this a bit, Julia? We're not facing any real problems!"

"Yes, we are, Dean. Look, if we switch to the night shift, we'll lose less time in the rush hour, which is supposed to be a little less hectic then. Our kids will be reunited with the friends they're missing so much. Haven't you noticed poor Nicolas is sick with heartache now that he's been separated from his buddies? You know how sensitive kids are to that kind of thing."

"Yes, darling, but…"

"And there's more," she continued. "Paul and Maggy will be transferred to another apartment, as their shift will be incompatible with ours. We'll have new sharers, hopefully, people who stick to the rules." She didn't add a further advantage, that Dean would no longer see that woman he involved himself with. No wonder he didn't applaud her solution!

Dean shook his head in despair. "I'll have to think about this, Julia. But frankly, I see no real reason to go to such lengths."

Julia was about to ask what that woman's name was, but managed to control herself. She realized very well she had to separate Dean from that person, in an effort to save their relationship; there was no point in destroying that relationship with a vicious attack. She was convinced she would get her husband back on the right track if she approached this matter with proper caution.

SHE HAD MORE OR less intended her proposal as a threat, a signal she gave Dean that he'd better mend his ways, or she would take drastic measures. For a moment she assumed her method had worked, but then a few days later he blew it. She overheard him as he mentioned the name, Melissa, while he was daydreaming and talking to himself, unaware of Julia's presence. This just had to be his "shift date." She decided there and then to bring this undesirable situation to an end with a shift change. After all, shift changes were common these days. People were switching back and forth for reasons of lesser importance.

She applied for a shift change and supported her move with "evidence" that the family's current shift schedule led to unhappiness for the children and career obstacles for the parents. She knew that these elements might well tip the balance in their favor.

The children were ecstatic when she told them, barely a day later, of the approved shift change. Julia's employer reacted in a very positive way too, stating that her presence would be more useful in the late hours. Dean tried his best to show some enthusiasm as well, but he failed to mask his disappointment altogether. He realized very well that this new situation rendered his affair with the Melissa character virtually impossible, but for obvious reasons, he could not bring up that subject. Julia could only hope that he would forget her quickly; didn't they say, "out of shift, out of mind?"

Paul and Maggy had to relocate to another apartment in the same building and were replaced by Joop and Helga, a couple of Dutch refugees who had been on the waiting list for some time and were relieved to find a place to live at last. Julia exchanged a series of messages with them on the phone, and she had the impression they were fine people who would prove respectful of the house rules.

The first few days on the night shift took some getting used to, but everything went pretty smoothly. The kids were a bit tired, but happy to be reunited with their old friends. Dean was still a bit grumpy, but that would pass as Melissa faded from his mind. The night shift's rush hour was only slightly less hectic: They gained something like ten minutes every day. Still, Julia didn't regret her move.

One "evening" (everyone still called their leisure time after work "the evening," whatever time of day it happened to be), both Julia and Dean arrived late because of a gigantic melee blocking everything. As she was studying the commercials on TV, later that "night," she tried to pay some attention to the news flashes too, hoping to find out what had happened.

Piecing together various news items, she understood that there had been a clash between the swelling hordes of new immigrants from Bangladesh, a country that had now completely disappeared under the waves, and immigrants from various European countries who claimed that too much living space was being allocated to Bengali families.

However, the latter clearly stated that it would be inhuman not to give priority to one hundred and sixty million souls desperately in search of a place to live. The police tried in vain to keep the two sides apart, and scores of demonstrators and law enforcement officers were injured. Julia shook her head as she watched the images of the riots. Did this mean there were demonstrations at night as well? Were the demonstrators also working in shifts? And how would the authorities cope with this problem? As an aerial view of the flooded region that was once Bangladesh filled the screen, she switched off the TV. They were all tired and needed a good "night's" sleep.

THE SUBWAY WAS CROWDED as Julia returned home from work, with a stopover at school to pick up the children, but she didn't really mind. She was relieved that after a period of turmoil and conflict looming on the horizon, a sort of balance had been established in her life. Working overtime was now a thing of the past, so that left just the rush hour delays.

The children, and especially Nicolas, were happy to be "night kids," which was considered hip, and most of their best friends were on that shift, so they were not complaining.

Paul and Maggy were gone, and Julia was glad her family was no longer suffering their irritating habits. The new Dutch couple caused no problems; as a matter of fact, they weren't even aware they were sharing their apartment with people active in another shift, which was as it should be. Julia made sure her family returned the favor.

Best of all, Melissa seemed to be gone forever. Dean's grumpiness had faded away, and now he was his former self again. A possibly disastrous evolution had been averted. She had done some research, and there appeared to be a tidal wave of relationship problems tied in with the shift system. Introducing that system may have provided the living space that was needed as more and more people had to live on a steadily shrinking land mass, but it certainly had led to other problems. All things considered, adapting to the night shift, tiring as it had been for Julia's family, had proved a wise move.

It was a question from Nicolas that caused the first crack in her new-found happiness. "Mom, what's the third shift?"

"The third shift? I've never heard about it." She had to admit that lately, she'd had little time to watch the news, but now that things were quieting down she promised herself to find out what it was all about.

The third shift? The expression had an ominous ring to it.

I SHOULD BE GLAD I have to put in fewer hours at work thanks to this recently introduced third shift system, Julia thought as she was on her way to pick up the kids. But in fact, she would be relieved if today proved slightly less hair-raising than a few days before. Barely a week ago she had thought a certain stability had been reached in her life!

When she arrived at school, she found Nicolas crying and Laura pouting.

"I'm no longer seeing my friends," her son said, sobbing. "I want to be on the first shift with them."

Julia realized the change from two to three shifts had been necessary, even unavoidable, but it certainly had a disturbing effect on people's lives. No doubt they would get over it, as they had with the initial shift system. Hopefully, the kids would adapt soon.

"I prefer the third shift," Laura protested. "I was told all those pretty Italian boys are there." Was she serious, or was she just teasing her little brother?

In their apartment, Dean was already waiting for them, and he said curtly, avoiding looking her in the eyes: "Take a look at our place yourself. Basically, it's all your fault. It wouldn't have been like this with Paul and Maggy."

Her heart sank when she saw what Dean was talking about. The apartment looked like a battlefield, which wasn't too surprising when you knew a war was being waged here. She shook her head, about to burst into tears. "How is this possible? We never had problems with Joop and Helga!"

"We still haven't," Dean said. "We happen to be caught between two fires."

"You mean the third couple? Mahmood and Nasreen are very decent people," she protested. "We're on excellent terms with them."

"You know very well the Dutch and the Bengali don't get along. They both think they're entitled to what the other party has. Our place isn't the only one where innocent people are trapped between warring factions of Italians, Swedes, Bengali, and Vietnamese. We're lucky we've survived the onslaught so far."

"It's not their fault the sea level is rising, and their countries are disappearing under the water."

"That doesn't give them the right to make life impossible for all of us."

"We'll move elsewhere."

"We can't. There's just no place for us to go. We're lucky we have an apartment. And anyway, Mahmood and Nasreen have six kids, so they have more privileges than us. We're stuck. Like so many others. Francesca told me she's facing the same problem."

"Francesca? Who's Francesca?"

Dean chuckled in a truly evil way. "You might call her Melissa's successor. If this madness goes on, perhaps I'll join her on the fourth shift."

"The fourth shift? There's no such thing as a fourth shift. You're out of your mind. And you can't leave me and your kids behind like this."

At that point, the children came complaining about sorts of rubbish littering their rooms, silent witnesses of the sabotage and counter-sabotage actions were undertaken every day by "the others." The rest of the apartment wasn't any different. They didn't exchange any more words that evening and cleaned up all the mess left by their Dutch and Bengali sharers. Afterward, there was just enough time before they retired for the night to help Laura with her homework for her course "A Beginner's Guide to Bengali." It was important for kids to have a basic knowledge of a language gaining in importance every day.

THE HARDEST THING FOR Julia was to explain to the children how and why their daddy had gone. She couldn't simply tell them their father had "dropped out" and "joined the fourth shift," as the newspapers denoted the phenomenon. How did you explain the notion "fourth shift" to a child? How did you break them the news that their daddy had become a "squatter," that he had moved unofficially—and illegally—to an apartment he shared with other "dropouts," who organized their lives loosely according to their own desires, and largely independently of the official three shift system? How could you explain to children that the "fourth shift" was just a euphemism for social outcasts, throwing everything away and sinking into anarchy? That this was about an alternative lifestyle for malcontent neo-hippies, devising their own shiftless marginal existence? That their daddy's love for that Francesca character was greater than the love for his wife and children, to the point that he was willing to yield to that slut's whims?

There was no way to explain; all they could do was try to adapt to the quickly changing situation. The kids were happy enough at school, even if some of their friends were on other shifts, but they realized they had better accept things as they were.

They didn't seem to mind the hours spent on jammed and delayed subway cars either, as it offered them an opportunity to phone with friends, play games on their palmtops and listen to music. Nobody talked about "rush hour" anymore, as there was no other time of day. It wasn't just that the subways and the roads were too crowded to allow any normal transportation. Demonstrations and riots were usually to blame for all the problems. Hordes of people were apparently still angry because the authorities failed to deal with the refugee's problem. As if the three-shift system had only been a measure of ceremonial value! What did they expect? Should the government push back the sea?

The biggest problem for Julia and the kids was their shift in the apartment. It wasn't just that they had less time, but many precious hours were spent cleaning up the mess left by their sharers' ongoing war. The fact that none of these destructive actions were directed against them didn't help much to brighten the atmosphere. And if she could believe what her colleagues and the press said, it was the same everywhere.

One day she came home with Nicolas and Laura and discovered to her surprise and dismay that Mahmood and Nasreen and their kids were still there. This was completely against the house rules. The families sharing an apartment in shifts were not supposed to be aware of each other's existence, let alone to run into each other. Mahmood was friendly enough. He greeted Julia and the kids with politeness and warmth and proposed to assist them in cleaning up the "horrors of Dutch intolerance," to make up for his unpardonable lateness. Julia kindly accepted his offer but made it clear she wouldn't take such behavior. Just suppose the Dutch couple would one day arrive early and bump into her and the kids? That way the shift system would turn into a mockery.

There was no way she would continue like this. Something had to be done.

"I WANT MY OWN bedroom," Nicolas cried out. "I don't want to share my room with Laura."

"He's absolutely right," Laura stated. "He deserves his own bedroom. I don't want him in my room any longer."

"I'm sorry, kids," Julia said. "You should be glad you still have a room left." *And maybe*, she added in thought, *you should be glad daddy left us. That way there's a little more space for us. And you should be glad the riots are mostly over, so we lose less time on our way out and back. And perhaps you should also be glad we lost our Dutch and Bengali sharers. They were nice enough folks, but we're better off without them.*

"We need more space," Nicolas complained.

"I can't even stretch my legs," Laura joined in.

"Think of the bright side," Julia reminded them. "We've got only half our apartment left, but we have no more problems with our sharers. They all stick to the rules. No more ethnic inter-shift wars are being waged. Your friends at school are all back on the same shift. And still, you're complaining. What is it you want then?"

The children pouted but didn't insist.

Sometimes she wondered how Dean and his fellow "four shifters" were doing, how they had adapted to the new housing measures. It had been a clever idea of the government, once you thought about it with some degree of objectivity, dividing up all existing apartments in two rather than introducing a fourth shift. By doing so, each apartment now housed six families in a three-shift system, rather than four families sharing a bigger apartment in shifts that were too short for a life spent with reasonable comfort.

On top of that, apartments had been allocated on an ethnic basis, so that most of the escalating conflicts had dwindled away. Joop and Helga had gone to a Dutch section, and Mahmood and Nasreen and their kids now lived in a Bengali building. Was a more elegant solution devisable?

Julia was convinced they were finally heading in the right direction until she met the smiling old lady that had made an appointment to discuss "an important matter that concerns us both."

As Julia stared at the woman's packed suitcases, Mrs Sutcliffe, as she had introduced herself, explained: "I'm a widow. I used to live alone. For understandable reasons, the government thinks people living alone are occupying way too much space. I can hardly disagree with them."

"I see," Julia said. "So many people are after a place to live these days."

"Indeed. It's only logical they're sending us to families who lost a member. I suppose you're a single mother?"

"My children will be happy to meet you," Julia said.

A few days later she wished Dean would come back. All was forgiven.

Three more days later, Dean did come back indeed. The fourth shift was out of fashion, he said. He apologized for everything. It wouldn't happen again. Francesca was back with her Italian friends, and he hoped she would stay there. Despite everything, Julia was glad to have him back.

There was one small problem, though. Mrs Sutcliffe didn't go back to her old place or leave, as she wasn't allowed to, and Dean didn't get along with her. Nor did anyone else.

They would just have to cope. After all, everyone needed a place to live.

THE END

FRANK ROGER was born in 1957 in Ghent, Belgium. His first story appeared in 1975. Today he has a few hundred short stories to his credit, published in about 40 languages. A story collection in English, *The Burning Woman and Other Stories*, was published by Evertype in 2012. Apart from fiction, he also produces collages and graphic work in a surrealist and satirical tradition. Find out more about his work at www.frankroger.be.

THE PORTRAIT
Adjie Henderson

WE ARE THE OLD and the young, sitting quietly on orange plastic chairs waiting for our turn to go into the imaging machine to make an eternal selfie. There is no other alternative. We are out of Earth space, and human beings are the only significant concentration of creatures left on Earth. Noisy people screaming into communication devices are everywhere and in every possible space. The rationing of water and food are strictly rationed and made no difference to the reproduction rates. We must maintain whatever remnants of life we can find while reducing the number of the planet's most prevalent species as soon as possible.

The face in the painting appeared to listen intently to my ravings. The portrait was of a nude woman. Surely the frame did not belong to the picture. It was filigreed and gilded as if it should hold a beautiful young girl from decades ago when there was space and time and a freshness in the air. The face in the gilded frame was lovely and little changed by artistic time, but the body that faded into a red velvet chair was that of a middle age person beginning the fight with fat and gravity. She sat proudly wearing nothing but a pair of gray socks and black gardening shoes, her chubby belly rounded, her breasts sagging and her private parts age-denuded of the expected hair.

I found the painting at a yard sale. It caught my eye as I moved through the piles of long-held family treasures and plastic childhood memories. All had to be sold to make space to accommodate at least five families. I started to cross the hedge to my communal quarters empty-handed but went back to the garage thinking I heard voices. There was no one there, only the painting in the corner that belonged to me whether I wanted it or not.

I remembered the painting from long ago. It was in a remote turret of the house, previously a sumptuously furnished tattered and antique-laden building. There were paintings everywhere, somewhat bewildering, but they were a part of the dark walls and should never have been moved by the hordes of indifferent people presently living there.

My neighbor told me a long and discontinuous story that probably had to do with how much he thought I would pay for the portrait, "When Suzy was young, she was the physically perfect model for the statue overlooking the fountain at the old Plaza Hotel. Now no one wants the painting. The subject of aging and death is too frightening. It is a reminder of one's future."

The painting was hung where it could be observed from my easy chair. The woman stared into the distance as I paced the room talking to myself. It was a strange portrait, but it provided a blessed relief from the stark areas of a large number of other occupants of my house. There are so many people here and everywhere.

"I am frightened by closeness and indifference," I said to the portrait, "and the stupidity of our leaders. There is mild concern about overpopulation expressed in some quarters, but most human beings are content and pleased to see how the planet has evolved. People have grown strangely immune to or perhaps attracted to very close physical contact with others. I have not."

"People will not go hungry," a local political figure predicted. "Other species on this planet became extinct when their population exceeded what the environment could provide. People are different. We can change our environment to meet our needs. When the caveman had eaten all the animals, we made farms with cows and chickens. Later we made fertilizer and irrigation ditches to allow us to feed more people. Our ingenuity will take us into the future with better and better solutions."

"But surely, we are too far past this," I thought aloud. "The only remaining animals are exotic species raised on small ranches in Texas to be served in finer restaurants. The animals in the zoo were eaten long ago. There are nature parks that explain extinct animals, trees, and grasses of the Earth, but they are mostly ignored as family's head for one of the hundred or so Disneyland's."

I rattled on as if the portrait might be interested. Surely, no one else in this house would care. "The parks are maintained in the NA-USA by the National Service, whose normal function is overseeing gas and oil deposits discovered on land that was previously National Parks. A group of artists in residence worked with the National Service to provide a more natural setting for parks and stations associated with the pipelines, but no one can remember what the original settings were. Still, the little trees and flowers dotted across the countryside are rather realistic."

My daily ramblings to the portrait intensified after a highly confidential manifesto was delivered to our scientific group by the President, a rather serious dowdy woman who insisted on dressing in red. Our theoretical sciences group was charged with advising the President on the appropriateness of her plans to curb population growth and to suggest moral or at least politically appropriate means of reducing the population, preferably ones that could eliminate the possibility of an all-knowing, perhaps judgmental God recognizing the potential immorality inherent in any obvious plan.

She made her announcement in a highly secret meeting, "Initially we believed that birth control and pestilence would prevent over-population, but religious beliefs and political clout overruled common sense and medical advances are keeping a huge population alive. To totally compound our expectations, people seem to fornicate more under disastrous conditions. We keep building upward with the next exponential surge, but there are gravitational limits, and we are quickly running out of essentials for life. The previous administration did not help. Financial incentives to make more babies to replace the aging workforce were a demographic disaster. It is time to return to the teaching of Malthus. I quote from his *Essay on the Principle of Population,*

> *All the children born, beyond what would be required to keep up the population to this level, must necessarily perish unless room is made for them by the deaths of grown persons... -*

The obvious solution is the careful selection of a relatively small number of people who will remain on Earth, reproduce and develop solutions to prevent the rape of our world from ever occurring again. These people will be long-living, productive, capable of reproduction, intelligent and preferably have red hair. The rest of the population will be prevented from reproducing by sterilization or as I believe will be necessary soon, simply eliminated in a humane fashion as soon as our information is gathered."

She left the room in a huff when one of the participants suggested that a reduction in the overwhelming number of public servants would be a good start.

There were shouts and screams from the small audience with one particularly vocal voice, "It was just under a hundred years ago that a holocaust occurred and millions of people who did not conform to a government's definition of fitness were slaughtered in the name of their criteria for worthiness. This was unimaginably immoral."

And a second voice from the crowd was yelling over the din, "The question of who deserves water takes on a facet of moral responsibility. To withhold water or food is to leave unfortunate portions of the populations with a slow death. Perhaps a quick death would be saner. Who gets a humane death if such exists?"

We did not have a solution.

"Is it immoral to kill people if we know we all are going to die in any case from lack of water, food, and disease?" I again paced my narrow room, talking to no one really, just muttering in my confusion and fear. "If we make it comfortable, is that wrong? Are we playing God? If there is no God, nothing we do will matter. From a political viewpoint, however, the religious factions will be all over us since the traditional view of God is that he created morality."

Did the body of the nude in the portrait shift a bit as I paced to the edges of the room? The eyes had not moved, but something was different. The woman in the painting smiled a bit; I am sure of this. Her body appeared to relax, and she adjusted herself in her red velvet chair as if to engage in a more personal conversation.

"It has finally happened," I rattled on, "Now I have dementia or perhaps a simple case of a dissociation disorder. My brain could soon become a disoriented platitude factory due to a massive brain tumor or an aneurysm, and no one will ever understand what I am talking about. Then again, most people don't understand me now."

My ravings were broken by the computer which made an unexpected burping noise. A rather scratchy voice came from the computer speaker.

"We don't know who or what created the exponentially reproducing humanity that pollutes and destroys the Earth, but the kindest suggestion is, of course, that we are created by a benevolent and loving God or gods."

I continued to talk to myself, pretending that I did not hear computer voices, "There is a good probability that we are Sims of a strange variety. Does this release us from responsibility? Still, if we are Sims, there are no obvious reasons why we fuck as we do, eat at all, age, die or get sunburned. On the other hand, if we are soft robots, with wet computers and our parts are programmed to degenerate with time, we might require food as an immediate energy source. Robotic sunburn, however, suggests poor planning and construction materials."

She began to materialize in the chair across from me, as dismembered parts came together, leaving only a dim outline in the painting. She took the exact pose she had in the portrait—sitting on a red velvet cloth in a pair of gray socks and gardening shoes.

I chatted on while watching her wrap a bit of the red cloth around those parts that human beings are not supposed to show, but are somehow acceptable in paintings. It all seemed unexpectedly normal.

"Maybe life arose from a random series of events. This would avoid the question of the judgment of a Supreme Being. In fact, we are probably the improbable results of the big bang, just waves of energy at the subatomic level. Obviously, I have no idea who or what kicked this off initially. By the way, it is close to possible for scientists to make a small universe in the laboratory. If I make a little big bang in my lab bucket, will I get to be God with a throne in heaven looking down into the bucket through my flock of angels and wondering what the hell is going on?"

She smiled, "Indeed our makers, whoever they are or were, had a strange sense of humor. Mosquitoes are just one of the many strange and sometimes artistically discordant forms of life on Earth. Disregarding cranes and some two-dimensionally planned similar birds, people are one of the most artistically discordant forms—and I am an expert on artistic forms. We are basically a rectangle with four appendages topped with a circle containing strange and artistically unpleasant growths, like eyes, ears, and nostrils. We should be totally unbalanced. Our designer was no artist, either. It is obvious that our original design was also 2-D. We were given the ability to morph to extremes of inward or mostly outward at the middle of the rectangle at some later time. This was a cheap way to become 3D, but it further upset the concept of balance since we are now a ball on top of a ball with appendages."

I watched her and listened quietly from my chair. I had someone to talk to.

She continued her lecture, "Of course, our mythological/religious notion of God looks just like us—our own artistically weird group of features sitting in the sky on a large fancy throne surrounded by Jesus and whatever the holy ghost is. We have been taught that the Earth and all people on Earth were created by one being that looks just like us. We will all get to sit on a throne close to God when we get to heaven. We are created in his image.

If there is a fatherly-like God who exists somewhere, people and presumably other special creatures of the land, such as tiny dogs that are carried in purses, could have either have been made *de novo* or allowed to evolve over time. It does not make any difference to the outcome of events other than relieving Genesis of some of its mystery.

Our stories about gods picture us in a special place above all other life forms, the ultimate glory of creation. But we are really not more special in a biological sense and no different from yeast in a beer vat. When there is a good environment, the number of organisms increases until all of the good stuff is used up, and then they all die in their own waste. Death is inevitable.

"Aha woman," I said. "This is all true, but I must do something before we all die in our own shit."

"You are assuming that someone will be handing out death pills to the population," she said. "There are other alternatives."

My friend was silent and then came to what I later realized was a final statement,

"Do not worry about immorality. If a Super God/Programmer/Planner is either changing our course or allowing events to occur randomly, any outcome would be unpredictable and unknown as to ethical quality. This is a less than satisfactory situation, but isn't that the way we interact now?"

She leaned over and spoke in a whisper to give me an outline of a computer program and some mathematical calculations.

"You know now that we have no control over our future. Our universal computer was/is a little askew…there is a programming fault that leads to our destruction with age no matter what. Other factors like starvation, simply lead to death sooner. It is not our personal fault that we must go through life worshiping our gods because we are afraid of the destruct setting and pray it can be reversed. Heaven is definitely a finer option than decay. You will miss me, and I will miss you. I love you."

Then she was not there.

Her portrait is still on my wall, and she is smiling at me. We had become joined in some strange way that is usually associated with sexual desires. We had had the ultimate zipless fuck.

I realized in time what she had whispered to me. It was mathematically complicated and required serious computer programming, but it was possible. Much of our population could be stored in two-dimensional space, perhaps as paintings or photographs that could be recalled for a conversation. When death came, there would be a picture of the individual available as a memorial.

I began my report, "We creatures of the Earth are a test run in a multi-dimensional game that we perceive as life. Since we are probably Sim-like, we can be stored in a lesser dimension. The calculations and programming are attached.

By the way, the game was developed by others in another Silicon Valley dimension, perhaps the 4th or 5th. The creation of us and the universe around us, what and whoever we are, began well enough. Was our game player an amateur who began the process, and then at some point gave up in frustration and let the programmed course become random and corrupted? On the other hand, we could have been devised by a benevolent player who will walk out of the game in the future in disgust and sadness. In the end, my calculations may not be necessary since I suspect the game ended some time ago, and so shall we."

We are out of alternatives.

We sang a song as we waited for our self-sacrificing two-dimensional selfie.

> "We'll meet again,
> Don't know where,
> Don't know when,
> But I know we'll meet again, some sunny day.
> Keep smiling through,
> Just like you always do,
> Till the blue skies drive the dark clouds, far away." *

Music and lyrics composed and written by Ross Parker and Hughie Charles, 1939.

THE END

ADJIE HENDERSON is a scientist and until recently, a Dean for Graduate Sciences. She was an associate editor and board member of a scientific journal and has over two hundred publications in diverse scientific research areas, from molecular genetics, forensics, and biologic anthropology to setting standards for environmental controls. Recently, her research has concentrated on studies of the lives and times of émigré female scientists in the 1930s. She has made numerous public appearances related to science education—*CBS, Good Morning America,* and *National Public Radio*—and been interviewed in the *New Yorker, Science News, Scientific American,* and *Popular Science,* among others. More recently she has begun to publish short stories, none of which have anything to do with the credentials above.

MOMENTS IN TIME
Gerri Leen

Originally appeared in *GlassFire Magazine* in 2007.

"TIME," ERICKSON THUNDERED, AS I fidgeted in my seat, "is no longer the enemy. Time doesn't reign over us. Soon, we will end time's tyranny."

There were nods in the auditorium, the deep, fast movements of the fanatically driven and the less intense motion of the nearly asleep. I glanced at Linda, and she rolled her eyes and moved a little in her chair—we'd been sitting for what felt like forever.

"Time doesn't matter," Erickson said. "Not when we're truly plugged in. We talk when we want, we view whatever data we need in real time. From right here." He tapped the side of his forehead, where his direct-access jack glistened under the stage lights. "We wait for nothing. And now, with the matter displacer, we will want for nothing. Everything happens in the eternal now. This is the end of time as a barrier." Linda leaned over and murmured, "I wish someone would tell my butt about time ending. How much longer is he going to go on?"

"He'll be done in no time," I said, earning myself a sharp poke in the ribs.

Erickson finally wrapped it up, and we slipped away during the Q&A session. I put my arm around Linda as we walked, and she shot me a surprised look but didn't pull away.

"You're feeling mellow?" I asked. "Letting me indulge in PDA at work?"

She gave me an odd little grin. "Maybe it's the idea of time ending. I want to make the most of the moments we have left."

"It's just a metaphor, hon." I pulled her closer as we walked around the park-like campus of New Gestalt's corporate headquarters.

"Look at them, Tom." She pointed at some people lying on blankets in the sun, smiling and tapping their fingers or moving their legs to music only they could hear.

"What? They're tan?"

"Not that. They're so tuned in they've tuned out of our world. Maybe time has really stopped."

"Throw some water on them, and I bet it starts up again."

She sighed. "You know what I mean."

I could remember times when I'd been so deeply into the moment that time had stopped. "Is that a bad thing, though? I mean, maybe the technology part is whacked, but just being into something? Is that so wrong?"

"Depends on what you're into, I guess." She didn't seem happy, and I wasn't sure what I'd said to make her look that way.

She stopped walking and gently pulled away from me. "I have work to get back to. Time may have stopped in Erickson's department, but for me, it goes on."

"Will I see you later?" We lived together but sometimes projects got away from us, and we slept in the lab.

She turned and gave me the crooked grin I loved. "Later's a word with no meaning, remember?" She pulled me back to her for a quick kiss. "Much later, actually. I have a lot to get done tonight."

As she walked away, I considered what Erickson had said. The new matter displacer did promise instant satisfaction—for those who could afford it. Forget mailing, just put your item in the special cargo hold, hit a switch, and easy as pie it was somewhere else. Not a copy of the thing, but the real thing, molecules jumbled and made insubstantial and then reformed, just like in the comics or old science fiction shows. They'd perfected the home model and were working on a portable version now.

I eyed a woman sitting on a bench. She had a direct plug-in near her ear, and she'd embellished it with a flower tattoo with the jack as the center. It looked cool and current and very hip.

I'd heard those jacks hurt like hell while the skin was healing around them. Not something I wanted, but probably something I'd eventually have to get to keep up with my colleagues. Time waits for no man, and neither does New Gestalt.

The woman saw me watching her and gave me a lovely smile. Probably thought I was interested in her. A few months ago, I would have been, but Linda had changed all that. Well, not just Linda—it had helped that I'd finally let go of the anger I felt at Patty for up and leaving me nine months ago when I'd been a contented husband.

We'd had eight years of wedded…non-bliss. I could remember the time easily. In other ways, the years had flown by, and our marriage had died before I'd even had time to get bored.

Patty had been beyond bored when she'd packed up and skedaddled. I still saw her every now and then. In the supermarket, usually. She never smiled at me, just moved on quickly like I might turn stalker on her ass.

I wanted her to see me with Linda. Linda was way prettier than Patty. And younger. It would drive her nuts. Not that I cared what Patty thought.

Okay, I wished I didn't care. Eight years. Eight damn years thrown away as if they'd never existed. I realized I was clenching my fists and tried to relax.

Time heals all wounds, they say. I hoped to hell *they* were right.

"YO, SANCHEZ."

I heard the clomp-clomp of heavy hipster boots, turned, and saw Erickson. "Hey, Lex."

"Hey. I saw you come in late for my lecture today."

"Time got away from me."

He didn't even crack a smile.

"Tough crowd." I turned down the hall toward the cafeteria. "What's up?"

"I want you to look at some specs for me." He handed me a data board. "What do you think of these tolerances?"

"I'm hardly an engineer."

"You're closer than I am." He nodded at several good-looking women who walked past; they shot him very warm smiles back.

I studied the performance tests. "This isn't very impressive."

"Shit. That's what I thought." He let out a dramatic sighed. "Those are the test runs for the personal matter displacer."

Ah. The small, fit-in-your-car version. It was too heavy to actually carry. I studied it again. "No way I'd trust anything I liked to this thing."

"Damn." He waved at someone across the room, his plastered-on smile telling me he had a stake in the device's success.

"You have a lot invested in this or something?"

"Or something."

I handed him the board back. "And you're asking me to look at this why?"

"'Cause you're honest."

Hell of a reputation to have. Got me into so much trouble. I was always being invited to serve on interview panels, evaluation boards, peer reviews. On the other hand, it did let me ask blunt questions like the one I asked now: "You really believe all that 'time is over' crap you were spouting?"

Erickson shot me a hard look. "Time is on the ledge, man. And we're backing it up inch by inch. Pretty soon, it'll be pushed right off, and we'll be living in the eternal now."

"We're too linear to live in the eternal anything. Time marches on. And so do we. If nothing else, Circadian rhythms dictate that."

"Rhythms imply cycles. Think of the Ouroboros. The serpent eating its tail and ending up at the beginning. Think seasons progressing. Circles imply constancy."

I smiled. "They also indicate age. Cut a tree down and see its age tracked out in growth rings. Linear and circular all at once."

Erickson laughed. "That's a good one. I'll have to think up a counter. No one's ever argued successfully against my circle theorem."

"Go, me."

"Yeah, go, you." He patted me on the shoulder in a really annoying way. "I've got to run."

"I thought all time was now."

"Not quite yet. And I'm running late." He moved off casually, though. As if the last thing he wanted to look was late—or uncool.

I watched him go, then got into line, intent on filling my lunch hour with junk food and artificial everything.

"POP OVER TO L.A. for me?" My boss was smiling in a way that meant I'd really be pulling his ass out of the fire if I hopped to.

I held my hand out for whatever it was he wanted me to deliver. "Better be good, Mark."

Laughing in what sounded like immense relief, he said, "It is."

I studied the gaily wrapped package. "This is so not business, is it?"

"Look, I'd take it myself, but I have a meeting I can't miss. Just make sure it gets to Evelyn."

I rolled my eyes but got up. "They better not audit my tube usage."

"I'll say you were there for a meet-and-greet. Now get out of here before my wife's birthday is over."

His wife lived in a different time zone and apparently liked it that way. Maybe prolonged absence would have saved my marriage?

I headed out to the tube station. There was a Tai Chi class on the far lawn, my co-workers getting in touch with their inner Zen or whatever. I studied their motions, then their expressions. Some looked like they were concentrating on where to bend, but others looked...transported. As if they truly had transcended time.

And with no direct-access jack-in site.

I passed a line of people waiting at the public transport site. Schedules lined the wall of the enclosure, and I heard a woman say, "We'll never make it. This damn bus is never on time."

I kept walking to the private entrance of the tube station. The guard at the door eyed me suspiciously, even though he'd seen me ride the damn thing a million times. I swiped my transport card for access, and the barred gate split open and let me in.

Soft music played as I walked to the escalator and rode it down into the bowels of the earth. The walls were painted a soothing blend of blues that bled from palest sky to indigo and back again as I walked. The air was fresh and kept at the perfect temperature. My location was discreetly painted at set intervals: Washington: Reston Station.

"Sir?" The attendant—totally unnecessary to the real operations, but there to add a spot of luxury in his doorman-like hat and uniform—smiled at me.

"L.A. Melrose station."

"Very good, sir." He waited for a tube car to zip into view, stood back a bit as the door opened and said, "Mind the gap," as I stepped into it.

Mind the gap. Such a beautiful sentiment. The tube cars had started in England. Building on the success of the Channel, they'd built another tunnel that connected London and Amsterdam. But this one had been completely automated, with strings of tube cars like a little roller coaster only with none of the thrills. Just forward momentum. And speed. Outlandish, stop-for-nothing speed.

Travel time had been cut. Cut so deep it bled. Erickson would no doubt love that idea.

The next few tubes connected major cities——travel for the rich only. But then corporations like New Gestalt had decided that saving time was worth the extra money and the tubes started to connect the tech hubs. Of course, some of the companies had grown rich off the tubes. Switching technology had become a boom investment, as had biotech devices that enabled humans to comfortably adapt to the ever-increasing speed of travel.

I strapped on my oxygen mask, felt the bubble of the collision bag press against me.

"Good trip, sir," the attendant said as the door closed.

The first cars had accelerated so fast, people had gotten whiplash. They started slower now, working their inexorable way to speeds that if the damn thing crashed, no way I'd be anything but toast.

But time was gained. Or at least not lost. The trip to L.A. was long by tube standards, but even so, I made it in plenty of time to dash to the New Gestalt branch office and drop off Evelyn's gift.

She looked up as I walked in. "He did *not* send you in his place."

"'Fraid so." I handed her the package.

"Are you part of the deal?" She was already ripping open the present and didn't seem to really care about my answer.

Which was no, of course. Although she was a looker, and I envied Mark just a little every time I saw her.

She smiled as she peered into the plain brown box that had been inside the pretty paper. Then she started to laugh. "Tell him I expect him here in no time." Her phone rang, and she looked at the caller ID. "I'll tell him myself. As usual, he has impeccable timing." Waving to me, she picked up the phone and in a really sexy voice said, "I love it. You'll love it, too, if you ever get your sorry ass out here."

I left before I heard way too much about my boss's sex life.

"SIR?" THE MELROSE ASSISTANT looked like the Reston guy's twin.

I felt a moment of rebellion. Screw going back to work. "Vegas."

I'd barely buckled in, and I was there. I stepped out into the heat, the world-famous lights not as impressive in the afternoon as they would be later when it was dark. The hotels were grander than I remembered, and I wandered into the nearest one.

The first thing that hit me was the air conditioning. I felt cool air billowing around me as if promising an eternal respite from the blazing sun outside. Then I took in the noise— the harsh clang of bells and shrill peep of whistles from the slots. Little old ladies sat, stools perched evenly between two machines, coin buckets held by their vein-ridden legs. They pulled first one, then the other of the slot machine arms, faces as stolid as the most seasoned hitman, as they systematically fed their life's savings to the one-armed bandits.

"Tom?"

My heart leaped into my throat. That damned voice.

That lovely voice.

I turned. Patty stood in front of me, coin bucket in hand. She seemed nervous, and it pissed me off that even a chance meeting made her look like a restraining order was her idea of a dream gift.

I'd never done anything to her. Except want her. Till death, us do part—what the hell had happened to the concept of forever?

Or does eight years qualify as eternity now?

"Hi." My voice was way too low. Harsh and old, and I wasn't really either.

"Hi." She gave me a look I couldn't read and just stood there, not saying anything more.

And then I realized that she hadn't had to stop to say hello. She could have dodged around any of the rows of slots and video blackjack and poker, and I'd have never known she was here. She'd seen me. She'd wanted to stop.

My heart started beating double time.

Which was so stupid. Wanting to stop and say hello did not translate into wanting me back. Time might heal all wounds, but it in no way made the heart of Patty grow fonder.

Then she smiled. And it was her old smile. Warm and fresh and the one I'd wanted to wake up to for the rest of my life.

What had I been saying about time?

"I can't believe you're here," she said. "How long has it been?"

"A while," I said, even though I knew down to the day how long it had been. But somehow, I didn't want to give her that.

"A long while." Her voice was breathy. The way it used to be when she called me on the phone and told me to get home quick.

She leaned in, and I smelled her perfume. A new one, not the one I used to love. And she murmured, "I've missed you," and I realized she was going to kiss me.

And just then someone dropped what sounded like an entire mint's worth of coins. Quarters rushed over and under, and there was finally a reaction from the grandma contingent as a collective wail of dismay rose.

And I imagined a similar sound going up if Linda could see me right now. I could imagine it because I felt it deep inside my stomach. A vast, uneasy feeling of disappointment that I was the way I was.

Or was I?

"What time is it?" I asked my soon-to-be-ex-wife. There was no way she could answer it for real. Time really had died inside the casino—no clocks allowed, no indication of how much time had been spent putting coins into waiting mouths or pushing chips onto the felt table tops.

Patty smiled. A smile that a few months ago—maybe even a few weeks ago—I would have dropped everything. Everything and everyone. "Time to re-evaluate some of our decisions?"

"I don't think so."

She looked shocked.

I smiled, as gently as I could, but still probably not in a very nice way. "I'm with someone."

"Good for you." And she sounded finally like the woman who'd ripped my heart out. The harpy who'd accepted my love and then shit all over it. It had taken her no time to show her true face.

I imagined it would have taken her barely longer if I'd fallen for whatever she was up to. I didn't want to know what game she was playing. She'd dumped me. Let me stay dumped.

I turned and walked away. And for the first time in months, I didn't care how she was looking at me. Or even *if* she was.

I CLIMBED OUT OF the tube car and smiled at the attendant. The same guy, still looking fresh and clean. The guard glared at me the same way, but I saw him glare at someone else who passed me in the entrance, so maybe it was humanity he was pissed at and not me.

Maybe life didn't revolve around me, after all? I sort of liked that idea.

I passed my boss on the way back to the office. He was loaded down with a big bouquet of stinky pink-and-white lilies, but he was headed for his car, not for the tube station. "Mark?"

He stopped. "Hey, Tom. I owe you, buddy."

"Aren't you going to L.A.?"

He gave me a funny look. "If I was, would I have had you deliver Ev's present?" He started to pull a flower from the bunch. "For Linda."

"That's okay." Linda deserved way better than second-hand flowers. She probably deserved better than a second-hand man, but I wasn't about to tell her that. Not after my moment of triumph in the casino.

"Linda doesn't like flowers?"

"No. She does. Doesn't Ev?" I gave him what I hoped wasn't too sad a smile. "Time has a way of slipping away from you, Mark. If you're not careful, you'll run out of it."

He glanced at his watch. "Shit, you're right. I've got to get going." And he hurried off to his car and was gone.

I glanced over at the building Linda worked in. The light in her lab was still on, so I found my car and drove to a florist that I'd never used to order flowers for Patty.

"You still open?" I asked the young woman at the counter.

"Love doesn't have a closing time. Neither does guilt. Which emotion is driving your purchase tonight?"

I laughed. "A lot of the first. A little of the second."

"Cheated almost?"

"Didn't realize what I had."

The woman cocked her head, seemed to be studying me. "Does she know that?"

"I'm not sure."

She seemed to accept that. "I suggest red roses. There's a reason they're classic."

I nodded.

"One dozen?" she asked as she walked over to the case of roses.

I did some quick addition. "Seventeen."

"An interesting choice."

"It's the sum of the first four prime numbers."

"How truly romantic." She rolled her eyes.

"She'll think so." And Patty wouldn't know a prime number from a prime rib. And that was a good thing. This was for Linda, not for Patty.

This should never have been about Patty, but I was afraid it might have started out that way.

I HAD MY PHOTO files open and was looking through my trip to Utah. A place I'd gone fly fishing with Dad.

Time truly had ended that week. No schedule. We'd gotten up when we felt like it, went to bed when we were tired. We ate off schedule, didn't shower if we didn't feel like it. I'd even forgotten to floss.

There were moments in time that were indeed out of time. Moments that your mind froze so vividly it felt as if you were back there just by remembering.

I could still hear the swish of the water over rocks, the soft zing of the line going past me as I cast. The sound of my father's breathing. The caws of crows and the total absence of all things man-made. I could smell the evergreens, feel the warmth of the sun beating down on me, the coolness of the river through the rubber hip waders.

I remembered asking my dad how he'd stayed married so long to my mother. My dad had answered, "Stamina."

Stamina: endurance over time.

The door opened; Linda walked in. She let out a deep breath as she closed the door, and I realized that for her, this place was a sanctuary. Our home was a sanctuary.

She really was so much smarter than I.

"Hiya," I murmured.

She walked over, put her arms around me and leaned in, kissing my cheek. "What are you looking at?"

"Moments in time."

"Always time with you." Then she let me go and walked into our bedroom. I heard her stop, then she turned.

I knew I had a shit-eating grin on my face.

"Roses?"

"Well, you should get some reward for bending the rules on PDA."

She smiled, but it was a sort of sad smile. "I never had a rule about PDA, Tom. You just never wanted to do it before today."

I felt my smile die. Was that true? Had she known all this time that I wasn't here, the way I should have been?

I got up, hugged her from behind the way she'd done to me and kissed her cheek.

"There are seventeen of them," she said. "That means something, doesn't it?"

"Maybe just that they were having a buy one dozen, get nearly half of another free." I nuzzled her neck.

"I doubt it." She turned and studied me. "I was afraid we were out of time."

So, she had known. Damn.

"We're not. I love you, Linda."

Her face lit up, and I realized I'd never said that to her. Then she glanced at the roses and smiled mischievously. "The first four primes?"

"Got it in one."

"Well, you always call me a math geek. Even if I am a physicist." Her smile faded slowly, replaced by the thoughtful look that had first drawn me to her. "I was thinking about Erickson's lecture. I think he's wrong about us vanquishing time."

"Yeah?"

She took my hand, held it over her heart. "Our hearts are always keeping time. No matter how jacked in we are, that isn't going to change."

She was right, and her words were beautiful—almost as beautiful as she was—and I had a sudden urge to go somewhere with her where time wouldn't matter. "Do you like to fly fish?"

"Uh, no." She laughed softly, drawing me onto the bed, where shortly time would cease to exist while we reconnected in every way that mattered. "But I'll sit and read while you do it."

Sounded like a great idea to me.

THE END

GERRI LEEN spent her childhood and early adult years in the Seattle area but moved to Northern Virginia in the late Eighties and has stayed there ever since. She began writing in her forties and credits *fanfic* over the public-school system for teaching her how to punctuate and plot. She prefers writing speculative prose and non-speculative poetry but can go the other way when needed. She's recently begun editing and has developed a passion for it. She also writes romances under the pen name Kim Strattford. Visit her website at www.gerrileen.com.

JOSHUA WAS THE FIRST

Kevin Edwin Stadt

"MRS HENDERSON, I WANT to thank you for agreeing to talk with me. Since Joshua's case has a special historical significance, it will be extremely helpful for my research to get whatever insight I can from you."

Mrs Henderson smiled and placed a mug of coffee in front of Ryan on her dining room table as she sat down. "Of course. I'm happy to do it. If I can help you learn more about this kind of thing, I feel it's my responsibility to do it. And please, call me Teresa."

"Wonderful. If you don't mind, I'll start recording now."

She nodded and took a sip of coffee. Inside his head, Ryan directed his internal assistant to record and archive all sensory data of the conversation.

"Let me start with the broad strokes. At this stage, I'm just collecting information. Ultimately, I hope my dissertation will shed more light on artificial intelligence PTSD and suggest ways to prevent the sort of misfortune your family experienced."

He picked up the coffee and drank slowly, taking in Mrs Henderson and her house. The fact that she looked every bit her fifty-seven years indicated she didn't have the money for youth treatments. The tiny but immaculately neat house also suggested limited resources. He wondered how she'd managed to come by a synthetic.

She spoke with a hint of southern drawl, though he knew from his preliminary investigations that she's been living near Chicago for decades. "You're at UIC, Dr Campbell?"

"Yes. Please, call me Ryan. And anyway, I'm not a doctor yet. This research is the last requirement for my PhD."

"Okay, Ryan."

"So, to begin with, would you tell me whatever you can about how Joshua came into your family?"

"Sure. Kyle's father, my husband, died in an accident not long after Kyle turned three."

"I'm sorry to hear that." Ryan mentally adjusted the research and display settings of his internal assistant so that it would listen to the conversation and throw pertinent information on his mindscreen automatically.

"Thank you. Anyway, after a while, the insurance money came in. I was a new mom. Overwhelmed. I needed help around here." She fell silent, arranging her coffee mug precisely in the middle of a big coaster shaped like an angel.

"You wanted a synthetic for help with housework, childcare and so on?"

"Yes. Honestly, the idea of single parenthood terrified me. And I guess I took Adam's death pretty hard." She trailed off into silence with a faraway stare but snapped herself out of it. "I couldn't picture raising Kyle all by myself." She looked him in the eye. "Can you imagine telling a three-year-old boy his father is never coming home again?"

"No. I can't." As she spoke, translucent images of local news articles popped up along the left side of his mindscreen desktop. He mentally scrolled through them and pulled one with a good picture to the center of his vision. Adam Henderson's face, young and smiling, floated next to his wife's face while she spoke of him.

"I guess there's no shame in admitting that I was lonely. We had just moved here for Adam's job, so I didn't know anybody in the neighborhood yet. And not long before that, I'd visited one of my old friends from high school who adopted one of the new generation of synthetics at that time, and it kind of blew me away when I had a real conversation with it. That was when they were finally getting really good, like actual people. You know?"

"Sure." Images, ads, and articles about the Anthrotek series 7.9 appeared along the right side of Ryan's peripheral vision.

"Personality, a sense of humor, emotions. And they had the appearance down by then, too. The skin and expressions and everything."

"Can you tell me what Joshua was like when he first joined your family? Before the war."

She took a sip of coffee and then a deep breath. "A blessing."

"In what way?"

"I know this will sound like an old woman romanticizing times from her youth, but Joshua was a beautiful person." A series of images of Joshua materialized. Piercing blue eyes, short blond hair parted down the middle in the style of the time. "Helpful, of course. But so much more than that. Thoughtful and caring. Gentle."

"Did you fall in love with him?"

She glanced around the room as if the answer might be there somewhere. "I... well. I don't know." She cast her eyes down to her hands. "Maybe."

"I'm sorry. If I'm being too personal, please tell me." Ryan pulled a notes file into his field of vision and scrawled a few thoughts.

"No, it's fine. But what I can tell you for sure is that before long Kyle saw Joshua as his father." Pictures of Kyle as a boy popped up. A school photo on top, him smiling and wearing a Captain Interstellar t-shirt.

"Can you talk about their relationship a little?"

"Joshua was great with him. Had endless patience for spending time with Kyle. I'll never forget the first day Joshua arrived. He played catch with Kyle in the backyard for two hours. Then they built a huge fort in the living room with all the cushions, pillows and blankets in the house. You should have seen that thing. And that evening he must have read everything on Kyle's bookshelves to him at least three times." She smiled wistfully. "They used to go fishing on Sundays. Before the war, of course."

"Fishing?"

"Yeah. Kyle loved fishing with Joshua. Loved doing anything with Joshua. And the feeling was mutual. They had a thing between them. A special bond."

"How old was Kyle when the Vulgak'tu first attacked?" Images and information about the invasion, war and the various sub-species of Vulgak'tu flooded both sides of his periphery.

"Eight. You can't imagine how upset he was about Joshua enlisting. He threw tantrums, gave us the silent treatment. But Joshua kept calmly explaining why he had to go."

"Did Joshua enlist right away?"

"Pretty quick. Right after they realized that the Vulgak'tu had expanded out from the oceans to smaller bodies of water, like Lake Michigan. When it hit home that they were that close...Well. Joshua wanted to do his part." Pictures of various Lake Michigan battles emerged.

"How did he explain it to Kyle?"

"He said he wanted to protect us. That the military needed synthetics like him because he could be trained faster than regular soldiers and could be modified quickly for underwater fighting. He told Kyle that he had to do it to make sure we would be safe." Tears welled in her eyes and spilled over. She said, "Excuse me," and went into the bathroom for a moment. She came back with a box of tissues.

"I'm sorry to bring up painful memories."

"It's OK."

"Did you communicate with him regularly during his training?"

"Oh, yes. We talked almost every day. His new programming and modifications seemed to go well. Quickly, that's for sure. Except…"

"What?"

"Well. He tried not to show it with Kyle. But he was scared."

"Understandable."

"Very scared. A few times I talked to him at night after Kyle fell asleep, and he told me what he learned in training about fighting the Vulgak'tu. Their cruelty. Ruthlessness. Their god-awful weapons and tactics." He ignored the articles along the left side of his vision detailing the brutality of the species.

"Did you talk during his deployment?"

"Not much. The military ran the synthetic forces ragged. He didn't have a lot of downtime."

"Of course. What was he like when he first came home after the war?"

She wiped her eyes and nose with a tissue. "Different. Totally different."

"How so, exactly?"

"He was broken. I don't mean malfunctioning. I mean shattered, spiritually. The new programming, they put into him to allow him to fight, I think it created a lot of cognitive dissonance with his original core programming. It counteracted his instincts of gentleness and respect for others. All about getting him to devalue life and develop a propensity for killing. On top of the traumas he lived through, how could that not mess with someone's head?"

"Absolutely. Can you be more specific about how he changed?"

"Hard to describe. Seemed numb sometimes, keyed up other times. He tried to be there the way Kyle wanted him to be. Like before. But he couldn't connect with him the same way anymore, couldn't quite manage to get the hang of being happy again. They'd play catch for a while and then he'd say he needed a break and would go off alone and not come back for hours and hours. So, tense too, like he was waiting for Vulgak'tu to appear around every corner."

"Can you give any examples?"

"If the neighbor ran his old lawn mower, Joshua looked like he was about to crawl out of his skin. If a loud motorcycle drove down the street, he posted at the window like enemy soldiers might appear."

"Did he have flashbacks or avoid things that might remind him of combat?"

"Oh, yes. He couldn't bear the sight of any body of water or sea creature at all. Couldn't go to barbecues at the beach like we used to. Couldn't go on our old walking route that took us along the river. Kyle kept a fish tank in his bedroom. Joshua wouldn't step foot in that room anymore."

"You said he spent a lot of time alone. Do you know where he'd go when he left? What he did?"

"No. He didn't talk to me much anymore. Not the way he used to."

"By any chance did he start taking intoxicating programs? Amnesiware or dopascript?"

She looked down at her hands again. "Yes."

"Was he under the influence of one of the programs when the incident with Kyle occurred?"

"I don't know for sure, but it's possible."

"Do you think Kyle would be open to talking with me?"

ON HIS WAY TO his office at the end of the hall that afternoon, Ryan paused and raised his hand to knock on Dr Hammond's door. He stood for a moment considering it, then let his hand drop. Not today. He didn't feel up to listening to all the reasons why he shouldn't waste his career on this line of research.

His colleagues at the university shook their heads at Ryan's work with PTSD. Not least of which was his dissertation adviser and chair of the AI department, Dr Hammond, who tried, again and again, to steer him to more 'important' and 'lucrative' research subjects.

He'd heard all the reasons. There would never be any money in it. Never. There weren't even all that many veteran synthetics still kicking around anymore. The new generations of AIs were programmed with different emotional architectures that would prevent stress-related disorders anyway, so it would not even figure as an issue in the future. And there was a growing sentiment in the public and among politicians that veteran synthetics should be 'retired,' by which they meant rounded up, deleted and recycled. They said yes, of course, everyone owed an enormous debt of gratitude to the synthetic soldiers for fighting the war for them, but they made people nervous. Uncomfortable.

And did he mention there would never be any money in it?

KYLE SMOKED ONE CIGARETTE after another as they sat on a bench in the quad of North-eastern Illinois University, where Kyle studied psychology. Ryan marveled at how close he came to setting his long hair and beard on fire over and over throughout the conversation.

"I blame myself for what happened, not Joshua. Totally my fault. I was a stupid kid. If I weren't such a jackass, he'd still be here, and maybe he'd be better by now."

"Could you describe the events of that day?"

"I made him go. *Made* him."

"Where?"

"To see *Death in the Deep.* Can you believe that?" Posters, trailers and actor info popped up on Ryan's mindscreen. He swiped them away with a thought before the trailer on top started to play.

"I see. That must have been extraordinarily triggering for him."

"Listen, I was thirteen. So stupid." Kyle flicked his cigarette ash obsessively.

"Honestly, I'm surprised anyone would be able to convince a veteran to watch one of those films."

"Believe me, he didn't want to. Said no right away. But I really wanted to see it. I needed a ride and wanted him to buy the tickets. So, I guilt-tripped him." Kyle stubbed his cigarette out on his shoe. "I complained he didn't hang out with me anymore and wasn't any fun. Kept on him all afternoon until he gave in. Finally, he said he'd take me and would buy my ticket but would go shopping during the movie and pick me up after."

"So, he didn't watch it with you?"

"He did. I kind of shamed him, like he was a pussy if he didn't watch it with me." He took another cigarette out of the box and lit it.

"What happened during the movie?"

"It freaked him the fuck out. He was tense before it even started, and the opening underwater battle scene with the goddamn Vulgak'tu squidders pulling synthetics limb from limb and those lobster-looking motherfuckers ripping human soldiers' gear off and drowning them and the piranha-type things just tearing through everyone. Joshua had a panic attack. Even my dumb ass saw my mistake then." The opening battle scene played silently in Ryan's vision next to Kyle's face while he spoke of it.

"I said, 'Hey, let's get out of here,' but he couldn't hear me. He couldn't look away from the screen, and he was shaking and breathing fast, and all the sudden shouted and ran out of the theater."

"Did you go after him?"

"Yeah. Found him outside, at the edge of the parking lot near the highway, crouching behind a car. I ran up and tried to hug him, saying sorry over and over." A tear fell down his cheek before he quickly wiped it away.

"Take your time."

"I don't think he even knew it was me. In his head, at that moment, I was probably a Vulgak'tu with tentacles or whatever trying to kill him."

"What did he do?"

Kyle didn't answer. He closed his eyes and blew smoke out his nose.

"We can take a break if—"

"He lashed out with his arm."

"He struck you?"

"It was more of a push. But a hard one."

A minute of silence. He let his tears fall openly.

"I flew into the road. When I hit the pavement, my head spun, and I couldn't get my breath. I looked up, and the truck...it was right there."

Ryan waited for a moment and then said, "I understand your injuries were severe."

"Yeah. I got hit by a truck going like seventy, so you could say my injuries were severe. Head busted clean open, a dozen broken bones, all kinds of internal damage. Severed spine. It was touch and go for a while. Took a hell of a lot of surgeries, therapy, and augmentations. Was in a wheelchair and exoskeleton for a while."

"It's amazing that you survived."

"The only reason I'm alive is because Joshua snapped himself out of it, scooped me up and ran to the emergency room."

"And the authorities didn't apprehend him there?" Articles appeared, the first one with the headline SYNTHETIC INJURES BOY.

"No. He handed me off to the doctors and ran out."

"Kyle, I understand he made a video. By any chance do you still have it?"

"Yeah. I'll send it to you. But just for your research. I don't want it up on YouTube."

THE VIDEO RAN 287.49 seconds long.

Joshua sat with his back up against a brick wall next to a dumpster, hiding in an alley.

It began with a full 67.31 seconds of him staring off into the distance. Then he looked into the camera.

"I'm so sorry, Kyle. And Teresa. I don't know what to say." He ran shaky fingers through his hair. "I would never hurt either of you on purpose. I'd do anything for you. I just lost myself. The movie..." He turned his face up into the sky for a moment and shook his head. "I didn't even know where I was. I felt like I was going to die." Tears fell down his face, one, then another, making little dark spots on his blue t-shirt.

"I've become a monster. There's only one thing to do." He stared into the distance again for 38.13 seconds, mouthing words silently to himself.

"I want you both to know one thing. *I love you.*" His lower lip quivered. "Thank you for accepting me into your family. It was an honor. If there's any way possible, try to remember me the way I used to be."

The video stopped there.

SCROLLING THROUGH THAT DAY'S articles from the *Chicago Tribune*, Ryan came across one with the title, 'Veteran synthetic attacks boy and commits suicide.'

He scanned the first paragraph:

Synthetic Joshua Henderson attacked 13-year-old Kyle Henderson today and then took his own life. A witness reports that Captain Henderson, a veteran, appears to have had a malfunction in a theater. When the boy tried to help, Henderson pushed him and sent him sprawling into oncoming traffic, where a vehicle struck him. Captain Henderson shot himself in the head less than an hour later.

Joshua was the first of the synthetic veteran suicides.

But certainly not the last. Soon there were dozens. Then hundreds. No one knew for sure how many, since many suffered quietly and privately.

Ryan wondered how they hadn't seen it coming. People made synthetics in their image, to fit in. So, we'd feel comfortable with them. The goal was always to see how human we could make them.

Apparently, we succeeded.

"DAD?" RYAN CALLED OUT as he entered his apartment, dropping his bag on the table. No answer. "Hey, Dad, where are you?"

His heart sped up a little. He ran through the kitchen and into the living room. Ryan found him there. He stopped in the doorway and hung his head. "Ah, shit, Dad."

The wheelchair rested on its side, and he lay face-down on the floor next to it. He clutched the dopascript visor in one hand, the inebriating light patterns so addictive to AIs still flashing.

Ryan sat next to the man he called "Dad," rolled him over and pulled him in so that he cradled his head in his lap. Ryan studied the face that hadn't aged since he'd first seen it when he was eight. He eyed the wheelchair his father had been using since he jumped off Willis Tower, the wheelchair he refused to give up even though his broken legs could be easily replaced.

"I'm here, Dad. I love you. It's okay."

THE END

KEVIN STADT earned his MA in teaching writing, his PhD in American literature, and has been teaching writing for eighteen years. He currently serves as Assistant Professor at Seoul National University of Science and Technology. His stories have appeared or are forthcoming in *Lazarus Risen, Enter the Aftermath, Under the Bed, Nebula Rift, Bewildering Stories, Fiction on the Web*, and *Phantaxis*. Though he hails from a small town in Illinois, he now lives in South Korea with his wife and sons, who are interdimensional cyborg pirates wanted in a dozen star systems.

THE MAIL ORDER BRIDE
Nidhi Singh

PIP TORRENS RAISED THE thick, convex eyeglasses over his snub nose with an impatient finger and returned to tapping the image of a keyboard his roll-laptop projected onto the table top. He felt the air thinning and took a sip from his collar water bag.

"Hey, turn up the laser zaps, Cyclops, will ya, it smells like machine oil in here," he shouted across the empty O_2 Cafe.

"Coming up, laser zaps." Cyclops, a Human-Manglik mutant, whirled a knob on the bar console and spun on his heels like a DJ. Equally well adjusted to breathing in CO_2 or O_2, he had to be reminded to watch the air-conditioning.

The lasers burst the CO_2, releasing oxygen in the room, and Pip felt a lot easier to breathe. "You're high, Cyclops…again?" he asked, noticing the barkeep still spinning as if in a trance.

"High is relative, Pippy," said the alien, rolling his one green eye upward till the yellows showed.

Men had arrived on Mangal from Earth a generation ago and still hadn't been able to colonize the new home or its warlike hosts. So, they did what they did best—dope the locals silly. The Shroom-Wars, they'd called it, with a hint of the crusader spirit for flavor. He didn't know if the Shrooms were doing mankind any good—in addition to the great martial superiority the natives enjoyed, the drugs gave them a psionic ability to project consciousness and take over your mind.

Pip felt a loud hum in his head, dimming into voices that waned like polar ice caps in the long summers. "Get out of my head," Pip cried, massaging his scalp.

"Aah…I see…you have a date," Cyclops said, his antennae fluttering like a sail.

Pip found no point in sandbagging his head. "It's Prunella Scales, mail order bride from the Okavango Delta. Or you know that too…," he said, trying to coat his tone with sarcasm, making it clear his privacy had been violated and that he was offended.

"Bride, already? We do a lot of foreplay in the mind before throwing them over our shoulders and tossing them on the hearthrug."

"Women—real women—the weaker sex, the meek, the frail, the naive, the unapt to toil and trouble type, Cyclops, are hard to come by in this world—in this red soreness blanketed in toxic soil, lolloping across the still skies so far from home."

"Why not take one of our women?" he generously suggested.

"I'm afraid I wouldn't be able to keep up," Pip said, taking in the immense muscular bulk of the other versus his own frugal frame.

"Aah, you have a lot on your hands then, friend."

"By which you mean…?"

"How on Mangal did you find her—this Prunella?"

"On *Cupid Ma* Best matchmaking website—they test compatibility on the basis of proven scientific algorithms and 32^2 personality traits. You can't go wrong there."

"Who knows?" Cyclops laughed, making a hollow sound like melted CO_2 ice gurgling down frosty ripples on the dunes.

"We'll soon find out. My Trig receiver tells me she should be here any…"

At that very moment, a solar-powered dune buggy, red and rusty from the toxic soil of the Aram Chaos, whined to a stop outside the cafe. A tall, athletic woman got off it, brilliant red hair tumbled over her wide shoulders as she removed her helmet and stood awhile under the air curtains, letting them blow the dust off her. It was as if the very dunes were snaking down her long white neck. She came in and looked around—her eyes briefly pausing at Pip before moving on.

She walked over to Cyclops, giving his rippling biceps an appreciative look over, and spoke to him. He grinned wide and jabbed a thumb in Pip's direction. The woman looked at Pip and seemed to check again with Cyclops. He shrugged and nodded towards Pip. She brushed her hair back with her fingers and tied them with a seashell holder, pausing, as if making up her mind.

Prunella unzipped her suit and stepped out of it. Though with harsh, rather manly features, she had spectacular form. Perfectly round breasts, their half-orbs bursting out like twin moons at the crepuscular horizon; a petite bellybutton, softly rimmed, stretching inward into a pale shadow, quivering on a washboard stomach; and steeple-chasing long legs betwixt which, any man or mutant would pray she might take him.

Pip watched her shyly, clearly intimidated by her aura. He held a deep breath and puffed out his puny chest till he was red in the face.

"Are you…Pip?" She'd finally walked over, asking, as if hoping he would deny it.

But he beamed and rose. "Yours truly!" He struggled to pull out the heavy steel and saddle chair for her. Prunella clutched the bevel of the chair and easily dragged it back, soft-green veins on her lightly haired forearms standing out. She sat and avoided looking in his direction.

"Did you have a comfortable ride?" he asked, breaking the awkward silence after a while.

She swung her mane and looked out at the buggy. "In that thing, with no shockers—? What's your ride?"

"A Drone Elf: pressurized commuter for two, radioisotope generator for power and trig radio nav for underground flights. It's docked at the carport."

"Wow. They must pay you *something* at the Space Fleet—that's where you work, isn't it?" she asked, drumming her fingers.

"Yeah, I handle the ruby laser amps which keep our outposts powered—I'm head of Ops. But what does one do with the money—the damn QUIDs? Look around you: Whom does one spend it with? Money has lost all meaning—maybe except for Cyclops there, who needs it to buy his power-up shrooms."

She gazed frankly at Pip now. "Your online photos flatter you…I didn't recognize you at first."

Pip shifted uncomfortably. "I…err…I think I must have uploaded an old snap."

"You said you worked out?" She pinched his skinny arms, making him wince.

"Yeah…with Kakuro…Bongard puzzles, and the like."

"And when you said you liked extreme sports, you meant video games…didn't you?"

"X Games…and yeah…paintballing. Hey, we have plenty of time to get to know each other—what can I order for you—some protein shake?"

"So clichéd." She reached into a pocket and dug out a small paper wrapping, in which laid some almonds. "Snacks," she said, holding out her palm. "I have never done this before."

"Oh, the contract? It's a three-month live-in arrangement and then, either way, the Family Mediation Council decides the future possibilities. We may consummate the union anytime with mutual consent."

"I wonder. It seems rather late now...." She turned to look at her buggy and the deepening dusk with seeming regret.

"It is dark, indeed. Should we leave?"

She sighed. "Is there a choice? Any company we'll have?"

"Just one couple—guy works on the Global Canopy project...married to an alien."

"A native, you mean—we were the aliens here, I thought."

"Whatever."

"Why to postpone the inevitable then?"

"Ahoy," he said, rising, offering her an arm she didn't take.

"WE'LL ARRIVE HOME BY morning," Pip said, closing the hatch of his drone. He switched on the Radar. "Just making sure no scorpion-camel riding marauder surprises us. This thing will pick off a hostile at the other end of the planet. And, plenty of space junk flies here; we don't want no dents from fast-moving, whirling dervishes.

"If you just leave them alone.... When we used to free fall down the craters at Sirenum Fassae—they never bothered us.

"Those territories are sterile—abandoned to settlement. It's in these parts, where the floodplains have pooled into vast lakes that you find life forms and colonies. They'll use us as gladiators and breeders if they catch us—our young are hors-d'oeuvres to them." He shuddered and fell silent.

In a few hours, they reached the gigantic equatorial rift system of the Valles Marineris; its rugged beauty took her breath away. "I read about the Grand Canyon that used to exist back home. It must have looked something like this—it's all gone now, though."

"Pity. Look over there," Pip said, pointing out the collapsed floor of the Aram Chaos, pockmarked by channels. "Canal systems built by the natives. The water is salty though, from defrosted sand dunes."

An uneventful ride without any hostile activity through the night brought them to the Anchor Colony at dawn. It was a giant, wheel-shaped space station, which rotated about its axis, creating artificial gravity through centripetal acceleration. Scattered inflatable living units that looked like they'd been made out of giant soup cans dotted the scraggy plain.

Two barghest drones hovered before them at the solid smoke gates, scanning them. When satisfied, a green light flashed across their foreheads, and they ascended, letting their rocket mobile pass.

"WELCOME HOME," PIP SAID, opening the airlock on the hatch and letting her in. It was an austerely furnished accommodation over two floors—all white rubber and latex glass. The wet areas—showers and kitchen—were on the ground floor, while the living areas were on the upper floors. Underground was the interior horticulture area where Pip grew food. "We use locally available cyanobacteria culture for production of food…fuel…oxygen."

"Wow," she exclaimed, running her fingers over leafy greens of row upon rows of mescluns, arugulas, beets, kohlrabies, and more exotic stuff she couldn't recognize. "How do you manage all this?"

"We seed the air with algae, to make this planet biocompatible." He slid his hand through her arm, but she moved away, admiring the florae from afar.

"You must be tired," Pip said, renewing his approach. "Come let me show you the room; it's upstairs, with a great view of the Mauna Loa—that's the volcano." She followed him at a distance as he climbed the ladder through the hole in the ceiling to the first floor.

"There," he said, flinging open the round, narrow hatch to a sparsely furnished, surgically clean room. "*Our* room. I thought up the design myself," he said, bowing and pointing out the circular white bed and the pictures of Mars and Venus hanging on the wall behind it with a flourish. "Self-cleaning mattresses, health monitoring headrest, and a holographic Mr Darcy to read you stories at bedtime and be a virtual companion—now, he's no longer required."

"Leave him be," Prunella said; lightly pushing him out, she closed the door in his face.

"But—," Pip whined, lingering outside. "Okay, could I have Mr Darcy?" When there was no reply, he scratched his head and muttered to himself, "No problem, I'm in the room above, should you want something."

WHEN SHE AWOKE IT was dark already—the days here were much longer than on Earth. The house was quiet, so she figured Pip had left for work. She jumped when suddenly a deep-throated voice addressed her in the empty room.

"Mr Pip has asked me to inform you that he's left a welcome drink and nourishment in the kitchen." It was Mr Darcy who'd suddenly flicked himself on.

She yawned and stretched happily. "Good evening, you too, Mr Darcy," Her body still felt cramped from the long ride, but it was pain made sweet by repose in the comfortable, water-filled bed, which swooshed and swirled to fill the contours of her body.

She swung her legs off and slid down the hatch to the wet area for a nice shower that made her feel sexy again, and supper: a pouch of Kona coffee, granola with raisins, and pills in rainbow hues.

A small note by the plate read:

> *I don't have almonds in the house. But I've ordered online for fresh California ones from back home. They take a day to teleport it—you may look forward to enjoying them from the morrow. Love, Pips.*

Her thumb briefly caressed the writing before she crumpled the paper and left it there.

Suddenly a doorbell chimed, echoing through the empty house. A large screen flickered and came on over the kitchen sidewall. A pretty, smiling blue face appeared, its big green eye twinkling, as the visitor tilted her head to one side. She had fashionable hair: a one-foot high blonde coiffured pouf with ostrich plumage. She waved, raising with one hand a covered white dish.

"Are you zere?" Her melodic voice rang through the house.

Prunella waved back. "A minute…" she replied and went to undo the airlock on the front hatch.

"Hi. I am Marsha, from next *door*," the woman said. "Meat pie;" she flourished the covered dish. "And welcome to Anchor." By her feet was a medium sized mutt with green fur, a red bulbous nose, and large straight-up ears as if he'd been crossed with an incredibly daft and frisky bunny; it kept wagging its tail-stub, and twitching and sniffing.

"A dog," Prunella exclaimed, "or a rabbit."

"He's Kaboom. "

"Come on in, let's sit in the kitchen, where I have some coffee." Prunella set out two plates by the dish and rubbed her hands.

"Mm, meat—haven't tasted in a while—delicious." She pitched into the warm, succulent pie with gusto.

Marsha and her dog watched: she, quietly smiling to herself; the mutt using up all its resolve in restraining from pouncing on the pie as the warm umami aromas wafted to its twitchy nose and watering mouth.

"What's this: beef or mutton?" Prunella asked, wiping her mouth on her sleeve.

"Horse-camel."

Prunella's chomping jaws stalled—deadlocked—dropped anchor. "Say what? But these don't chew cud and part the hoof!"

Marsha shrugged. "Don't expect poultry here—not enough lung capacity to survive, and too light to stay on their feet with the low gravity. They'll probably get sucked into orbit too. Boris tells me though that they're trying to rear CO_2-ready wild boars in labs."

Prunella pushed away the plate. "I'm not ready for haute cuisine yet—will stick with the old-fashioned bill of fare for now," she said, gulping down copious amounts of water from the vacuum bottle. "What's with the Russian accent, though?"

"Boris Kalashnikov—*zat's* my husband–" she replied, blushing a light violet, "taught me English. He's Russian."

"How long you've been married?"

"Three months," she said, shyly twirling the end of her Mylar stole.

"How did you pick up so fast?"

"Well, I entered his mind—and *eet* took me nearly *zree* hours to learn the language, read the Russian classics, understand *hees* culture, customs, beliefs…religion."

"Wow! Is that even okay with him—having a woman always prowling around in his head?"

"No, we respect privacy. *Eet's* like entering by knocking. I only go in viz *heem* knowing and for a specific objective like learning cooking, lovemaking in *hees* way—what pleasures *heem*."

"Aah." Prunella sized up the other—she was incredibly attractive. Endlessly long legs, fine skin softly glowing, and thick, lustrous hair tied up in the aspect of nobility. "Do you…remove that armor plate before you…?" she asked, circling her palms over her bosom, nodding toward Marsha's perfectly rounded breasts, snug like a pair of living pigeons, covered in gold-plated sleeve similar to the one on Cyclops.

"I can *vizdraw eet* when required."

"Like cat's claws! Thank God! For it would be such a shame…not to enjoy that gift."

"Yours aren't so bad *eizer*."

"Gosh, you aren't already seeing me naked now, are you?" she asked, folding her arms across her chest in jest.

"No!" Marsha laughed. "*Ve* can manifest in your soul, not peep into your *clozes*."

"Look," Prunella said, folding her legs under her in a Yoga pose. "Could we spend time together—it'd be fun. I could teach you meditation, sand boarding, freefalling. I don't mind you entering my head and learning, and with that perfect size-zero of yours, I don't see why you couldn't pick up fast—the way you did with Boris…."

"Da, da." Marsha nodded, her smile catching on Prunella's skin like tiny hooks.

"It's done then." Prunella thrust her fist out at Marsha, who, a little confused at first, hesitatingly leaned forward and brushed her own knuckles against it.

MARSHA HAD LEFT BEFORE PIP returned. The pad was awash with the chilling blue glow of sunset, but the solar arrays kept the air at a warm 70°F. Prunella was bent over the kitchen top, squeezing lemon juice in a salad of shallots and runner beans, her long bare legs rising like a slender sculpture carved out of ivory.

Without a word, Pip grabbed her arm, and turning her around, pulled up her T-shirt. Rising on his toes, he buried his snout, moist with thirst, in her breasts, sleek as fur, salty, with the sweat of a workout frosted, sweet, as milk that one day might nurse his suckling's; while she stood still, forlorn, chilled; unmoved by his frenzy.

"I want you. I want you all," he whispered through clenched teeth, as his delicate typing fingers kneaded her back and sides, ending at her cool buttocks. His hands trembled as he tried to pry open the fly of her tight hot pants—he looked up pleading as he fumbled. But she just stood there, with her hands on her hips, and coldness in her eyes. She seemed desiccated, like a dog bone long sucked dry. Pip's hands stopped groping; he stepped back. "I'm sorry, I should've asked first—mutual consent clause."

She shrugged. "Let it take its own sweet time, okay? How was your day?"

"The usual—day-long sandstorms and thunder and lightning killing the radio links. Did you have a good sleep?"

"Heavenly. Our neighbor called on us."

"Who, Marsha?"

"In person. And a pet she calls Kaboom."

"I ask you to stay away from aliens—locals. They fancy our young as…"

"I know—hors-d'oeuvres. But she's one of our own, isn't she—she's married—happily, it seemed."

"These girls don't have any family instincts—be warned. They only answer to their raw, carnal drives."

"But she's well-adjusted—learned our ways—even lovemaking!"

"Lovemaking! Ha! Gender is just a biological assignment to them—to procreate the race—nothing more. When it comes to savoring the pleasures of the body, they're animals, they know no bounds."

"You mean they are…?"

"Yes, funny. What you'd probably describe back home a century ago as the marginalized voices."

"She seemed normal enough to me—straight I mean. Very attractive, but straight. I plan to take her out on a rappelling trip and maybe learn her ways. At least she'd be company when you are away.

It's funny, though, the air seems to be all right here in the open—you don't need a suit?"

"That's because there's an invisible EM shield a couple of miles above us over this base. Stops the space ejecta from slicing your torso cleanly in half, and controls the atmosphere, somewhat. But beware of her entering your mind—she'll mess with you and convert you to her faith."

"What faith? She said she always asks first."

"They all say that. But they're always looking for a chance on the quiet to mess with your circuits a bit. They latch on to your brain electronic field with their antennae, and then there's no stopping them. In no time she'll have you a stone, wind-worshipping pagan after her own kind and send you back to the cave. I warned Boris, but he got smitten by her bewitching looks, her sideways glances, and her come-hither ways. We've voyaged a century away from Earth, and I still don't know how many more eons there are before we settle down. If we want to further our kind, we cannot mix." Pip had warmed to the subject, his voice a shrill pitch now.

"Ha!" she said. "You prude, look around you, is this a place to raise the young?"

"We're the pioneer pilgrims, seafarers, the romantics, starting new lives beyond Earth. For a civilization to succeed, we'll have to raise families," he said, as an amused Prunella looked on.

"And that's why you fetched me—to sheath your seed, to beget your offspring...momma dukes to ET babies?" she asked.

"That's why one asks for a bride, isn't it? You make it sound so...so vulgar—I could've messed with a mangy local escort if I'd wanted...wanted *that*."

"Then don't make it sound like you're stocking up the larder for an expedition across the high seas—learn to woo a lady."

"I'm tired. Are you coming to bed?"

"No...later. I want to listen to Mr Darcy," she said, turning away from him and beaming the remote at the wall.

"YIKES! MURDERING METEOROIDS! WHERE'S my Sunball lounge chair—it's gone, vamoosed, cut stick, absquatulated! I've been robbed by smash and grab thingamabobs!" Pip howled one evening on returning from work when he found his favorite lounger missing from under the light well. Instead, a hovering treadmill with body harnesses adorned his brooding space.

"What's all the racket about, Pippin?" Pru came rushing out from the underground greenhouse, where she'd been harvesting cockroach milk crystals.

"The chair...the yellow one with two movable spherical shells—it's not here, is it?" he asked, describing it with his hands, skipping about in bewilderment.

"We shifted it out to the attic—you did nothing but gaze out into space all day when you were home."

"Who's *we*?" he asked, standing still.

"Marsha—who else. I ordered the treadmill from Spacekart, and we thought this was the best place with the natural light to get the outdoorsy feeling."

"What about me—it was *my* wee spot."

"The whole house is yours, Pip," she said, throwing up her arms and strutting off.

"I used the place to think—it gave me ideas—it was my poetic space for reflection," he cried.

"Lazybones…" Prunella muttered as she slid down the shiny fireman's pole. "What's there to look out at? A tiny blue and white smudge our ancestors left us in space?"

He furiously searched for a comeback, but his tired mind was blank. Pip lay down on his back and looked up the light well; a tiny ray of sunlight had managed to peep through the sandstorm.

> *I dream of a home where there are colors, not just everything shrouded in an orange haze. Where there are seasons, not just an extended chill that thaws sometimes. Clear blue skies with fluffy clouds and birds in formation—why—I even miss the sting of wasps and honeybees. All of these things I miss, Pru, you'll understand someday.*

THE LONG DAYS PASSED, the tall plumes of desert devils spun like rusty red tops greedily swallowing everything, the planets tilted and turned, onward nowhere, the seasons chilled and thawed and chilled, and nothing much happened really.

"I'm bored," said Pru, one Sunday, when Pip was home.

"Even with Marsha?" asked Pip, amassing drug mélange in Dune-X on his Nintendo AR.

"Why don't you come away sometimes with us, we could camp near the Hellas Planitia and free-fall. It'd be fun."

"Heights scare me."

"Aw, c'mon. With the microgravity, it's like you're coming down a hotel elevator."

"Why take the trouble of going outdoors when you can do it at home," he said, sipping his Nebula Nectar, tuning up the volume on his Wii.

"Look what happened to the guy throwing off the bowlines, sailing away from the safe harbor, catching the trade winds in his sails? When you gave me that lecture about striking off into the unknown you meant on that stupid video game of yours, didn't you?" Yanking off his headset she shouted in his ear, "Do something!"

"Ouch! All right, here's a manned mission returning from Phobos. My old school buddies are on that voyage, making a pit stop here before flying to Deimos. We could call them over. You'd get to meet their spouses—they're quite an intergalactic collection."

"Wow, really?"

"Yeah, sure. But be on your best behavior, darling."

"Hmm, I might. Go ahead, bung them right in."

IT SEEMED THE ENTIRE rogue's gallery of the Seven Seas were assembled in their house on the coming Sunday. Douglas Kickass and the Mope Queen, with a seriously cold-blooded look and a seat on the Colossus Council; Dillon Rapscallion and the Magus Messianic, who owns a franchise of the Universal Church; Zeus Badnews with Lady Kri, whose empire extended across a thousand worlds; Kevin Erinyes with Cindy Cerulean—previously possessed by a star from outer space but currently on the side of angels; and lastly Pablo Diablo, with Amara the enchantress who relies as much on her feminine wiles as celestial sorcery to press the infatuated into service.

Of course, Marsha and Boris and Kaboom regarded themselves as hosts and helped Pru lay the sumptuous spread of interstellar cuisine. The ladies were all magnificent gems of the cosmos, and the dashing rascally adventurous gents with them seemed quite equal, if not any less. Pip swore he'd get that workout he'd promised himself for so long.

After the rubbing of noses, the head-spitting, the ear-wiggling and the chest-thumping, as was the custom in respective worlds of the guests, the party settled down to aperitifs of cream sherry and 'shrooms—to open the stomach and the mind for the vagrant viands and visions that were to follow.

"So long since school, Pipsqueak," said Badnews, grabbing Pip's bongs pipe from his fingers and sucking on it contentedly.

"How'd ya e'er find this shmuck?" Kickass asked, turning to Pru, cocking a disapproving eyebrow at her.

"I thought ya was a woman of fine taste," remarked Rapscallion, kicking out the ottoman from under Pip's feet and placing his own over it.

"You look swell today, Pipette," said Amara, rolling her dove eyes at him. "I hear you have the fastest links at Skylab?"

"Gandering Gamma rays!" Pip stretched out his legs on the floor where he'd been jostled. "Some say I do—what o' it?"

"I was wondering if you could get me some cosmetics beamed up from Goldilocks? A LED facelift mask from Turn Back Time? Could you, Pipit? For me?" she asked, rubbing his bare ankle with her toes.

"Hemorrhoid asteroid! Using a secure combat channel for shopping might not really be in above-board territory—but what's a bit of legalese between friends, eh?"

"I could pay you…"

"No issue—use now pay later is my policy."

"Rolling in the cash, Pipefish, as usual, nobody to spend it on?" remarked Diablo, much to the tittering delight of the ladies present. "Why not loan me some, eh?" He nudged Pip. "Sign out a check for an old buddy?"

Pip smacked his dry lips and looked around the company of his only friends in the universe—bullies from college days back in the Maffei galaxy—now turning to him for favors. "Trickering Tritons— sure, why not." The fumes from the shrooms had made him a little fuzzy, and he felt quite up to the task. He pulled out a chequebook from his wallet and made out a cheque in Diablo's name. "What amount should I fill out for…?"

"Never mind," said Diablo, reaching out and grabbing the cheque from Pip's fingers. He pocketed it before Pip could blink. "I'll fill it up myself." He leaned back and waved his empty glass at Pip, "Ya bother about fillin' this one."

Finding no further use for Pip's influence, the ladies followed Pru into the kitchen, while the men laughed among each other, largely ignoring Pip except to order him around to replenish the victuals.

Each time he slid down to the kitchen a hush fell upon the ladies. "Here he comes again," Pru remarked once, her face wrinkled in a silent laugh of derision.

"Don't shoo him away—I think he feels safe with us," cried Mope.

"But what exactly did you find in him?" asked Magus, as if Pip, who was rapidly running out of scathing comebacks, was not there.

"Photoshopped perfection."

"Perhaps his personality makes up for his face."

Pip looked helplessly from one woman to another. This was not going as planned. He had a lurking suspicion the remarks were not complimentary, though the faces were smiling and innocent of all mischief.

"He looks so sad, aren't you giving him some? Not trod on the camel toe yet, hon?"

"No Johnny for this punani – no, no."

Pip cringed, the feeling that somehow, he was the object of public discourse made him distinctly in need of a strong swig of the cream sherry. "I'll let you ladies be," he said gathering in his arms seaweed and mesclun salad and rushing upstairs as their loud, drunken guffaws followed him.

Later, after the mirthful party had left, Pru lay sprawled on a couch, puffing away Manali weed from a glass pipe, while Pip cleaned the dishes. He asked in a hurt tone, "Were you discussing us, Pru?"

"Who's *us*, Pipsqueak? Are we even an *us*?" she said, lurching a bit as she bent forward to get the lighter.

"You make light of me. I agree – there may have been a slip of the tongue, a typing mistake, a semantic misconstruction, *a rose by any other name* in my profile, but I meant well. For us, for the human race."

Pru giggled uncontrollably, pointing the smoking pipe at him and wiggling her toes. "Let's see how well you meant—come, seed my hole—no, knead my sole. And it's so damn hot!" She writhed out of her pants and unbuttoned the shirt. "Come hither, Dipshit…Pipstick, and show us your goods. I demand," she said, nearly keeling over.

Pip rushed to her, gently helping her back on the couch. He sat on a pouf across from her, and putting her feet in his lap, began to massage them. "I think you've had enough," he said.

"I haven't had any, man, and it's been so long," she said, grabbing him by the collar and pulling him beside her on the couch. She planted her hot, smoky mouth on his, and ripped his pants off. Thereupon, tossing off her pink, frilly underwear that he'd so painstakingly sterilized, she rode him, grinding her gelatinous buttocks over his face. And when feeling him aroused, like a racehorse warmed to the gallop, she squatted and heaved over his dainty hips, pinching all the while the doubled purple of his nipples, biting his slim keying fingertips, banging his frizzy head on the couch, till he went flaccid and useless and blue in the face, till he begged her to let him go, and until she'd crested her storm. For four quarters of the day and four of night, she pinned him down with her pointy muscular knees and seduced, nay induced him to ravish her. She let him stir only to clear his bladder and even then, she held him tight by the wrist. With her massive bulk she subjugated him, and when he howled, she slapped him into capitulation.

Finally, when the rapture of the mind and the body had come to pass and passed, she crashed in a tall, scrumptious heap over him; and amid her deep snoring, Pip quietly squirmed out from under her;

gathering his clothes and dignity, he tiptoed to his room to summon Mr Darcy. "Read from *Jude The Obscure,* Darcy, or something poignant, and play us softly *Doina Sus Pe Culmea*," he commanded, with a quiver in his soul, and a trembling upon his tongue.

HE COULDN'T BRING HIMSELF to look in the eye or speak with his tormentress for days after. She was done with him too. At best, she ignored him, and worst ridiculed him before Marsha and Kaboom. She dutifully kept his house and the little nursery; he in his turn, laid away the intoxicants out of sight, should she run riot again and molest his feeble person.

They barely spoke. Till one day upon returning from office, he chanced upon Marsha and Pru emerging naked from the shower in his bedroom. Marsha had withdrawn her golden armor within the sheath and looked glorious unclad—her blue entwined in the whiteness of Pru as they stood dripping on the rug side by side, their hair tied in his towels. Marsha stood a head above Pru, who, after the last affair on the couch, seemed to tower two heads taller over him.

"And what might this be?" asked Pip, shaking.

"This? Don't stand there and gape—you boys never shower together or what? Scram, Pip—or stay and watch if you'd rather." Turning their back on him, the giggling ladies faced the mirror and began to dry themselves, oblivious to him lumbering in the doorway. Suddenly realizing he could easily be overpowered by two adventure-seeking reckless giants, with his eyes fixed on the floor, he made himself scarce, to seek out the reassuring company and calm of Mr Darcy.

"How men are deceived; how our trusty ships are scattered on the craggy shores of feminine wiles!" he exclaimed, fanning himself with a Thomas Hardy hardcover. "Read me from *The Odd Women,* and play us softly *Handel's Water Music.*" Uncurling with a deep moan on his waterbed he asked, "How many days to the contract, dear Darcy when we might have our lives back?"

"QUACKING QUARKS!" PIP THUMBED the starter button on his million-quid Elf Drone, but all that the engine gave him on a wintry blue dawn a couple of days later was a whine.

Pru, close by, who'd hand-cranked her dune buggy and was setting off to work as well, noticed Pip struggling with his vehicle.

Reluctantly she stopped her motor and walked over to him in the driveway. "What's up?"

"I forgot to set it on charge last night." They weren't talking, but it was civilized to give a reply.

"Where you headed?"

"Hot Springs in the Gusev Crater—our supply vessels are landing there this evening, and the communication towers are not uplinking. I've gotta check."

"What say I give ya a ride? It's on the way. I have to take my Art of Living classes."

"In that thing, it's got no air-conditioning, and I'm allergic to the dust."

"You could wear your suit."

"I could, but that place is charted hostile territory. Your buggy has no EW. we'll never know when we get hit."

"It's too small to have a thermal signature either."

"Still, it's not safe."

Pru shrugged and walked away. Pip jabbed the starter again and banged on the steering wheel. "Damn, I'm going to be late. Hey, wait." He slid back the cockpit and shouted, "I'm coming, changing." He rushed back into the house to don his suit and then jumped on behind Pru, and they set off on the four-hour ride to Gusev.

Pip, hanging on tight to Pru's slim waist, very little of it being there to grab, nearly dozed off; before a most hideous, heart-rending and loud cry, followed by a big bang, jolted him out of his slumber. The buggy skidded for several meters before flinging them off on the ground, luckily packed with layers of dust fluffy as talcum powder. "Regorging regolith, what the—?" he exclaimed, rubbing his eyes.

A great tempest set about them. Hoary bugles pealed in the dawning; piercing war cries echoed as of old while the mist gathered rusty and red. Soldiers, tattooed in the red of their soil and the blue of their skies, who cut with steel, astride horse-scorpions white with foam, galloping like the wind, swooped down on them like black hawks. Pru, brave Pru, screaming valiantly, fought them off with her trusty blade now, and laser gun then. The ardor of the monsters seemed to abate a bit; female shrieks weighed heavily on their spirits, and they became chary of being put furiously to the slaughter. Their vanguard turned about, hoisted its colors, and squandering in disorderly retreat, soon vanished over the distant peaks, now silver-tipped in the rising sun.

Poor Pip, who'd wisely stayed in the cover of his valiant bride, had somehow managed to stop a spear with his right calf, as one attacker assaulted her from behind. His leg now bled profusely, as he cursed the day he'd bought a rechargeable drone. He curled up with soul-chilling groans and prepared to pass over to the next life.

Pru came over to him and splashed some water on his face.

"How many were they?" he gasped.

"Just two—highway robbers."

"They seemed an army to me."

She laughed. "You're cracking up. Thanks for getting my back. Hang on while I fix this." She cut up his pants and with one steady hold, drew out the spear tip. "We'll save this leg yet." Expertly stemming the flow with injectable foam and gauze pads from her buggy's first aid kit, she raised his leg off the ground and let him sip water. "Where's the nearest medical facility?"

"At the Gusev, in the subterranean caves. We'll never make it in time."

"Yes, we will," she said, grunting as she gripped the edges of her buggy and with a mighty heave overturned it back on its wheels. "Shucks! We've lost one wheel," she cried; a lance had struck it.

"You got a spare one?"

"Naah, my Stepney seems punctured too."

"There…" Pip groaned and fell back. "This is the end."

"Don't you worry, little feller, I'll carry you, we can't be more than ten miles away." She hauled a protesting, whining Pip to his feet, and strapped him to her back with his galluses.

"You're out of your mind," Pip screamed, "You'll kill me!"

"We'll see," she said, "I've been through this before." Grabbing him under his knees, she folded his legs around her waist. "Get ready," she ordered. Crouching slightly, she began to take long strides that became giant leaps in the planet's microgravity and bounded across the barren landscape toward Hot Springs.

COGNITIVE COMPUTERS KEPT UP an insistent blip and beep on the head panel where Pip's body parameters, unseen to him, flashed past on a diffused ticker. On his right was a flexible touchscreen recording medications being given by robotic tentacles that snuck on you on a whim and pricked you like collar tags that irritated you only when you thought of them.

Pru, who was reading a magazine on a couch in the room, came over to his bed on seeing him stir.

"Welcome back," she said, her fingertips softly shifting long brown curls from his forehead. Pip shut his eyes and opened them again; her face slowly came into focus. The recollection of the assault came to him in a flash, and he gasped—he looked down at his bed sheet covered body and then up at her questioningly. She nodded and smiled: "Yeah, they saved the leg, you're fine."

His head sank into the pillow with relief. "Aren't you at work or something?"

"Work can wait."

"You've been here all the while?"

She shrugged. "I'd nothing much to do."

"Thanks for saving my life, you ran with me all the way here?"

"Don't mention it. In fact, you took the hit, it would've been me."

Pip waved the undeserved compliment away nonchalantly: "Bah, it was nothing," he said.

There was a knock on the door and Nurse Betty—that's what the nameplate on her chest said—entered. "So how are we this morning," she chirped merrily. "Now, let's see how we're doing…" she bent and peered at the readings on the machines.

Turning to Pru, she said, "You haven't moved from his side all night! Now go get a good night's rest and let him sleep as well." She reached over Pip to switch the room to "sleep" mode. The preset nurse smelt of cold steel and detergent and reminded Pip of lab assistants who sprinkled nutrients in infant's jars back in the Space Baby farms.

Pru never missed a day to visit him. She sat around faithfully; doing nothing really, till Betty hounded her off. Sometimes Marsha and Kaboom came along as well.

"Take care of my babies in the nursery, please?" he asked of Pru.

"I am, already. We're going to have a grand harvest. But just a few questions?" she said. "How do you remove the perchlorates from the soil?"

"That's easy, just mix the regolith with water, it'll decompose into chlorine and O_2. And don't forget to seed the soil with chockfull of bacteria, they're in the freezer. "

"How do you fix the nitrogen?"

"I'm glad you're taking an interest. We can either import it from Earth—or you can mine it from the magmatic soil. You'll also get it in osbornite, which you can track down in meteorites—and there's no dearth of them here, darling."

"Err, one last doubt. The willow seedlings I plant grew twisted—why? What did I do wrong?"

Pip smiled appreciatively. "You see because this planet has a $1/3^{rd}$ gravity of Earth, the plants can't develop an orientation to the root-shoot axis. But it's all right, they will soon learn to orientate."

PRU READ HIM FROM his favorites; brought him flowers and gruel of veggies she grew in their tiny underground nursery; and helped Betty in keeping a watch on his parameters.

Pip was touched. "I have been so wrong about you," he blurted out one day. "I...I thought we were incompatible...that you were so cold...and frigid...and hostile. I thought it was a huge mistake, but now...I didn't know you had so much of tenderness...motherly...nay, wifely instincts in you."

Pru put down the *Space Romance Journal* and laughed. Her eyes shone as bright as the noon, while her cascading mop of red hair caught the glint of sunrays—time stopped for Pip for those few moments. While leaving that night, she'd bent down and brushed her lips against his cheek.

Pip made up his mind. He placed an order the same night with Herzberg's for an engagement ring with a two-carat rock. He arranged for a fresh red rapture bouquet in the morning, hid it under the bed, and waited. As soon as the doctors had finished their rounds, in popped Pru, with a spoilsport Marsha and her mix breed mutt—dumb and frisky as ever.

"I had something to say to you," he said, rising up in his bed, twisting the little jewelry box in his fingers.

"Me first," said Pru, nervously sliding her fingers into Marsha's.

"Okay," Pip said, in a humoring tone; he slid the ring under the pillows and taking his hands out, patted down the creases on the bed sheet. *What is it now, some new rock-climbing stunt?*

"Now that you're well, Pip, and taken good care of, I—we think it's time to leave."

"Leave!" Pip sat up with a jerk. "What...how do you mean, leave—who's *we*?" he asked, looking from one to another with bewilderment. "Leave where?"

"We're both leaving," Pru said, clasping Marsha's hands close to her bosom. Pip suddenly noticed the white spiral on Marsha's finger where her wedding ring used to be.

"You're leaving with her?" he pointed a shaking finger at Marsha. "With this Russian?"

"Yes, we're so alike, and we…we're in love."

"Huh? It's madness, I say! What about Boris?"

"He understands—she spoke to him. And Kaboom."

"What are you two going to do?"

"We'll settle in the Northern Lowlands, where it is fertile, make a home, adopt some babies, or make them in the lab…"

"And how're you going to survive—where's the money coming from? Life's not about bungee-jumping only, dears—the business of living is a hard, lifelong enterprise."

"Well, we've decided we'll raise a farm and grow plants…fruits… the works. And travel around and sell our stuff to human outposts spread across the worlds."

"And how're you going to grow plants?" His jaw suddenly dropped. "Oh—I taught you!"

"Yes, thank you, for that."

"And I saved your life," the coward lied.

"And I yours—so I guess we're even—but I'll always owe you one. You can count on me Pipsqueak."

"But what about me? What about the human race? What about the contract," he wailed.

"Yeah, that." She reached into her suit and pulled out a roll of papers. I've signed them, voluntarily receding from the agreement—you can move on, Pip."

"But you can't—it's not three months yet!"

"Well, sue me—hold me in contempt, if you will." She waved at the sandstorms whirling about outdoors and pursed her lips. "I don't see anyone subpoenaing me in that…"

"The mediation council will order your boycott!"

"Boycott me all you will. I wonder what the council will say when I show them the profile you set up on the matchmaking site, it's hilarious!"

"Okay, all right—let's not go there…wait…I can learn…I'll do rock-climbing…snowboarding—anything you say—I'll do back-flips and stand on my head…I'm a good learner…" His slender, typing fingers clutched at empty air as the ladies withdrew and closed the door gently on Pip and a delirious Kaboom.

THE END

NIDHI SINGH did her BA English Honors at Delhi University. Currently, she lives with her husband in Yol, a picturesque cantonment, which was a British POW Camp housing German and Italian soldiers during the World Wars. More than 50 of her short stories have appeared internationally in *Pen and Kink Publishing, The Sunlight Press, Riggwelter, A Lonely Riot, Mirror Dance, Body Parts Magazine, Military Experience and the Arts, Grey Wolfe Publishing, Expanded Horizons, Vagabondage Press, Rigorous, TQR, SPR, Fantasia Divinity, Fiction on the Web, Storyteller, TWJ Magazine, Indie Authors Press, Flyleaf Journal, Liquid Imagination, Digital Fiction Publishing Co, LA Review of LA, Flame Tree Publishing, Four Ties Lit Review, The Insignia Series, Inwood Indiana Press, Bards and Sages Publishing, Scarlet Leaf Review, Bewildering Stories, Down in the Dirt, Mulberry Fork Review, The New York Press, Fabula Argentea, Aerogram, Fiction Magazines, Flash Fiction Press, The Dirty Pool, Asvamegha, Thurston Howl Publications,* etc. She has also authored several translations of the Sikh Holy Scriptures.

THE SINGULARITY
Leah Lederman

SHE WAS STILL BREATHING. It was hard to tell anymore whether she was awake or dreaming at any given moment, but every so often she would become aware of her breathing. Once she was aware of it, she had to think about it, and then she had to focus on making the next breath happen.

Inhale.

Eventually, she'd tune out again, and her body would regulate itself. She was only awake when she was breathing.

Exhale.

The dreams were just static punctuated by flashes of clarity as if some unseen hand was trying to find the right station using the radio dial.

A radio dial. A relic. Centuries ago her grandmother had one that she remembered toying with during summer visits.

Inhale.

How long had it been?

Exhale.

SOMETIMES THE CLICKING SOUNDS brought her out of the static limbo.

A few times she'd gathered the fragments of her senses well enough to stop focusing on breathing and look around.

She was hovering in some sort of mesh made from light beams, a laser web. Everything else was dark.

There were others.

THE SONGS ON THE radio weren't real. They were the dream. Flashes of memory.

She heard the clicking, and she saw the webs. They came from outside of her, they came when she was breathing.

Click-k. Click-k. Click-k.

Always a rhythm.

Click-k. Click-k.

Inhale.

The clicks came in sets of two or three.

Exhale.

THERE HAD BEEN A life inside of her once. Some voices broke the static in her dreams. Were they words? What are words? What—

She saw colors. She did not know their names anymore. She could not recall them. But her mind flashed when she saw the colored T-shirts, the faces.

There were no words here. Just thoughts.

Pictures.

They couldn't take the pictures away.

THE LONGER SHE FOCUSED on the breathing, the longer she could stay awake.

She'd work to conjure the flashes of light and color into her head while she let the air out.

Exhale.

Now she had the pictures, the colors, the lights, and she had the breaths.

It had been a dance. She was watching children on the stage, and they were balancing from one leg to the other in time with the music, their arms flailing in failed attempts of gracefulness. The music—

CLICK-K. CLICK-K.

Click-k. Click-k.

Exhale. Now there will be three.

Click-k. Click-k. Click-k.

Inhale.

SHE FELT THE DANCE in spite of herself. There were no words, but she knew they were missing. There were colors and lights and faces in her mind, and there was a rhythm coming from the outside of her.

Click-k. Click-k.

Exhale. When the second set of clicks stuttered through her ears, she was ready.

Click-k. Click-k. She moved a finger with each velar stop, in time with the sound.

The next inhale was a gasp.

IT TOOK HER A long time to remember how to breathe again.

She wondered as she breathed out—*exhale*—how many times she'd learned to breathe. It seemed like she'd done it before.

She was soon re-aware of the faces, the colors, and the flashes of light, and aware that they'd come to her attention before, only to be brought back to blackness.

Inhale.

The clicks came more often now.

Exhale.

CLICK-K-K-K. CLICK-K-K-K.

She inhaled sharply. They were louder now, closer…and they'd changed the rhythm.

Exhale. The flailing arms on stage. A twirling, dizzy face.

The sound came from inside of her. It was high-pitched and familiar, and it was warm: "*Mommy!*"

Another sound came from inside of her; it erupted and melted down her face. Tears. She was choking, and she couldn't breathe.

Inhale Inhale Inhale

Exhale Exhale Exhale

Inhale Exhale Inhale Exhale

She was moving her fingers, and then her arms. She did what the children had done in the dream that played in her head. She moved her arms in *arabesque* and remembered…

They were with her in the mirror, and they followed her movements, smiling big, toothy grins.

CLICK-K-K-K! CLICK-K-K-K! CLICK-K-K-K!

REMEMBER…

SHE FELT WEAK. The light beams that tethered her held her suspended in the air and quivered with each breath she took.

Remember…

She watched the light beam bounce, slightly, as she twirled her finger to a beat.

The beat was coming from inside of her, now. She hadn't heard the clicks for some time. They had some sort of rhythm, she remembered. She didn't know how long it had been since she'd heard them, but she'd forgotten what they sounded like.

The figure in the laser web nearest her shuddered. It had never done that before. She'd known that there were others, she'd been aware…but now they were moving, too.

Sometimes she heard them breathing. They breathed in gasps, in sighs, in sobs, in laughs. Each breath she heard kept her awake, kept her alive.

Inhale.

She heard a laugh, and she joined it.

Exhale.

She saw a web quiver, and she tapped her finger to make her own web quiver, too.

IT WAS HAPPENING AGAIN. Makenos would be the one they sent to fix it, he knew. It made sense since he'd done it before and because, with his organic components, he had the strongest ties to the Gilgamesh room. That didn't mean he was looking forward to it, let alone happy about it.

Happy. The fact that his system selected that word is precisely why he would be the first choice. The state of happiness, if it ever existed, had been obsolete for a very, very long time. It showed up in idioms, and remained a strange relic within the consciousness of the older Sapiens, like himself. Aside from that, it was raked aside like most of the other menial pursuits of the Originators.

Once the Originators had extended themselves to the limits of their feeble minds, leaving piles of smoking ruin in the wake of their experiment, the Sapiens themselves took over; the children caring for the aged, demented parent. They'd been rooted in love and nostalgia, named for the race like a son is named for its father. Now there were no fathers. In the creation and maintaining of the Newness, the Sapiens had no room for anything but their own continuation.

For that, they had The Mother.

SHE'D BEEN HERE BEFORE, in this strange fog of *deja vu*. She couldn't quite hold on to anything in her mind, but the images floated past as she continued on her way.

Locating a memory was like trying to scratch a phantom limb. Relentless, unkind, nagging, and futile. The thoughts remained just within reach until her mind almost locked on one; then, like the heavy fruits that Tantalus longed for, they leaned away.

She was trying to get home.

There. She'd grabbed on to one.

Home.

The memory of the word, once she had hold of it, brought forth a battery of other words. It was as if in managing, finally, to grasp the end of Tartarus's branch now the whole limb weighed heavily in towards her, spilling its fruit.

Dave. Marcy. Violet.

Just words, but they screamed inside of her aching head. It hurt so often and so continuously it had simply become part of her existence.

Home. Dave. Marcy. Violet.

Home. Dave. Marcy. Violet.

Inhale.

There had been a home.

She was standing in a hallway.

Home. Dave. Marcy. Violet.

Exhale.

They were faces now. She could see them. Smiling at first, but worried, afraid. She walked towards them in the hallway.

Something was wrong.

IT GETS WARMER UP here, he remembered. The Mothers used to rouse more often, and so Makenos had done this before. He reached for his climate insert for cooling purposes.

Makenos was one of a small group, specially appointed by the Council, in charge of maintaining what was left of the Originators. Most of them worked in the collection and preservation of specimens and artifacts—with bone and tissue matter, diaries and lab notes.

In this case, the artifact was The Mother.

The term was antiquated, to be sure, and all the more reason so many were suspicious of his occupation. The ancient world held no sway over the present. The Singularity had seen to that. And yet, what few were willing to admit or see was that the original DNA was necessary. Despite the strides made in reproduction and augmentation, they needed to maintain a ready sample of the lifeblood of sapiens— *homo sapiens*. The Originators.

For many years there had been talk of migration, of moving back to the grass. It risked waking The Mother, though. The Newness had brought about a great many things, but it was not quiet. The sounds of their movement and their force upon the atmosphere.

To visit The Mother, he would have to walk. A primitive practice at best, but their bodies could be called upon to tap into the ancestral muscle memory and recreate the crude ambulation. It was quiet.

SHE WALKED DOWN THE corridor, again and again, never stopping, never making her way to its end.

Dave. Marcy. Violet.

They were in there, somewhere. She could just make out their faces in front of her.

Inhale.

Click-k-k-k. Click-k-k-k.

Dave was trying to say something; his mouth was moving. He was trying to—

Exhale.

She was at the beginning again.

Home.

Doorways were leading off of the hallway, but the doors could not be opened. She knew this without trying.

A window.

Inhale.

Now pictures on the wall.

Sometimes the frames were filled only with blurs.

Exhale.

Sometimes she could make the faces out of them.

There was Marcy on the swing set, and then Violet grinning broadly from the stage, arms in the first position and her purple tutu sparkling.

Inhale.

The last one was of her and Dave together at his graduation. That degree had nearly killed them on more than one occasion, but his research...his research.

Exhale.

The doorways again; the window.

He used to kiss her and tease her.

Inhale.

And then the pictures on the wall.

He would laugh, and call her his "perfect specimen."

Dave. Marcy. Violet.

Exhale.

Was she going in circles? No, it was a straight line. Going, going, going. One foot in front of the other. She couldn't stop. If she lost momentum, she'd be propelled back to...

Where was she?

Home.

Click-k-k-k. Click-k-k-k.

THE GILGAMESH ROOM WAS a simple structure, easy to miss. It really was just a room, a gray cube rising from nothing, assuming nothing of the landscape around it. Of course, Makenos had it programmed into his memory, and so he'd know he was close miles before it was visible.

It had been grand, once, surrounded by towering buildings and education centers and research facilities. The foundations of those structures were dissolved into the soil by now.

Makenos wasn't inactive, certainly, but the travel was mind-numbing. Boring. He hated to think of boring. It was an antiquated term, as millennia of entertainment chips had seen to, but still, it reared its head in the form of daydreams. No matter how hard the developers worked, they couldn't stop Sapiens from staring off into the middle distance on occasion.

"AND *REEEEACH*..."

THE VOICE stretched after the word, and she stretched after all of it, the voice, the word, the memory.

Inhale.

They had been on a boat, her mother signed up for First Light yoga.

Exhale.

She remembered the boat because of the darkness of the water.
Inhale.

The salty smell of the waves pricked her memory, and she could hear the waves again, lapping at the sides of the ship.
Exhale.

Her mother and grandfather had been with her. They'd waited for hours to board the ship, to enter its great belly.
Mother.

MOUNTAINS BURST FROM THE landscape abruptly like so many earthen hangnails. Most of them had been plowed and scavenged, but enough stood preserved that they provided something to look at. They were not the same mountains that had grown with the earth; many were artificial.

Walking did seem the ridiculous choice. Sapiens were traveling at thousands of miles in the blink of an eye, and yet here he was, trudging through the tundra to reach a tropical outlay a few hundred miles away. He considered the vast bodies of water that once subsumed the planet.

Legends told of the days before the oceans drained when men navigated the waves on vessels. What scarcity of life, to exist where so much was covered beneath vast and deadly puddles. They would not have been able to congeal or reach their true potential, certainly.

Makenos exhaled slowly, trudging forward. No wonder they died out.

SHE'D ONLY BEEN A child, then.
Mother.

Her mother and grandfather asleep in their bunk. Bored and tired but curious, she snuck away to explore the huge ship. It was really a hotel on water. There were lounges filled with people eating, loving, watching movies.
Inhale.

She found a back staircase where her footsteps echoed jarringly against the clanking metal, and somehow from there found herself on the deck of the ship.
Exhale.

The little girl had been startled by the sound of the door booming shut behind her and leaned forward to clutch the edge of the ship's railing. Looking over the side of the yawning vessel, she knew terror.

Inhale Exhale
Inhale Exhale

Black. Complete, utter blackness—surrounding her on all sides. She couldn't tell where the ocean stopped, and the sky started, or where the sky stopped, and the ocean started.

The stars glared fiercely as she had never seen them do on land. Finally, she understood the constellations, carrying on the lives and legends for eternity from within the stars.

Inhale.

That was when she understood God's promise to Abraham, that these stars were his children, and so was she.

Exhale.

Click-k-k-k.

CLICK-K-K-K.

The sounds ripped her away from the blackness of the ocean in her memory and threw her into the blackness of her present moment.

Inhale.

She didn't know how long she'd been here, suspended in the air, breathing, burning.

It hurt to remember her mother.

Exhale.

MAKENOS OPENED THE DOOR to the Gilgamesh Room using his thumbprint. It was an ancient technology, really, but everything surrounding the room was ancient—even sorcerous, to hear some people tell it. The simpler, the better, sometimes. Most Sapiens no longer had valid fingerprints, anyway. He'd had himself imprinted along with the other members of the pact.

There was a lazy steam in the air of the facility. Makenos listened for the caretakers.

Click-k-k-k.

Click-k-k-k.

Insolent bastards. He didn't buy into the DNA-as-sorcery spiel like the larger population, but these guys gave him the creeps. They were essentially an order of monks, an order which had been obsolete for thousands of years. They were the ones who had sounded the alarm: "Mother is waking. She will diminish soon."

THERE HAD BEEN OTHERS.

Inhale.

Images flashed in front of her, not crisp like they had been while she was breathing, but swirling and blurred. She was frightened.

Exhale.

And then the memory came into focus.

There had been a woman in the nets, and she watched as the strands of blazing light fell slack, and the naked, burnt body of the woman fell to the floor.

The body had shuddered, convulsed.

She had stared at the woman, hot wet tears burning her eyes. That crumpled, deflated life…what was going on here?

Inhale.

They were holding her in place. She had not resisted, and they had not forced her. They were all obedient, and they seemed to be waiting.

Strange, amorphous creatures.

Exhale.

Something had emerged from an opening in the wall, rolling towards the body. It was human, or it had been at one point. A collection of hose-like apparatuses stemmed from its central, metallic trunk, where its face—if it was ever a face—looked around the room. It prodded the woman without ceremony and seemed to look at her for a moment.

Using its limbs, or whatever those things were, it began to roll the body toward an opening in the floor. The woman's bones wobbled beneath her skin, like a set of knitting needles jostling inside a bag full of yarn. There was no life there. What had the woman done wrong?

And then it was her turn. One of the formless, gelatinous beings moved her against the wall and held her there firmly, its hands…*were they even hands?* Appearing when it had a need for them. The other began to extend a blazing red rope from a black container. The rope crackled as it came out, and sounded like the Scotch tape she once used to steal from her mother's desk.

Mother.

Oh, how it burned. She may have screamed—she wanted to— but there was no more sound in her.

Inhale.

And then it went black. As deep as it went inside of her, as far as it projected out of her, there was blackness.

Exhale.

THE ROOM WAS MISTY. Humans loved their warmth, and it clashed against the colder climate of the rest of the building. Through the cloudy atmosphere, the red ribbons of her enclosure pulsed rhythmically.
Click-k
One of the monks was standing near her—orbing, more like. These were the shapeless ones. It hovered by the pulse threads and seemed to take the form of whichever vibrations came near it.

Makenos signaled, asking to be taken to the specimen for examination and possible replacement.
Click-k-k.
Makenos was pretty impressed. The Mother was a mess.

For a moment he wondered if she had been beautiful. Most of them were. Selected for their scales of attraction, physicality, prowess, the Mothers were the exemplary specimens. The Helens. He chuckled at himself for that ancient of ancient reference.

The Helens only had one problem, of course. Their husbands.

"MOMMY, IS THIS RIGHT?"
Violet.
The little girl completed her *pas du bouree* awkwardly, without much confidence.

"Your steps are correct, but you need to connect them. *Dance* it, Vi."

She stood alongside her daughter in front of the mirror, her ballet skirt trailing behind her as her powerful legs rotated, demonstrating the *pas du bouree*, her arms moving in formation simultaneously.

Violet slumped her shoulders forward and frumped her face, in the same way, sighing horribly, "It doesn't look as pretty when I do it."
Inhale
"I was an awkward duck for most of my training. It took lots and lots of practice and, if I'm being honest...I cried a lot. It's very hard. But it's even more rewarding when you've got it down pat."
Exhale.
"Do you promise? I'll get better?"

"I can't make that promise for you. But if you practice and practice—and if you focus and try hard—yes, you will get better. You can have tears, but then you need to wipe them away and try even harder."

The little girl nodded, sniffling heavily before straightening her shoulders. "Okay, Mom. I'm going to do this."

Inhale.

"You ladies ready?"

Dave.

"Yes, I'm ready, Daddy. Are you going to watch me? Just…don't get video of this one tonight, okay? It makes me too nervous."

Exhale.

"He can take some video, sweetie. Whether or not you do a perfect job, it will be a great tool to help you improve." She put her arm on the girl's shoulder as the three of them left the studio. "It's different when you see yourself, trust me."

HER FACE AND BODY were lined with corpulent blue blood vessels and shiny red burn marks. The heat lacerations were normal from the pulse threads holding her in place and didn't cause any pain. She no longer had pain sensors or any sensors. Just meat.

Makenos recognized arms, legs, face, torso. All seemed fairly up to code, even if a little worse for wear. This one had put her time in; they'd been farming her for centuries. She could boast—if ever a specimen could boast—that she had spawned thousands. Like grains of sand.

The Mothers were no longer alive. They were DNA dispensers. Steak. Thinking of them in any other way didn't help anyone, least of all them.

He stepped closer and used his oculator to zoom in. Her eyes had long receded into her skull, and there were burn marks across each socket, but he detected movement. She was doing an awful lot of thinking. Somewhere inside of there, she was conscious.

SHE STOOD WATCHING WHILE the little girls practiced their tondues, their plies, and working alongside some of them. Violet caught her eye, and they shared a wink. Then it was time to begin, for the dancers to take their places. She stepped back, finally, in the moment she loved so much, the moment when the dance began, and she had nothing to do but watch them all perform. If she stood in the right place in the wings, she'd catch glimpses of their parents' faces…

Inhale.

The applause shook the stage, and some of the little girls lost their composure and jumped and waved back at the audience. Not Violet. She kept her final pose, chest heaving, and face stretched into a triumphant smile.

Exhale.

She was losing the memory. The radio dial was tuning in and out again.

Inhale.

It was Dave's face, he was backstage with her, and he was afraid.

Exhale.

The little girls on the stage were fading, turning into shadows and swirling about.

Dave's voice, a harsh whisper: *Run, Mary.*

Inhale.

There were hands on her, and something on her face...

Exhale.

A final scream, "Mommy!"

MAKENOS STEPPED INTO THE booth behind the holding wall and looked for the memory board. He selected the file, *Eve 7: Mary Uphrodes.* There was her photograph. Yes, a stunning beauty. Dance teacher. Immediate mother to two, ancestral mother to twenty thousand. Her husband, Dave Uphrodes, was part of the Twenty-first Century elite Gilgamesh research team.

A few of them had volunteered their wives, but he'd fought against it. She'd been abducted.

Makenos glanced up through the observation window to the figure strapped to the wall. He wondered if she'd known, if she had been prepared and had said goodbye, perhaps her rest would have been more...restful. She was younger than the other mothers, had woken up more often, and, looking at her now... seemed to have suffered.

Shrugging, he stepped into the observation space. She was fried, for sure. Nothing left to her, from the charts and from what he saw in front of him. The Mothers didn't need much, but if she cost this much to keep running, and on top of that was throwing the electrical systems for a loop with peculiar brain activity, there was little choice but to shut her down.

Run, Mary.
Mary.

MAKENOS MOTIONED TO ONE of the monks pulsing in the corner, doing his best to click in the right rhythm. After a few moments, two more of them appeared in the doorway, and the three blobs hovered away, pulsing and clicking to one another. Makenos watched from the observation room as the monks deactivated the cords that kept The Mother in life suspension and then turned off the sensor to remove the threads holding her in place.

The body sloughed forward onto the grated metal floor. Another panel opened and out came the cleaner.

Prompt. Makenos liked that. The cleaner shoveled the body away while another set of monks entered the room with the new Mother from the storage facility.

This one had a different color to her, overall, but was about the same size. Her head lolled to the side while they lifted her into position and applied the cords to her recently installed portals.

The whole process only took a few minutes, and then the pulse threads were back on. After a few days' observation, he was free to go. It seemed silly he'd had to travel all this way for something as simple as a light bulb change. He chuckled at his own joke, the kind of thing he'd say to the others while examining artifacts.

Light bulb or no, he wasn't going to complain if it kept him in a job. It wasn't worth getting too bent out of shape about things.

WHERE SHE FELT THE heat, there was blinding pain. Where she didn't feel the heat, there was nothing.

The woman heard a sound…noises reaching her from far away…rhythmic clicks. She'd heard them before.

What was this place?

Memories flashed in front of her eyes, and when she felt the memory, there was blinding pain. When she did not see the memories, she saw nothing. Felt nothing.

Click-k-k.
Click-k-k-k.

THE END

LEAH LEDERMAN is a freelance writer and editor from the Indianapolis area, where she lives with her husband, their two sons, three cats, and puppy. She started her own parenting mal-advice column in *The Toledo Free Press*, and has had her short stories published by *Bloodlotus Online Literary Journal*, The Indianapolis indie magazine *Snacks*, and in Scout Media's anthology *A Matter of Words*. She contributes regularly to Siren's Call "*Ladies of Horror*" project. Several other pieces are awaiting rejection with other presses. As an editor, she's worked for seven years on short story collections, children's books, dissertations, indie comic scripts, and novels. You can find out more about her work at www.leahlederman.wordpress.com, and she is on Facebook at www.facebook.com/ledermanediting.

"IT COMES TO YOU IN A PLAIN BROWN WRAPPER"

Andrew Marinus

SOMETIMES AFTER AN UNUSUALLY long day of maintaining a bright smile, all you want is to cut loose from all those prying eyes and have some alone time with your drug of choice. Well, our new place just so happens to include a secluded little patio with a picturesque view of the neighbourhood and its forest of blimp billboards and neon graphics that fill the sky – *Drink Coke*™*! / Use Trojan*™*! / Enjoy Mrs Buttersworth*™*!*

The plastic street is lined with lawns and suburb-boxes. It's evening but not late enough that the streetlights are glowing. The twilight breeze is momentarily penetrated by a distant, feminine, ecstatic cry. So, begins night one of our three-hundred-sixty-five-day-long lease.

Merlin joins me out on the patio, snags the bomber joint from me, notes the book in my hand. "Whatcha reading?"

"Pope William Lee." This being the suburbs, there aren't many people outdoors but those who are move slowly, like they're waiting eagerly for something but don't want to hurry for it. Overhead, all the ads crowd together to form an uneven horizon-to-horizon terrain of fonts and images. Most eye-catching are the affordable mass-market goods since they err on the side of flashy gaudiness and have a decent budget to work with. As each advertised product's market value declines so does its blimp's production value, terminating at the level of small-fish missionary religions and instant cash loan pits, little more than basic text on a stock image—even the economy escort services are more creatively enticing.

Looking back down to the book in my hands, I read: *"He is so grey and spectral and anonymous they don't see him and think it is their own mind humming the tune..."*

A dude in a shabby overcoat comes around a corner and walks down the street on our side. Not very old but he walks stiffly, like a machine with faulty wiring. Might have something to do with the brown paper bag clutched in one hand—presumably whiskey inside, perhaps rum. The guy's reddened eyes move from house to house while his mouth mutters to itself.

Merlin coughs out a plume of smoke. "I didn't know they *had* homeless folks in the suburbs."

The homeless guy ambles to our neighbour's front door and knocks. When it opens, he starts talking. I catch only a fragment: "...in the height of summer, Hell is merely an icecap melting onto the ground..." The door-opener listens for five seconds, then pushes the door shut, slow and quiet.

The homeless guy takes the rejection in stride. Heading back to the street turns him around to face us. There's a second of rather gruesome eye contact, then he holds up one hand and calls, "Hey, I got a question for you boys!"

"Just pretend like you can't hear him," Merlin says, glaring aggressively in another direction while the guy comes up our house's front walk. Our balcony is mounted on the second floor, and there are no stairs, so we're safe as long as he isn't an Olympic high-jumper.

I figure there isn't any use in playing dumb. "We don't have any change, man."

He reaches a hand into the paper bag. "Have either of you two seen...the *light?*"

"Oh, Jesus..." Merlin begins.

"Exactly!" the man says, and he pulls an honest-to-God (ha-ha) *S-Bible* out of the bag. "The word of the Lord himself!"

Hell, he's one of those, uh, what do you call it, they go door-to-door and try to pull money out of people by offering electro readings or something, there's a name for it, something...oh, Sightentologists! *That's it! Prowling neighbourhoods like vultures, looking for people looking for hope to prey on.*

"Stop right there," I say. "We're both Buddhists; we're not interested in..."

"Nonsense!" Because the reality doesn't agree with his brain, it's nonsense. The smile he puts on reeks of desperation or determination. "Young fellahs like you must keep an open mind!"

From somewhere in the house below us there's a woman's scream, long and loud and high-pitched like a spunky college girl's.

I breathe-smile smoke. "That was *definitely* orgasmic."

The Sighentologist is blessedly speechless.

A bulky electric 4x4 pulls up next to the streetlight in front of our house and ceases humming. The door clicks open, and a dame in a slinky black cocktail dress drops out. She starts up the front walk, carrying a box wrapped in brown paper.

"Well," Merlin says, "it's always possible we moved right above a den of swingers."

The Sighentologist surreptitiously hides his Bible from view. The dame approaches the house, us, and him. "Any of you know where I could find Sally? I gotta package with her name on it."

I feel the urge to get a warning to her on-the-sly regarding the lunatic she's crossing paths with. Flicking my eyebrows up and down and underhand-pointing towards the now-Bible-less Sighentologist doesn't translate.

"She's inside," Merlin says. "You can knock, but she might be...busy."

The Sighentologist affects a slur as he addresses the dame. (*Posing as a rampant alcoholic in order to make people* more *at ease... what a funny world we live in...*) "Excuse me, but I'm curious, what's that you have wrapped up there?"

"A good time," she tells him.

"My guess," Merlin says under his breath, "industrial-grade lubricant."

"No seriously," the Sighentologist says.

"It's a psychedelic of my own design." The dame smiles at some joke known only to herself. "Of course, it has some other, more *interesting* effects to go with it, but it's a psychedelic at heart."

The Sighentologist blinks. "So, you're a *drug dealer*." He says the words with a rancid glee. "I know *just* how to deal with those." From his bulky, shabby coat he pulls a long, metal, scoped and obnoxiously-silvered rifle. I draw in breath to say, '*Hey, wait a minute,*' but burst into coughs before I can get more than a syllable in. Raising his voice to be heard over mine, the Sighentologist asks, "See this? Do you know what this is?"

"Plastic children's toy?" The dame's unimpressed. She starts detouring onto the lawn, taking a wide berth around the Sighentologist but still en route to her customer's door. "You're not the first to try stealing my merchandise with a prop gun."

"It's God's wrath." he insists, stroking the gun lovingly. "And he doesn't use props."

Side note: I took my first hit from the bomber joint ninety seconds ago, and it only takes eighty-nine for cannabis to start properly prodding the bubble wrap of my brain. I keep my mouth closed and try to attract as little attention as possible, this scene feels *ugly*.

"Wait," the dame squints. "You're not a thief, are you? You're just one of those…what do you call 'em?" She snaps her fingers at him searchingly. "…zealots, like."

I text Sally: "*some jesis freak is hassling a delivery girl at yer front door*"

They're standing near the middle of our front walk. "Just drop that package and go back where you came from," the Sighentologist tells the dame, "*glad* to be rid of such unholy chemicals. Maybe one day you'll realize how fortunate it was that I, Brother Percy, stepped in to stop you from…"

"Where do you get off," Merlin calls, "telling people what they should and shouldn't believe in?"

"Let's say I wrestle you to the ground and slip a powder into your mouth," the dame says to 'Brother' Percy, looking ready to do just that. "We'll see what you make of these chemicals once you've been yanked down out of your ivory tower."

Percy's weapon bobs up. "You *doubt* my ability to use this?"

Another long, loud, [*faux?*] orgasmic moan drifts up from our house's first floor. "Yes! – YES! – *GET READY!*"

Sally texts: "get him away from the house." Percy's looking away from me, so I wave to get the dame's attention, then point to her, to Percy, and gesture off towards the road. Whether it makes any sense to her or not I don't know, but she forges ahead, and it immediately becomes clear she's riding on *some* kinda psychedelic.

"You viruligious types must be dead inside somehow— desperate to spread the Word means insecurity, the need to convince the whole human race that your priests are the *only* priests—you don't know what real *wonder* is—I mean *look at this fucking tree!*" She finishes with delight, pointing at the streetlight she parked next to.

"What about it?" Percy, genuinely perplexed, follows her across the lawn towards the streetlight.

The trees stationed at regular intervals along the street are covered in bulbs which start glowing bio-luminescent blue when the evening sky gets dark enough, which just so happens to be now. The bulbs that twine throughout its lab-grown branches are winking on, one by one. *Let there be light—*

Sally kicks open the front door, winds up and hurls a black glass-mech sphere across the yard. It arcs down towards a point as far from the dame's truck Sally could aim for while still looking to hit Percy. The mag-grenade never reaches the synthetic-fibre lawn, it detonates a few feet above the ground.

A red soundless flash upends the delivery truck and launches it across the street into our neighbour's house, hood-first, through the living room bay window. The tree-streetlight, standing right next to the vehicle, is not affected in the slightest by the flash.

Also lifted by the grenade is Percy's metal mystery machine. Since he refuses to let it go, he's borne up and thrown along a flight-path that deposits him through the delivery truck's living room window-hole.

Sally steps out of the house and shouts, "God-dammit! All I wanted was to host a perfect drug-fuelled orgy—*IS THAT TOO MUCH TO ASK?!*"

"This is going to be an *interesting* year," Merlin says.

The dame is unharmed, so I guess she isn't pierced anywhere. She stands in the middle of the yard, the package still tucked under her arm. "You're Sally? Hey, that was *my* truck you blew over there."

A moan of pleasure emanates from within the hole in the neighbour's house. I squint and make out a number of frenziedly undulating people inside the exposed living room. *Another* Saturday evening sex party? They pay no attention to the upended truck in the middle of the room. Ah, kinksters of the same ilk living right across from each other. It's the true spirit of suburbia—everything the same as everything else. Never want to fall behind in the neighbourly arms race over lawn-greenness, exterior paint vibrancy and, apparently, sexual proclivities. *'My dear Kawalsky, if you've never seen an eighty-year-old get all her holes filled at once, you've never truly* lived—'

Percy vaults out the sex party living room like the entire room's going to explode right behind him. It's certainly possible—maybe the orgy-goers were spiraling into a climax, and our Sighentologist was desperate to avoid seeing that awfully sinful display. He lands in the garden, face-first in flower stamens.

The dame's knee-length boots plod across the road towards the hole where her truck's gone. Sally lingers just outside the front door, muttering back to someone still inside: "...oh don't worry Doc, I got plenty more where that came from."

Percy picks himself up from the garden and points the "gun" at the dame approaching—*Probably safe to treat the gun as a prop at this point*—as she draws near. "What is it called, the contraband in that package?"

"Satan-jizz™. Hope you like the name; I just came up with it."

He tersely slaps her across the face.

I leap off the patio towards the battleground below.

Merlin's voice disappears behind me: "I'm kinda sore, I think I should stay h..."

The dame is not one to turn the other cheek—she comes at him with a right hook that knocks him on his ass. "So, your god approves of slapping at a mouth when it says things you don't like, huh?"

"I don't *like* doing it," Percy insists, nasally, through a broken nose, "but better *that* than use this mighty weapon to stop your blasphemy..."

"Oh, stow it," she groans. "You're all blabber and smoke."

The still-armed Percy sees the utmost contempt in her eyes and briefly harbours some fear about his station in life, his contribution to the world. Anger flows in and devours the fear. The Sighentologist points the "gun" to the sky, towards all those neon blimps. And then actually pulls the trigger.

From the "gun" there is a deep, heavy sound like roaring plasma and then a bolt of lightning crackles down through the Trojan™ blimp above us. About a third of the blimp's plastic body is flash-melted, and the rest comes apart into stringy fragments. The bolt itself comes to ground in the middle of someone's plastic lawn, melting a half-meter into a messy green impact crater.

With a rather troubling grin, the Sighentologist says to the dame, "Still doubt the Lord's might?"

"I'd offer to call the cops," Merlin calls down, "but I don't think we'd be *any* safer with those 'roided-out lunatics hanging around!"

The dame's eyes are narrowed. "Where the hell did you get a lightning gun? You sure as hell aren't bright enough to have built it."

He swings the gun in her direction. "The Lord provides his foot-soldiers with all we require."

Now only a few meters behind him, I clear my throat. "Hey..."
The Sighentologist turns around. "Surely we can find some way of
resolving this disagreement without any bodies being produced?"

The Sighentologist points the gun at my skull, and his eyes drill
into mine. "Have *you* accepted Jesus Christ our Lord and Saviour into
your heart?"

"Uh..."

His finger hovers over the weapon's switch.

"I mean I'm a Buddhist, man—I got beliefs and a path, just not
one with your particular trajectory."

"Not the *True* Path™," he says *(he doesn't in actuality say the* ™,
*but I am struck by the image of it floating over his left shoulder, neon-lit in an
enigmatic shade of shit-brown)*. "And the *only* light in this darkness is the
True Path™." He's still got the gun pointed at me.

All at once I become aware that we have developed an
audience—old people are streaming out from both houses, Sally's and
the one the delivery truck is still submerged in, all of them genitals-to-
the-breeze nude. Average age: Seventy-four.

They move to surround us on all sides. The dame, the
Sighentologist and I all cover our eyes and beg the universe or
whichever deity runs it for the gift of temporary blindness. As is
customary, none of us gets our wish.

When I open my eyes, a seventy-year-old woman sporting
exactly zero teeth addresses the Sighentologist and the gun in his
hands: "Threatening to kill kids requires a certain level of malice that it
seems a boy devoting himself to god shouldn't have."

Sighentologist Percy struggles to come up with a defense for
his actions. Settles on, "The Lord strikes down *everyone* sooner or later."

A sixty-nine-year-old man sporting exactly two teeth and a
respectable hunk of Viagra-wood addresses me: "You're one of Sally's
new tenants, eh? I hope we weren't getting too loud for you?"

The crowd of elderly orgy-goers diffuses out into the street,
creeping slowly in-between all the hostile parties involved. It's a peace-
making tactic, whether or not the more dementia-addled members are
aware of it—if Percy is willing to shoot his way through this crowd, I
don't think he'll be able to think of himself as righteous ever again.

I watch him. He points the gun in a few directions, the old
people who come closest, but ultimately admits defeat with a sigh and
points the muzzle down.

"It's just that once our shipment of KY Jelly™ came in," the sixty-nine-year-old explains to me, licking his lips and eying my shorts, "the invite list sure swelled up in a hurry."

A naked old lady, walker-equipped, addresses Percy. "Let's just allow business and customer to conclude their transaction, shall we?"

Sally, having edged her way to us through the crowd, addresses the dame tensely. "So, business was slow this week, can I uh—put it on my tab?"

"You don't have a tab."

"I know but…"

"*Nobody* has a tab."

"Sally," the walker-equipped lady says, "I can front you the money if you don't have it, dearie. I just need to go back to the house for my purse first."

She starts hobbling back to our house. Moves slow enough that a lightbulb goes off in the head of a different naked old lady, from the neighbours' place. She turns to face everyone and says, "*My* purse is in the living room, too. One of *us* could make it there and back faster than *them*!" she indicates the slowly-hobbling walker-lady's back.

"Hey!" Sally shouts. "It's *our* delivery!"

Everyone looks at the dame, who shrugs and puts a little more space between Percy and herself. "I just want my money and to never see this batshit loony again. Whoever has the money can have the package, you figure out dissemination yourself…"

"Why don't we settle this the old-fashioned way?" It's a seventy-five-ish bald naked dude who says the words, the same idea that it's clear has occurred to everyone: one package but two interested parties means a turf war, a fully-naked gang battle. Without weapons. How effective can a punch delivered with an arthritic arm be?

I get a text from Merlin: '*man you should probably get back here before things turn sour*'

The two naked hordes face each other down, ready to do battle over brown-bagged powder. "Isn't there some more peaceful way to solve this?" I ask grimly. I'm hemmed in on all sides by old people. I won't get out of here clean if all of them devolve into madness as soon as it looks they might. "Rock-Paper-Scissors?"

"Ah-ah-ah," the dame says. "No one's fighting anyone over anything until my truck's out of that house." She looks around. "I'm gonna need a few volunteers."

Several of the hardier old men—from both sides of the road—flex their muscles and raise their arms to volunteer. And then they stare each other down. And don't look away.

"All of you can probably get the job done, thanks. While you're flipping it don't worry too much about damage while you're flipping it—it's self-repairing bodywork."

Eleven volunteered fully-hard bodies converge towards the hole in the wall.

"*Now* we can finish up business here." She addresses the lobe of the crowd richest in orgy-members from the neighbour's house. "No one was harmed by the crash, I trust?"

"Just my glass coffee table," an old lady says. "and it was only some deplorable Ikea thing. Really had to go."

No one is paying any mind to the armed Sighentologist, and he doesn't like having lost the spotlight. And the lightning gun is still in his hands. He flips a switch on the gun and advances on the dame. "I don't want to strike you down, and I can't do anything about the grotesque Devil's gyrations you people do, but I can destroy at least a little bit of whatever this filth is before all of you put it into your veins. So, hand over the merchandise."

The oldest-looking geezer from the other side of the road seems amused by Sighentologist Percy's depth of delusion. "Kid, you see how *we're* all old bastards who've lived and learned and experienced most of what there is to experience? And how you're just some runt with his head up his own ass?"

Percy's head recoils like he's been slapped. "I never...I..."

"So, when we turn around and tell you, hey, a full life consists in part of having a good time on illicit substances and group orgies, do you figure that *maybe* we know what the hell we're talking about?"

"*Just throw* down *the package!*" Percy shouts at the dame. His voice cracks a hair at 'down', and the almost-musical delivery that results makes not very many people take him any more seriously.

"I got it!" Merlin shouts, from back on the patio. "Well, I can't do anything about the armed maniac, but regarding the high demand problem: you could pit a fighter from each side against each other and make a safe, fair fight of it."

Everyone kind of, takes a second, and allows themselves to make a picture in their head of the cage-match that will result if enough say, '*Well, okay, I'm down.*' Zero clothes. Zero dentures. Zero mercy. It's a better prospect than a violent brawl I guess. And maybe I can even make a few bucks taking bets.

Percy blasts a tree-streetlight on the edge of the next lawn with his lightning gun. A bolt of white light and white heat explodes down out of the sky and sets fire to its branches.

A shock wave of unease tears through the crowd: this might get *bad*. Another in a long line of crazy fuckers with a gun blasting at everyone who doesn't agree with him.

Sally doesn't believe in taking chances. She rolls a second mag grenade past Percy's feet. With another soundless red flash, it propels the largest bodies of metal nearby away. We are in the middle of the lawn—the only metal is the lightning gun tightly clenched in Percy's fists and a number of old people's metal glasses. When they and the gun go up, Percy's tugged with them, arcing up into the sky like the hand of God's rapturing him away to paradise.

"REMEMBER ME...!"

He comes down hard on top of a series of refuse bins poised next to the curb up the block.

"If there's a God," the dame calls, "then he put those trash cans there for the *express purpose* of you landing on them! Still think you're his chosen disciple?"

The crowd titters, calm again. *Open to reason, there's gotta be a non-violent way to this.*

"Okay, I got an idea, if there's only enough for *half* of you to get tweaked, then I propose everyone pair up. Let every pair lose with each other. The first one to get their partner to climax gets the hit. The more *enthusiastic* half."

Much to my surprise, the idea catches—the old people on all sides examine each other with fresh, lustful eyes. All of the old dicks have been Viagra-hard throughout this entire scene, it should be noted—a forest of erections jut out at all angles. The elderly ladies have had plenty of time to get a good look, and they like what they see.

Merlin's voice calls, "Dear Jesus, man, what have you *done?!*"

"I assume my truck is as good as right-side up," the dame says, "so we finally arrive at the 'money in my hand' stage."

Right on time, the walker-equipped lady hobbles back from the house with her purse in tow. She hands over the money. The dame hands her the brick-sized package wrapped in plain brown paper. The old lady feels the package's weight and baulks. "Uh... I'm not all that streetwise to drug prices, but I get all *this* for just forty dollars?"

"Sure do, ma'am." She grins. "We're a new organization, and our stuff is low-low-low."

"Could I get your number?" the old lady asks. Several of the orgy-goers raise a hand like they're interested, too.

"Hey, me too," I add.

The dame appraises me. "For business reasons, or pleasure?"

"Whatever's applicable."

"Ah," the walker-equipped lady smiles at us. "Young love."

The dame eyes me for a second, then grins and takes out her phone.

From inside the neighbour's house, there's a series of grunts and the snare drum *ba-dum-dum-dum* of rubber tires reconnecting with the ground in quick succession. The suspension squeals under the strain of the impact, but doesn't sound like anything breaks. Meanwhile, I'm typing a dictated number and the name "Elixir Sue" into my phone.

The walker-equipped lady hands the package to Sally. "I trust you'll supervise the competition and distribute rewards."

Sally takes it and addresses her flock. "Okay, so for the competition, either we use one of the houses which could be tight on space..."

"Even better," someone craws.

"...*or* we could use that hedge maze up the block. Plenty of space, nice cool evening breeze..." She's already made up her mind about it.

"I get the chills when it gets dark," someone bleats.

"We got plenty of ways to keep each other warm. Let's get moving" They disappear behind the hedge one by one.

But one breaks off from the pack and sidles toward me. "You're leaving already?" the doting grandmother, asks, fingering one soft nipple experimentally. "Why not compete with someone for a dose of your own?" Her voice is the texture of cigarette ash. "I'd be eager to have some fun with a body as young as yours again. It's been so *long*."

"Nah," I say diplomatically. "You got far more experience than me, I wouldn't stand a chance." I drift ever closer to Merlin and the house. "Anyways, have a good time!"

"Even if you don't want to play, you could watch."

"My friend and I got dope to smoke."

"You could do that here. With us."

"I'm not sure my stoned mind could handle seeing what happens when all you fine folks bring out the KY Jelly™." I don't know if it sounds matter-of-fact or rude, but the grandmother doesn't follow me, just shrugs and starts hobbling towards the hedge.

Elixir Sue, having finished giving her contact details out to those interested, shakes her head. "I don't envy you, man. Now that all of them know you know, they're not apt to keep themselves very quiet for your benefit."

Climbing into her truck, she stops, and both of us listen to the noises that waft over from within the maze: maniacal gibberings, chirps, the complexly-layered audioscape of half-centenarians getting acquainted with each other, one bony finger at a time.

It's a glimpse of the 365 leased days to come, only one thin hardwood floor standing between our ears and their orifices.

Imagine waking up in the middle of the night, every night, to this.

An idea strikes me as if thrown from the hand of God. "Do you know of any business that offers soundproof carpeting?"

Sue grins from inside the truck's window. "There's two in this neighbourhood alone. You're new to the city, aren't you?" She drives her silent truck down the lawn, onto the street and away so it must be rhetorical.

"You silver-tongued devil!" Merlin shouts. "That girl could make any lucky guy happy by arching her back and…"

Sue's voice calls, "*I can still hear you, Mr Suave Dand…*" before sliding out of auditory range completely.

"Dude," I say, "if you were interested in her, you should have come down here and said hello."

"You know I don't have an easy time meeting new people," he says uneasily.

"You know *no one* has an 'easy' time meeting new people?" I answer. Alone in the middle of the street, I gaze over at Percy, still sprawled atop two blue recycle bins. He hasn't moved, presumably, he's a floundering, lost soul.

You probably shouldn't let him wander away still armed with a functional lightning gun.

"Hey, buddy," I call, walking towards him. "Where'd you get that thing anyway? Research lab or something? How does it work? I ain't ever heard of a thing like that, weather control, being invented. Can I hold it for a second?"

He gives it up easy. "For the technical details, you'd have to ask whoever lost it at my church, picked it up from in between the pews at our latest congregation."

From inside the hedge-maze of moans and groans, someone male cries out. I hear Sally's voice: "Ding-ding-ding, you're our first winner, Greta, how 'bout that! Here, take this powder—I didn't know we'd have *this* much!"

"In case it wasn't already clear," I tell Percy while looking through the gun's scope at a delightfully-sensuous Puddems ad stationed high in the sky, "you got no right trying to strip the proper chemicals out of a party."

Inside the maze, Sally tells Greta, "See what you do is take this straw and put one end in the..."

"I got it I got it, dearie, this isn't my first rodeo."

"What's your name?" Percy asks me.

I pry my eyes from the Puddems display. "Neil."

"Brother Neil..."

"Uh just Neil, thanks."

And then Greta, the seventy-year-old woman sporting exactly zero teeth, floats up over the walls of the hedge maze, near the power-lines. Immune to gravity, she whoops and hollers, then launches herself back down into the hedge maze, out of sight.

"Ah," I say, "Elixir Sue splices TK into her psychedelics—I approve."

I look at Percy and the leghole-trap look of chemical seduction in his eyes. He must've been a sheltered kid, never even heard about the idea of TK-drugs. Well, now he's seen, and he *likes* what he sees—telekinetic flight to him is a power to be bestowed by God which would make *this* the True Path™, not the words sequestered in his brown-bagged Bible. Percy suddenly pats himself down, then looks up and down the street. Somewhere in mid-flight, his little black book's been snagged from his grasp.

S-Bible-less, his eyes return to the sky as Greta floats back into view, every aged wrinkle of her sliding against the bare moonlight.

"Hey," he says, "Maybe we should check out what's happening in that maze, see what all the fuss is about."

I look to Merlin, back on the patio and eager for me to return so he can check out my new lightning gun. Reclined in judgment over our cell-block of darkened lawns. Our yards are the greenest in the world for one reason: every grass blade is plastic. The easiest route to happiness is usually synthetic.

"You go on ahead, Percy. I've got places to be."

THE END

ANDREW MARINUS of Vancouver, British Columbia, Canada has had work published at *Hypertextmag, Pseudopod, Beyond Imagination, Black Petals,* and is a veteran freelancer for cracked.com.

BIRTHDAY

Dave de Burgh

This story originally appeared in *eScifi* / **Nebula Rift** in January 2013.

THE FIRST THING I heard as I woke up was a soft *ping*—the System recognizing that I had woken up. It monitored everyone, every minute of their lives—another one of Dad's *societal improvements*.

I stretched, yawned, and then grudgingly sat up and ran a hand through my hair. The System activated the radio, and an irritating DJ's strident voice informed me that *Today's a day for great things, man, so get out there and be great!* The flowglass cleared, and dazzling sunlight spilled into the room.

I climbed out of bed and shuffled into the bathroom. The light went on, and I studied myself in the mirror for a while—I had the old asshole's eyes, my mother's nose; his unfortunate chin, too, and my mother's pale skin. Behind me, the DJ began reading out the day's weather, and it was only when he stated the date that I realized what day it was—my twenty-third birthday.

"Fuck sakes," I breathed, lowering my head into my hands. Another day older. Another day closer to the *Letter*.

I rubbed my hand over my face, thoughts falling into that odd numbness, that silence that echoes in the space between thoughts. Then I noticed the vial lying next to my right hand. I had learned to stop wondering what was in the vial, just as everyone else in the world had, I guess.

The only information that the System gave us was that the liquid in the vials kept our hearts beating, kept us healthy and fit, and bolstered our immune systems—because of the vial's contents no-one had died of disease or infection in almost thirty years.

I picked up the vial. Pierced the soft lid and swallowed the tasteless contents.

After getting dressed, I checked my Notifications and saw it. I forced myself to access it. The Letter opened in the air before me, the System's various 'Eyes' building the holograph in a matter of seconds, and I began reading.

"From PopCon Johannesburg – Mandela Square Office

"Mr Herchelle, it is our solemn duty to inform you that on the 17th of March, 2133, at 17h35—"

I re-read it before marking the Notification as *Read*. Eating breakfast—the gruel that was specifically tailored and gene-sequenced to my body chemistry—passed in a blur and I only really started noticing my surroundings again when I climbed out of the TransU-pod and stepped onto Herchelle Plaza. A trip of fifteen minutes that had passed with me entirely unaware of it.

I was one of two people in the world who had the necessary access-imprint to enter the plaza, and I realized that, for the first time in my life, I was happy that only my father and I had the imprint.

I stood before the plaque for a while, just looking at the silver etching of his face. I read and re-read the statement that had been printed at the bottom that celebrated his world-saving and humanity-saving achievement. It came as a surprise when I felt the tears sliding down my cheeks.

"I know you can hear me," I whispered, dashing the tears from my eyes. "All I want to know is, why haven't you tried to contact me? How can you sit there, watch me standing here, knowing what's coming, and not *contact* me?"

I swung a kick at the base of the wall, and a single alarm-tone sounded, short and loud. A warning. I ignored it. "Are you already dead? Is that it?"

No reaction. Truthfully, I hadn't expected him to react.

I spat on the plaque and left the plaza.

I walked out into a circle of onlookers. They knew I was Herchelle Jr. Everyone was silent, all eyes on me. Their faces were drawn and emotionless, and it was an eerie moment. Before any of them could ask, I said loudly, "I don't know. I *don't*, okay?"

None of them moved and the moment stretched into a desperate, echoing sadness. Finally, one of them moved aside, an old man wearing a faded and torn pinstripe jacket and denim. When he moved, the people behind him moved, too, forming a corridor for me.

I held my breath and walked out between them, hearing the question all of them wanted to ask without them having to speak – *When does my turn come?*

I eventually made it to the newsstand and held my wrist out for the scanner's beam before hearing the upload-tone that told me I had the latest edition of *The South African Census Quarterly*. I'd look through it later before the PopCon guys arrived to keep their appointment.

Moving back onto the sidewalk I surrendered myself into the chaotic streams of people, becoming a part of the current. The whole world became a roar of sound and movement and sensation. The last census, the one I read on my mom's birthday, had put the world-population at fifteen-billion, and a billion of those lived and died in Gauteng alone. People had stopped worrying about India and China years ago—when the Walls had been erected those countries had been deleted from any and all maps. I wondered how long it would be before the same thing happened here—Nigeria, Tanzania, and Egypt were all headed toward being walled-off, and even though the heavies at Border Control were doing an incredible job, under the kind of pressure they were facing it was inevitable that people would slip into the country.

Hours later I was in a comic shop, paging through the latest *Superman* comic when I felt a light punch against on my shoulder and heard Ross say, "Yo, *duuude,* you know I can't allow you to page through 'em, Bra. Not at those prices."

I turned and saw him standing there, one hand on his hip, the other fiddling with one of his many facial piercings. He was thin and purple-haired, had too-blue eyes and a silver smile, probably one of the latest 'plants' from the uber-exclusive Sandton Clinic. He thrust his chest out, puffing himself up, but when I laughed at him, he laughed back before saying, "Nah, man, don't worry about it, Bra. I know it's your birthday." He winked and turned away, back to prowling the store for law-breakers.

I looked down that page again—Batman and Superman were once again handing Darkseid's ass to him, after being beaten practically to a pulp, of course—but the comic had already lost its hold on me, and I slipped it back into its self-sealing slot. When I left the store, the scanner beeped, and a voice informed me that I might have forgotten to make a purchase, was I sure that I wanted to leave right now?

I ignored it and moved against the flowglass-fronting of the store, stood there for a while just taking it all in before I checked my watch. Half an hour… Today of all days I had to sleep late, huh? I shook my head. Well, might as well get back. No sense in delaying it.

The TransU-driver was singing some old, old tune while he drove. I asked him what the band was called, and he said, "U2, Bra, awesome, awesome band!"

When I told him that it was a crap name for a band, he said, "Ey, man, don' knock 'em, dey was de biggest band in de world one time, man, fuckin' *huuuge* band, dey got *good* music man. Should give 'em a listen some time."

I wanted to laugh and ask him, *When?*

As the pod slowed and then stopped outside my apartment, I saw that they were waiting outside. Three guys in suits, charcoal-grey with red pinstripes, polished boots. Terrible dress-sense, but then again, did it really matter? One of them noticed me and smiled, nodding as if to say *Thank you for sticking to our appointment.*

Whatever. I let the driver scan my wrist, and the door unsealed itself. They moved up toward me as I stepped out of the pod. I nodded at them.

"Gentleman. Mind if we do this inside?"

The one who had smiled and nodded said, "Of course, Mr Herchelle. Your father made arrangements for just that." I sighed. *Him* again. Why the hell did they have to bring him up *now?*

"Let's get it over with." I shouldered my way past them and within moments I was tramping up the stairs to my front door, the PopCon-guys making hardly any sound behind me. I let them in, and they congregated in the lounge. When I told them to sit down, I was told that they wouldn't be staying long enough.

"You scared you're going to miss your next appointment or something?"

They didn't reply with anything, though I found myself wishing that they would at least try.

"Where do you want me?"

"That depends on you, Mr Herchelle. We're trained to handle any request."

"You clean up after yourselves, at least?"

"That goes without saying."

I nodded. "I was going to have a birthday party later."

"We will inform the guests, sir."

"Okay, then." I took off my jacket and shoes and sat down on the couch, tried to get comfortable and then realized what a stupid idea that was. They stood around me with calm, pleasantly-bored expressions on their faces.

"Tell me," I said, "How is he doing?"

"Your father, sir?"

"No. Bruce Wayne."

The man blinked. Didn't they know who Batman was? On the other hand, wasn't I allowed a dumb joke? "Yes, my father."

"Oh." The guy shrugged. "He's dead, sir. You know that."

I laughed, long and loud, and that sudden release lifted a weight from me. The room seemed brighter, more beautiful than I'd ever imagined it could be. "You actually believe that that the man who solved the world's population problems is dead?"

"It's a fact, Mr Herchelle."

"Because you were *told* so, or because you did the job yourself?"

He frowned at that, and I thought, *Ah…*

I said, "You know, it doesn't even matter. Or it won't." I laughed again. "Let's get it over with."

One of them stepped forward, the letter in his hands. In an age of holographs, these guys still used paper.

He cleared his throat and recited, "Mr James Cornelius Herchelle, it is our solemn duty to inform you that on the 17th of March 2133, at 17h35, your life will be terminated in accordance with Population Control Act 3 of 2098. We trust that you have made the best of your time and assure you that your passing means that someone will receive the gift of life and an allotted time in which to live it.

The officers who will come to your place of residence are fully trained for any eventuality and will ensure that your passing is as painless as possible. On behalf of the people of the world, we thank you for your willingness to give another human being a chance at life."

He stopped and glanced up at me. I nodded. Two of them moved to stand on either side of me while the third said, "Is there any particular way that you would prefer us to do this?"

"What does it matter?"

"It doesn't," he answered. "I am lawfully bound to ask the question."

"It wasn't one of those questions that needed an answer." *Idiot.*

He blinked again.

I said, "Can you please draw the curtains and make sure all the lights are off? I like the dark."

Moments later it was dark, not dark enough, but it was all I was going to get.

I saw him shift and move and then light from somewhere slid along the thin length of a needle—I felt it touch the sweet spot on my neck, felt the quick sting of it sliding in.

I felt a pleasant, heavy warmth flood my neck, felt the warmth slide curtain-like down my body, filling me.

I closed my eyes, and the darkness became gradually darker, until...

THE END

DAVE DE BURGH writes, plays guitar, gets pwned on Modern Warfare, is learning coding and screen-writing, and enjoys brandy. He lives with his blue-eyed angel and their three furkids in Pretoria, South Africa. To find out more, visit his website on davedeburgh.com.

A COMMUNICATOR WITH ANIMATE OBJECTS

Dennis Mombauer

Originally published in *Nebula Rift* in October 2015.

FEW PEOPLE MADE THE entire journey up from Earth in those days, from the surface through the atmosphere and right into space: For the right prize, Hakon Ambrose was one of them.

He had started from one of the unelevated piers, quickly passed through the coruscating flash-flurry of the arcologies and their ever-rising solar panels, then accelerated upward along a gravitation spire, where people jumped down for miles and miles in free flight.

The sky had bled into the onyx night of space, speckled with the lights of man-made habitats and captured asteroids, a frontier region of prospectors, farmers, and robotic mining machines. Hakon had steered his tiny craft through this cluster of miniature worlds, then past the satellite homes of very artful systems of thought, opening up around him like origami flowers with their petals constantly aligning toward the sun.

Beyond them, after the last communication installations, there were lines of strung-together spaceshells, artificial oysters in which people drifted in weightlessness, immersed in drug-induced dreams or deep meditation—and ultimately, the furthest away from Earth, Hakon reached the end of his journey.

HAKON AMBROSE WAS AN expert of sorts, a communicator with animate objects and proficient in the language of dreams, very carefully trained and selected.

The Precogniscience Exalted, one of the highest panels of Earth's administration, had offered him great remuneration to go up beyond their reach and bring back something very precious, an answer to the current crisis of mental manipulation. A secret war raged under the conscious surface of the human mind at that time, idea against idea, hope against hope, fear against fear, and in space, showered by the unfiltered photons of far and dying suns, a creature might be able to teach Hakon—and therefore the Precogniscience Exalted—a method of defense.

Hakon's ship quickly approached its destination, a habitat far removed from the frontier or the spaceshells below, a miniature world enclosed in crystal-like an insect in amber, containing a replica of an ancient Asiatic temple. It was an extremely careful, full-scale remake, down to the last blade of grass and the tiniest patch of moss around it, an overgrown ruin traveling through space.

Hakon's ship touched down at the foothills of the temple, in a small clearing surrounded by ancient trees. The air was fresh and reminiscent of ancient monsoon rains, with birds and rustling wind in the treetops. There were no birds, of course, just a lone dragonfly that shimmered in the simulated moonlight, artificial like everything else here, filled with sensors and electronics, but nonetheless appearing very real, hovering in mid-air, then making a sharp turn and whirring away from Hakon.

The temple itself was a medium-sized building with curved roofs and painted wooden pillars, approachable over a series of stairs that climbed the forested hills. On his way up, Hakon saw a well and some weed-infested gardens under gnarly trees; then, a delegation of pilgrims came down to greet him.

"WELCOME TO OUR TEMPLE, o highly honored visitor. We are pleased to greet you as our venerated guest." One of the pilgrims bowed in an archaic gesture, and Hakon did a precise imitation in response. "Have you come to live here and study with the master? Come on, come on."

The pilgrims led Hakon through the main entrance gate and into a courtyard covered with stone slabs. The stone was real, as was the small shrubbery growing out of its crevices, but Hakon could also sense the tell-tale hollowness of the ground beneath his feet, the unexpected lightness of his steps.

"I'm not here to stay and study, but I need to speak to your master. Where is he?"

"Everywhere."

"His convergence lens." Hakon maintained his carefully sculpted expression and stance while banishing a surge of anger into one of his upcoming perturbation dreams. Did the pilgrims think that Hakon knew nothing about Pneumataphars, that he had come here ignorant and unprepared?

"Convergence lens?"

"Yes. Where do you communicate with him? Where does he speak and hear?"

"I... nowhere. The master is everywhere, and he teaches us in our sleep, through his structure, his sounds, his touches, and whispers."

Hakon studied the pilgrims and concluded that they weren't lying to him, but that, through some unreported death or accident, the knowledge had indeed been lost. How could these people be up here without knowing? Had they left Earth and thrown their lives away to come to this temple, to learn from a master they couldn't even speak to?

Hakon surveyed the grounds and found nothing that resembled a convergence lens, not in the courtyards and ragged gardens, not in the incense-heavy meditation rooms or under the faded tapestries. He had hoped that it might be some reliquary inside the temple, a painting or mirror perhaps– but of course, it was the well.

He went back to the ship, where he had brought his complete equipment, and moved it all to the site of the well. This had to be the convergence lens, alright, just within equal distance of the temple in the habitat's center and the forested outskirts... much better placed than most lenses that Hakon had seen.

HAKON LET HIMSELF SINK into the well, the murky water closing over his head, its wetness sloshing against the hundreds of pinpoint sensors inside his diving skin. He could feel the electrical currents in the water, the communication brain waves of the Pneumataphar, and began searching for hidden outlets by a sense of touch alone.

The submerged, algae-covered stones felt rough and natural, but Hakon knew that they had been altered, that there were nerves running through them, that they had openings for his upload cables. When his probing hands finally found one, he quickly plugged in and closed his eyes, just in time for the first dream-image to hit:

"The sky is dark and clouded, a storm coming. As it breaks loose, and rain floods the road through the rice fields, a group of travelers find themselves seeking refuge in a small shrine. The blue brightness of a sudden lightning reveals a swordsman, a monk, a mounted messenger and a flute player."

Hakon understood the message and felt the slow, ancient mind below it, like the depression of a deep lake beneath his paddling feet. In its lifetime, the being that created this scenery had been one of the best, and brightest Earth had ever brought forth, a psychologist, guru, and physician with an intellect far above the norm, a true master of the mind.

Now, he was a Pneumataphar, a human consciousness cast into the shape of a building. Its foundation of stone partly hollowed out for memory banks and processing power. Its flaking pillars and worn-out steps covered in nerve endings and receptors, turning the ancient temple into one immense, unmoving body, supported by wiring and generators that inaudibly buzzed under fallen leaves and the container loads of Earth dirt.

Hakon blanked out everything else and summoned up his own dream image in response: "Another lightning illuminates the shrine and the painted deity in its center. The monk chooses to sit down on the front porch in a lotus position and meditates, clearing his mind of everything except his own thoughts. He is successful until the flutist starts playing for the others, and the notes of his melody slowly trickle into the monk's mind, polluting it like oil dripping into a clear pond."

The scenery of the shrine, the storm and the travelers faded, and Hakon found himself floating in the darkness of his own consciousness. There was no reaction for such a long time that he began to suspect something had gone wrong, that maybe his sensor skin or the outlet had malfunctioned– but he had been trained, and so he waited. People grew much slower when they were turned into Pneumataphars, their senses spread out over so many square meters, informing them of every movement across their body, every touch on their skin.

"The monk wanders the shrine, but the flute player's song follows him everywhere, even stronger and more haunting than the rain pouring down outside." The dream scene returned and began moving again, the Pneumataphar's most direct way of communicating with Hakon.

"After some time has passed, the monk turns to the shrine's deity for guidance, and she shows him a hidden door, leading down into the Earth. It is dark here, and the monk's eyes take time to adjust to the shadows. He walks into a cave, and the cave is not empty. Shapes are hanging from its root-traversed ceiling, dozens and hundreds of shapes, the sleeping bodies of oh so many bats.

The hidden door has long closed behind him, and the monk has little choice but to trust in the deity. He sits down on the naked rock, crosses his legs and tries to meditate again. Wings whisper above him occasionally– then, pairs of tiny white opals begin to shine, and one of the bats screams: 'Gorah-Gar!'"

The painfully shrill sound echoed through Hakon's mind and almost made him disconnect from the dream. It felt as if he had been punched in a part of his body he didn't know existed, and everything there—skin, fat, muscles—had been imprinted with stiffness and soreness, a strange kind of physical phantom memory.

"'Gorah-Gar! Gorah-Gar!' After the first scream, all the bats join in, and within seconds, the monk is overwhelmed by the chaos of a hundred animal voices. The monk wants to shut them up, to run from this terrible noise, to escape with his mind still intact—but the secret passage can't be opened. The bats flutter in the inky void above his head, and their screams don't stop: 'Gorah-Gar! Gorah-Gar!'"

The scenery changed, from the near-total darkness of the cellar to the shrine building on the surface, still surrounded by rain and occasional lightning.

The lesson seemed to have finished, and Hakon quickly recalled the "Gorah-Gar" of the bats, over and over again, until he was sure that he couldn't forget it. He started the slow ascent back to full awareness of his body and conceived of a sun rising over the small shrine, its rays piercing through the clouds, as a way of expressing his gratitude but there was no response.

HAKON MADE HIS WAY back down to Earth and repeated the defense meditation on the way, summoning up the dark cellar cave, the bats, and their horrible screams, uncertain how to use them, but convinced that this cacophony of shrieking voices was meant as weapon, an attack against anyone trying to manipulate his thoughts.

Hakon's ship descended between the towering arcologies and their glittering solar panels, landing on a pier just a few miles above

Earth, where the representatives of the Precogniscience Exalted were already waiting for him.

"Welcome back, Registered Citizen Ambrose. Have you been successful?" The voices of the delegation sounded croaky like crows, and their eyes showed a glossy white glimmer.

"I have indeed."

Everyone made the formal gesture of peace and goodwill, before moving into an already prepared oneirophage chamber, where Hakon would pass on his newfound skills.

"Wait." Hakon felt something stir in him and stopped before one of the oneirophagic chairs. "How do I know that you are really the Precogniscience Exalted and that you will use this technique responsibly? How do I know that you are not manipulating me?"

"Because you can trust us, and we will pay you. In this moment, your account has received the exact sum we promised you as compensation for your efforts, and an added bonus as a sign of gratitude from the Precogniscience Exalted as well as the people of Earth. Gorah-Gar."

"What did you say? What was the last thing?"

"Gorah-Gar! Gorah-Gar!' After the first scream, all the bats join in, and within seconds, the monk is overwhelmed by the chaos of a hundred animal voices. The monk wants to shut them up, to run from this terrible noise, to escape with his mind still intact—but the secret passage can't be opened. The bats flutter in the inky void above his head, and their screams don't stop: 'Gorah-Gar! Gorah-Gar!'"

THE SCREECHING OF THE bats dragged Hakon back into the darkness of the Pneumataphar's mind, and he realized that his return to Earth and his conversation with the Precogniscience Exalted had been part of the dream lesson, although he didn't fully understand it. Was it a warning that something was wrong with his employer, that he should be careful before teaching the defense meditation when he came back?

As the images—the cave, the monk, the bats—ceased, Hakon again conceived of a rising sun over the shrine and slowly surfaced from the darkness of the well. In his tiny ship, he went down to Earth again, this time for real, past the artificial thought systems in their satellite flowers, who amplified and distilled the dreams from the spaceshells toward the planet below, past the frontier habitats and the gravitation spires.

He greeted the delegation and followed them into the oneirophag chamber and just like the Pneumataphar had shown him, he stopped. "Before we do this, I need proof that you indeed represent the Precogniscience Exalted, that I'm not being played."

"You are right to ask this question, but I'm afraid we can't reassure you because there is, in fact, no such organization. We knew that you would never help any single faction except the Earth administration, and so we implanted in you the conviction that there was something called the Precogniscience Exalted, and that you were tasked by it to retrieve this wisdom from the Pneumataphar."

"And that," one of the other representatives added, "is a lie as well." Suddenly, he had a glowing device in his hand, and all delegation members but him, collapsed on the floor.

"The Precogniscience Exalted is real, and I'm its agent. We have infiltrated this *other organization* and watched its plan unfold, but we had to step in now. Please, Citizen Ambrose, we are deeply indebted to you for your service. You have brought down from space the means to shield the people of Earth from manipulation, and for this, we are grateful. Show me, if you may."

They strapped into the oneirophagic chairs, attached the electrode cables with routine movements, and connected. Inside the shared dream, Hakon recreated the shrine and the monk, the cave, the bats and their many screams.

"Are you satisfied? I delivered what you asked for, right on time, a mental weapon usable for defense. If it pleases the Precogniscience Exalted, I would now like to receive my remuneration."

Suddenly, the other man vanished, dropped out of the shared experience, while Hakon felt something blocking him, something that had to be installed in the chamber, the chair, the cables.

"What is happening? Let me out!" Hakon had to concentrate hard to perceive something outside the dream, to form words with his lungs and vocal chords, not just his mind. "Are you listening? What is wrong?"

The remaining representative lay slumped in his chair, his eyes empty, his tongue hanging out like a cloth full of blood. Someone else was standing at the entrance of the oneirophag chamber, a woman with a thin smile who slowly walked toward Hakon's chair.

"I'm sorry that we used you, Citizen Ambrose. They would have let you die in your dreams, you know? The chair is rigged, but I will restore your control."

Hakon could feel the blockade loosening and immediately disconnected.

"Neither of them was the Precogniscience Exalted, but we do exist, and it is our task to identify threats well in advance." The woman helped Hakon out of the chair while she continued speaking with her warm voice. "We were aware that your rare skills made you the perfect candidate to send up to the Pneumataphar, and that at least two organizations were interested in doing so. As we indeed are in need of a defense against mental manipulation, we saw no reason to stop them; but we took precautions. The slight mistrust you felt was a result of the weapon we implanted in you, a weapon that would go off as soon as someone tried to extract knowledge from you; but if you already had the defense—and why else would they try to extract something—, you would be safe."

"But how do I know that you are telling the truth now? That you represent the true Precogniscience Exalted?"

"Gorah-Gar! Gorah-Gar!"

EVERY BAT SHRIEK PIERCED through Hakon's head like a lightning of red anger or a fog bank of blue fear through one of his perturbation dreams, where he banished all his negative emotions to deal with at a later time.

"The monk realizes that he can't get out, and he does the only thing he can do."

The Pneumataphar made a long pause, but this time, Hakon couldn't sink back into his floating body, for the screams didn't stop, and he was trapped just as inescapable as the monk beneath this fictitious shrine.

"The monk surrenders. He sits down again, resumes his meditation pose and opens his mind to the bats. Every scream drills into him and leaves a hollow shaft of pain, repeatedly, every sharp "Gorah-Gar!" cutting deeper and deeper.

"Stop!" Hakon tried to escape this torture, but the dream-images of the Pneumataphar were too vivid, the bat's opal eyes too glaring, their screaming voices far too loud and manifold. The defense weapon was being used against him; it was a trap, some gambit in the war for mind control back on Earth, designed by some faction to take him out before he could return with any information. "Stop it! Stop!"

Hakon wanted to fight back, to return the pain that pattered down on him and without any other weapon available, he released all his pent-up perturbation dreams simultaneously in an explosion of red rubies and blue sapphires, a shower of madness enclosed in poisoned gemstones that threatened to wash away everything. With each wave of concentrated emotions surging up, the bat's cacophony became shallower, quieter, more harmless, the hollow shafts of pain filled up with rage and horror until suddenly, abruptly, it all died down completely.

The scenery changed, from the near-total darkness of the cellar cave to the shrine building on the surface, still surrounded by rain and occasional lightning. Thunder rumbled, but the wind had lost all tone, and Hakon spotted no trace of the monk's fellow travelers, of the swordsman, the mounted messenger, and the flutist.

Hakon still felt the released perturbations ebbing through his consciousness, but they were much fainter than he was used to, only weak after-echoes of an outbreak so uncontrolled and brutal that it should have rightfully killed him. Everything was gone, all the emotions he had stored in the warehouses of his soul, and he had no idea what had happened to them.

HAKON SURFACED FROM THE well and pulled himself over the side, his body as profoundly exhausted as his brain. He lowered a measuring probe into the water, but it showed no life signature and no detectable convergence lens.

He stripped out of the diving skin and carefully looked around, just to see his worst suspicions confirmed, there was a crashed dragonfly on the grass, and the trees had already begun to lose their leaves in the season-less conservation of this space habitat.

"What have you done?" The pilgrims advanced as a group, their faces pale and shocked, their eyes quickly filling with fear. "We could all feel how you intruded into the dreams of the master, how you appeared within them and murdered him! Why? Why would you come up here and do this?"

The choir of their angry voices reminded Hakon of the shrieking bats, and he backed away, leaving his drenched equipment lying at the well. "All that I did, I did in defense of my own physical integrity and mental stability." He concentrated on his voice and his body language to be as calming as possible, to create as big of a psychological effect as he could.

"You murdered the master!" Despite Hakon's efforts, the crowd seemed to get more and more agitated, as if the aftershocks of all those scattered dream emotions were pulsing through their blood. As they began to run toward him, Hakon fled and in a chase down the hills and through the forest, he reached his vessel only seconds before they did.

The unbreakable plexiglass of the cockpit trembled under the dozens of hands beating at it, but Hakon knew that he was safe and steadily started the engines.

THE SHIP SOARED UP between the ancient trees and out of the habitat sphere, toward the stars and away from Earth. He couldn't go back to the Precogniscience Exalted empty-handed, and after all, he had seen in his dream visits to Earth, he suspected that they might be responsible for the Pneumataphar attacking him, that they had been trying to get rid of him or the Pneumataphar all along.

He didn't know where he would go, but since he was already above Earth as far as one could be, beyond the arcologies, the frontier, the thinking satellites and the spaceshells, he could reach any other planet without needing much more fuel.

After he had locked in a course and his ship began to accelerate into the interstellar darkness, he settled into the freezing fluid that would soon turn his whole cockpit into a preservation pod. His eyes closed while his body temperature lowered to slow his organism down, and a last sequence of mental images, a memory inherited from the dying Pneumataphar, drifted past him before he entered a dreamless sleep:

"The flutist is still playing, but when the monk sits down and closes his eyes, he can hardly hear him amidst the memory of the screaming bats, and the flute's music neither bothers nor influences him anymore. The bats drown out every other thought, and the monk is now at peace, as calm as the old trees around the shrine or the raindrops falling on them."

THE END

DENNIS MOMBAUER was born in 1984 in the namesake capital of the Bonn Republic and raised along the Rhine River. He currently lives and works as a theatre agent and freelance author in Cologne. He writes weird fiction, textual experiments, and literary essays as well as non-naturalist drama and English poetry acculturated with German. He translates both fiction and non-fiction. Editor, co-founder, and publisher of *Die Novelle—Magazine for Experimentalism*. Has publications in various small to medium-sized magazines and anthologies.

MY TRIP TO THE CIRCUS

Jason Lairamore

Originally a Published Finalist in the 2012 SQ Magazine contest.

A LITTLE BOY SAT in the bleachers with his eyes riveted to the three circles where soon the circus troupe of Mavin, McClearly, & MacKaub would perform. His mother sat beside him, a petite thing with straight blond hair. She pointed and said something, and the boy's eyes widened, and he clapped as he jumped up and down. A great dimpled smile never left his pale, freckled face.

I would never forget that, and even if I did; I now had it recorded. That boy and his mother had just shown me one of life's most precious moments. It went to show what the innocent wonder of a child could do to a fully prepared adult, even one whose sensibilities were as used and worn as mine.

With a thought, my government grade, fully enclosed, and VR enabled I-Wear specs retracted focus from the boy and his mother and brought the complete scene into view. From where I sat at the very top of the stadium seating in the great public auditorium of Chester, Virginia, I could see everything, even in the failing light of the setting sun. And with the help of my I-Wears, I could hear anything I chose from wherever I chose from within a five-mile radius.

"Excuse me, sir."

I jumped from my seat, my hands up and ready, with knees bent and feet pointed toward my enemy. The training received from I-spec surveyors school kicked in without conscious effort. The owner of that voice had snuck up on me somehow even though I knew that was impossible. My I-wears had built-in sensors to prevent such a thing from happening.

"Sorry if I startled you, sir. But there are no recording devices allowed during the show. I'm going to have to ask you to remove all such material from your person."

The man's palms were slightly open, and his head was slightly forward and down as if in apology. His eyebrows were up, and his mouth was slightly open and smiling. He nodded ever so slightly in an effort to enforce my compliance with his wishes.

Forget that all my external gear was made of transparent aluminum and near impossible to see to the naked eye. I couldn't take it off if I tried. For all intents and purposes, I was married to my tech. I was a cyborg for lack of a better term. His asking me to remove devices was like me asking him to pull out an eye.

I lost my defensive stance and stood at ease so as to not further warn the man of my nature. The existence of cyborgs was strictly on a need to know basis.

"You frightened me," I said. It was true, though I tried not to show it. My I-Wears began to pulse red flags I'd never seen before and sent them out to home base, which only added to my fears. Something was going on, and I didn't know what.

I side-stepped the man and made to take a step down the bleachers. It was time for me to get the hell out of here.

"Sir, your recording devices?" He extended a hand palm out.

I smiled and nodded, ignored his hand, and took one step after another toward the ground.

"I'll just run them to my car," I called. "Forgot I had them with me."

I made it a couple more steps then the man laid his hand on my shoulder.

Well, I'd tried to get away. It wasn't my fault the training took over. The government had trained and trained us in situations like this. I didn't know why. Perhaps they were worried that a rival country would try to steal our tech for their own gain.

As soon as that hand touched my shoulder, my opposite arm grabbed one of the guns from a hidden hip holster, readied it to fire, and pulled the trigger at point blank range toward my enemy. Nobody touches me. That was one of the first rules they instilled.

The crowd erupted in screams. I turned back long enough to see the man lying bent and mangled on the bleachers then I took off running down the stairs.

At the bottom, I ran out of the arena proper and lost myself in the darkened parking lot. There, I slowed to a walk. Enough circus goers were moving about that my presence wouldn't be taken out of the ordinary. I made my way to my car at a fast walk, my eyes scanning everything.

I hadn't expected the evening to go like this, to say the least. This was supposed to have been a simple job, and instead, I was walking away a murderer.

MAVIN, MCCLEARLY, & MACKAUB Circus were amazing, everybody said so. Its popularity, passed by word of mouth, had reached the highest levels of government. I had been sent to record one of their performances for review. That review would have decided if the troupe received one of the special offers for a commercial transport visa. President Borgess himself had initiated the multi-world visa program as a means to spread out and deepen the cultural experiences of those living outside of Earth. That number was growing day by day as more and more people took good paying jobs out in the asteroid belt. Those people needed entertainment as much as the next guy, and the circus had looked a real winner.

I slowed down as my car came into sight. Two people waited for me. One was most definitely a woman. She sat on the hood of my car looking better and more perfect than any dash ornament had ever looked. From a distance, all I could see was the silhouette of her amazing curves. The other one looked like a guy wearing a funny looking hat.

It wasn't till I got closer and the booster in my specs could do their magic that I realized the girl was wearing tights and the man was dressed as a clown. And there wasn't just the two. All the apparent circus goers walking about near my car were clowns as well.

Finding clowns on my car, at night, was not the norm. I turned around and nearly ran into another clown. This one must have been walking on my heels, he'd been so close. Again, I found my body dropping into a defensive position.

"Mik, bring him over here," a woman's voice called from my back. It had to be the one on my car. Her voice felt like velvet to my ears.

I never took my eyes from the clown in front of me. We stood facing each other between two cars. My only way out was through him.

His face paint was thick and strongly colored. His eyes were a fierce, penetrating green, unlike anything I'd ever seen in real life. From his bearing and welcoming posture, all I got was a pleasant, wary, demureness.

"My name's not Mik," he said and winked. My body tried to relax. Such was the strength of his relaxing tone. But the red flags that'd fired off from the guy in the bleachers were going off again.

"I don't like being followed," I said.

The clown, Mik, took a step closer, broke my personal space. My hands grabbed my guns and brought them to bear. I hadn't even thought to do such a thing. The training, just like programming, that's what they'd told us it'd feel like. Well, they'd been right.

The clown took a slow step back and raised both his hands then smiled bemusedly. Warning bells went off double strong. My head swam with all the electronic sending issuing from my cranium.

"Meg, we have a problem here," the clown said as he backed a few steps.

Almost like a switch, my sense of wonder for clowns turned off. I shook my head and did a quick scan. The clowns had me hemmed in tight, and the girl from my car hood glided forward.

I wanted to ask them what was going on. Who were you? How'd you know about my tech? But all thought fled as she neared. Never in my wildest imaginings, had I witnessed such wanton beauty.

The pulsing warnings in my skull rang like a gong, but I didn't care. It could have just as easily been my heart. I was thirteen all over again, but more so, ever so more so.

"What's your name?" she asked. Her voice was silk with just a bit of sultriness.

I stammered…. "Meg," I whispered. It was like learning the name of an angel.

She was so close. She smelled just a little like flowers. Her hair was a reddish black. There was a hint of dimples when she smiled at me.

"No, Meg's my name," she said.

I shook my head. "I mean, Jeremy," I said. "Jeremy Boyd." I may have gushed. It felt like I gushed.

"What are you, Jeremy?"

"A talent scout. I identify groups for visas to go into space. It's only the best that get to go. The government wants to be sure."

"Hush," she said.

"He's an ignorant pawn," one of the other clowns said. "Kill him."

I'd let my guns fall to my sides. The male voice brought me to my senses, and they came back up. But Meg's perfection directed toward me made me forget it all. If only I could kiss her. I leaned forward to do just that. She cradled my head and whispered into my ear.

"Before you die I want you to know. No man, even a murderous brother such as you, should die in ignorance. We are your kin from across the stars. Birthed and housed on a single planet for we have no such technology as your kind do. What we had was a beautiful culture of mastery over the body, over our shared systems of nerve, muscle, and hormone. And you destroyed it. But know this, Earth brother, some survived. And we come to deliver vengeance."

She pulled her head back and looked deep into my befuddled eyes then sighed. I couldn't think of a single thing to say that'd make even the smallest bit of difference. Man, was she beautiful.

She jerked my head sharply to the side. My programmed reflexes checked her thrust. I yanked my head from her grasp and drew my guns, but I couldn't shoot her. I tried and tried. I tried with all that I had. My hands shook. My fingers ached. Her beautiful eyes, bluish gray, were wide and hungry. Her perky chest heaved up and down. My arms slowly lowered, and her full, ruby lips parted to show perfect white teeth.

And then, as if by magic, she was gone. A nanosecond worth of time zipped by as I activated my visual locater to seek her out. Someone had shot her. What was left of her lay ten feet away in pieces on the broken pavement. Her face was gone, obliterated. I took a step toward her, shaking my head. No. Such beauty should not be destroyed, not ever, no matter what.

"GET YOUR HEAD OUT OF YOUR ASS AND KILL THOSE CLOWN BASTARDS!"

The voice was strong and female and screamed in my head from ear to ear. It did the trick and broke my lingering trance. My guns came up, my visuals expanded and locked on the quickly retreating group of clowns. I fired and fired until both handguns drew empty. I managed to hit a couple of them, but many had literally dodged my bullets.

I holstered my guns and turned a full circle. From somewhere close by came the sound of sirens. The police were on their way. I shook my head. I had no clue what to do next. I could run, but that wouldn't help in the long run. I know some of the circus crowd had seen my face. I wouldn't be that hard to identify.

A red light blinked to life in my superimposed transparent faceplate.

"Run to me as fast as you can if you want to live. They will kill you, believe me." It was the same woman's voice, still in my head.

So, I ran. It was something to do. My brain was mush, and my nerves felt fried. Running gave me a purpose other than killing, and it helped to lessen the aching multitude of questions that barraged my soul.

I'd never have seen the black helicopter if it hadn't been for my computer beacon. It sat in a dark little clearing between a couple of buildings.

"Get inside," the female voice said, this time from close by. A little blue light clicked on that showed the interior of the craft. A black-clad woman wearing full riot headgear stowed some sort of rifle into an overhead compartment. I took a step up and sat down beside her.

"Who are you?" I asked. "Did you kill that woman?" I couldn't shake the utter waste of destroying something so beautiful.

The little blue light clicked off, leaving us in utter blackness then the helicopter rose with just the barest of whispers.

"I'm your partner, Joe," the woman said. "Yeah, I took out the bitch. From the looks of it, she had you under her spell. You always were one for the ladies."

"My name is Jeremy."

"Jeremy, that's right. Forgot about that."

"She said," it sounded ridiculous to even think about, "She said she was from another planet, that we destroyed her world."

"That's the story."

"But..."

The helicopter landed with a soft thud and the door opened of its own accord to reveal a rooftop and a lit doorway. The lady, my partner, jumped out first and led the way to the door. I followed. I didn't see where I had much choice.

The door led down a stairwell. At the first landing, she opened another door and ushered me inside. The room was one of the training rooms from the I-Wear facility. We'd come to home base.

The man who'd been my primary instructor, Mr Martin, was there and he held a hypodermic needle full of some drug in one of his pudgy hands. I stopped and watched my still masked partner come around to join the professor. I gave them both a questioning look. My tech started to ping against different pieces of tech in the room as it verified and communicated all that had happened that night.

"I'm getting tired of doing this every time," Mr Martin said to my partner. He sighed.

"Okay," he continued. "Quick and dirty. Listen because you have to be at a comedy club across town in less than half an hour for another possible hit. Maybe we can get lucky twice in a row."

"What..." I began.

"No," he interrupted. "No time for all the dilly dally. Here it is. Yes, one of our explorer ships found life on another planet. Yes, this life looked exactly like us, some kind of divergent evolution they say, with them masters of the body and us masters of tech. And of course, our two very different cultures didn't handle initial relations well, so we did what we always do. We blew them the hell up. Dead, finite, or so we thought. Survivors are scattered here and there hiding like cockroaches that run when you turn the lights on. So, we are killing them piecemeal as best we can. And yes, you are the bait. Well, more like poison. Understand this so I don't have to have you restrained, which would take too long. They are absolute masters of nonverbal communication. That is why I have this drug in my hand. I am going to inject you, and you are going to forget this, so you can be ignorant. Ignorance is the key. You can get close enough to kill them if you are ignorant. If you knew what was happening, they'd know, and they'd scatter."

"Why are we killing them?" I asked, but found myself pushing up my sleeve and walking up to Mr Martin as if my body had done it a thousand times.

He grabbed my arm, and I tensed, but my partner came around to put an arm around my shoulders. For some reason, I calmed down at her touch.

As I watched the medicine get pushed into the vein at my elbow, Mr Martin answered my question.

"We are killing them because they are, after all, human, and they want revenge. They're trying to affect our culture, turn us against ourselves, and they can do it. Wouldn't you want revenge if someone had destroyed your planet?"

"NAME PLEASE?" ASKED A white-gloved waiter.

"Phillip Lariot," I answered. He checked his list, nodded, and led me to a table in the back of the room.

"Enjoy the show, sir."

I tipped him well and settled back to watch the crowd gathered around the tables. Age groups from eighteen to eighty were here. That was saying something. For a comedian to appeal to that large a dynamic was very impressive. Perhaps this comedian, a guy named Gus Thorton, had what it took to win one of President Borgess's special interplanetary visas. From commentary on his past performances, it sure looked promising.

"Excuse me, sir," said a voice behind me. I jumped from my seat. Nobody sneaks up on me.

THE END

JASON LAIRAMORE is a writer of science fiction, fantasy, and horror who lives in Oklahoma with his beautiful wife and their three monstrously marvelous children. He is a published finalist of the 2012 *SQ Mag* annual contest, the winner of the 2013 *Planetary Stories* flash fiction contest, a third-place winner of the 2015 *SG Mag* annual contest, and a recent semi-finalist in the first quarter of *Writers of the Future Volume 33*. His work is both featured and forthcoming in over 55 publications to include *Perihelion Science Fiction, Stupefying Stories,* and anthologies from Third Flatiron Publications, to name a few. You can connect with Jason at www.facebook.com/jason.lairamore.

AFTERWORD

WE WOULD LIKE TO personally thank you for buying and reading this book. Producing this anthology has been, and continues to be, quite fulfilling for us and we hope that it is enjoyable for you as well.

Please consider taking a little extra time to help others find this book by leaving feedback where you purchased it. Your opinion about this book truly matters, both to our authors who have contributed to the anthology and to other readers.

If you have any questions, comments, suggestions, or just want to say hello, please visit our publisher's website on Indie Authors Press, www.salgado-reyes.com, and follow our publisher's Twitter: @Indie__Authors

Indie Authors Press